D0267845

CONSTABLE AROUND THE HOUSES

Sergeant Blaketon prepares to retire, but Aidensfield isn't free from crime... Geoffrey Cunningham reports the theft of his famous art collection of red-headed nudes, a burglar breaks into an isolated house to leave something behind and a builder discovers a human skeleton. There are problems with Greengrass's goat which loves butting motor vehicle headlights while Claude Jeremiah himself decides to establish the Greengrass School of Motoring. Constable Nick copes with all these, as well as the priest who photographed the Loch Ness Monster, and the aerial photograph which reveals a woman's secret...

CONSTABLE AROUND
THE HOUSES

For Derek Fowlds
With gratitude for bringing
Sergeant Oscar Blaketon
so perfectly to life in *Heartbeat*

CONSTABLE AROUND THE HOUSES

by

Nicholas Rhea

Magna Large Print Books
Long Preston, North Yorkshire,
BD23 4ND, England.

British Library Cataloguing in Publication Data.

Rhea, Nicholas
    Constable around the houses.

    A catalogue record of this book is
    available from the British Library

    ISBN   0-7505-1711-5

First published in Great Britain 2000 by Robert Hale Ltd.

Published in Large Print 2001 by arrangement with
Robert Hale Ltd.

Magna Large Print is an imprint of Library Magna Books Ltd.

Printed and bound in Great Britain by
T.J. (International) Ltd., Cornwall, PL28 8RW

Chapter 1

The fact that Sergeant Blaketon had confirmed his intention to retire was not unexpected. We knew he was approaching fifty-five, which was the age limit for service as a sergeant, but even so the reality of his impending departure was rather unsettling. I and the other constables of Ashfordly Section felt he was such a strong, enduring and rather calming presence that it didn't seem possible the police station or its personnel could function efficiently without him. I was sure his retirement would shock members of the public, too, whether it was those who had willingly entered the station during his stewardship or those who had entered less than willingly. And, of course, there was the Greengrass factor – how would the old rogue cope without his uniformed adversary? Would Claude Jeremiah celebrate by going berserk in an orgy of unrestrained law-breaking, poaching and minor motoring offences, or would he obtain his revenge by behaving like a normal law-abiding citizen? We felt that latter was too much to expect.

It was difficult to imagine Ashfordly and

district without the authoritative but re-assuring presence of Oscar Blaketon. In some ways, it marked the end of an era, the conclusion of an older and more personal-ized style of policing. The duration of the Blaketon era had been one where wisdom and experience were gained through long hours of working the beat and dealing with every problem created by the great British public.

That well-tested system had proved very effective and it took twelve or fifteen years' action-packed service before a constable was promoted to the rank of sergeant, and a further five or more to gain the exalted rank of inspector. Promotion was well and truly earned – police sergeants really did earn their stripes.

From a personal point of view there was an added dimension to Blaketon's retire-ment because he had expressed interest in purchasing the shop-cum-post office in Aidensfield. The idea of running that small village business was his retirement ideal, but I was not sure whether his perpetual pre-sence on my beat and in my own village would help or hinder my constabulary duties. It would be rather like having some-one permanently sitting on my shoulder and offering advice whether or not I wanted or needed it; he'd be like a guardian angel perhaps, or (more probably) the proverbial pain in the backside. I'd have to find ways of keeping him at a discreet distance from my daily duties.

It was with some personal trepidation, therefore, that I awaited the day of his departure while each of us wondered who would replace him. Various names cropped up in our speculative conversations but the odds-on favourite was Sergeant Raymond Craddock, the recently installed incumbent at Brantsford.

Brantsford was a small North Riding market town with cobbles upon its market place and a peaceful air that came through its position on the edge of the moor. With some interesting history and a charming rustic appearance, it was not plagued by tourists thanks to a fairly modern bypass. That road carried speeding traffic past Brantsford and along to the Yorkshire coast and moors.

Brantsford was only some eight miles from Ashfordly and due to the heralded amal-gamations of police forces, coupled with the subsequent merging and redrawing of boundaries of divisions, sub-divisions and sections – and, of course, thanks to modern means of communication and transport – it seemed inevitable that Brantsford and Ashfordly Sections would merge to become one larger unit supervised by a lone sergeant instead of the present two. As the sitting tenant, so to speak, Sergeant Craddock was the obvious choice, even if he was a bicycling, ballroom-dancing Welshman with no Yorkshire pedigree.

Visions of what the future might be buzzed around my head in the days following the news of Blaketon's impending retirement and it was Joe Steel, the current owner of the Aidensfield Stores and Post Office who confirmed my fears that Blaketon would soon become a villager upon my patch.

'Not long now, Nick!' he cheerfully told me one morning when I popped in for my customary visit. 'Just a few more months, then we're moving to the Lake District, Betty and me. It's our favourite place; we're going to Dockray, that's a village near Ullswater. Then we can spend our days pottering on the fells and walking by the lake beneath the trees...'

'Lucky you!' I said. 'It's one of our favourite places too, we go every summer with the children.'

'Then I hope you'll look us up next time you're there.' He sounded sincere.

'I will, that's a promise!' I would be pleased to keep in contact with Joe, adding, 'I understand Sergeant Blaketon has confirmed he's taking over your post office.'

I introduced the topic which would be the talking point of Aidensfield for weeks to come.

'He is. He's buying the house too. We've negotiated things so that he can move in immediately I move out – hopefully with a weekend in between. But the job can't stop.'

'Just like the police service,' I said somewhat inanely.

'He'll be fine.' I must have worn an expression of apprehension because Joe appeared to have read my thoughts.

'Blaketon the civilian will be a different person from Blaketon the police sergeant, you'll see. He's quite sociable when he's away from his job. I think he'll be a great help to you.'

'I might not be here all that long myself,' I said, and I think I must have looked rather wistful.

'You're leaving as well?' Joe sounded shocked.

'Not leaving the service, no,' and I explained the rumoured changes to the police service. 'It means there'll be no village constables. There'll be teams of constables operating in cars from a central place, like Ashfordly or Malton, Thirsk, Pickering and so forth. Round-the-clock mobile teams will be responsible for the supervision of rural areas instead of village constables. I'm not sure it's a good thing, we'll lose the personal touch.'

'There's talk of closing some rural post offices too,' Joe told me. 'Most people have

11

cars, even pensioners manage to run them, so the number of village post offices could be effectively reduced.'

'That won't please the locals!' I said.

'It won't, but that is the gospel according to some faceless bureaucrats in a city office somewhere. It's all to do with reducing costs. But it won't bother me or Betty! We'll be well away from red tape and government interference.'

'I forget who it was,' I smiled, 'but someone once said "Reforms are all right so long as they don't change anything" and I think I'd go along with that concept of things. But we can't and mustn't frustrate progress. Even if we don't like change, or can't understand it, it has to happen, Joe, and right now, you and me and Blaketon are part of that development.'

'Well, with Blaketon's appointment, it seems Aidensfield Post Office is secure for the foreseeable future, otherwise the powers-that-be wouldn't have sanctioned a new postmaster. Blaketon's got a few years left in him before he becomes an old age pensioner.'

'A good ten years,' I told him. 'Fifty-five might seem a bit early to put constables and sergeants out to grass, but it does give us chance to do something else with our lives. And some of the long-serving officers don't like change, it gives them chance to avoid the hassle that comes with change – and it stops them doing their best to halt change! One thing is for sure though – Ashfordly Police Station will merge with Brantsford for supervisory purposes,' I said. 'And I think Aidensfield rural beat will close, but perhaps not just yet.'

'Enjoy it while you can,' said Joe as a customer entered. 'And remember, there's one thing that your job and mine have in common.'

'What's that?' I asked.

'We deal with the public, every one of them, old, young, male, female, working and idle, nice and nasty; we see society in all its forms. And in a place like Aidensfield, it means we are given access to every house in the village. Not many professions can boast that kind of privilege. Not even the milkman calls at every house, neither does the nurse nor the doctor. Think about it. See you, Nick.'

'I will. 'Bye Joe.' When I left, his words lingered in my mind. It *was* a privilege to be allowed access to peoples' homes and even if the postman did visit every one of them during his rounds, I could not claim that kind of unrestricted access. There was a possibility I might visit every house at one time or another on very infrequent occasions, but to date I had been inside very few. That made me realize how little I really did know about the village in which I lived – and how little I knew about the people amongst whom I worked.

Who were all those people living their quiet lives behind closed doors and drawn curtains? What did their homes look like on the inside? Did the interior of a house give any indication of the personality of the owner or occupier? If so, what would it reveal to a policeman? Had I the right to intrude upon their privacy? I had not, I told myself – but that did not prevent me being intrigued by the variety of lives, worries, successes, fears, happiness and every other human emotion which lay behind the sturdy stone walls of the houses of Aidensfield and district.

With these thoughts in my mind, I realized that it was the vision of Blaketon living in Aidensfield which had prompted my speculation about others.

So he was already exerting some influence upon me … but it was true that his forthcoming arrival in our midst did encourage me to learn more about the people who lived and worked on my patch.

One of the houses I had never entered since my arrival was called Rookery Cottage, a surprising name because there was no rookery in the village nor had there been one here within living memory. The nearest

14

colony of rooks was several miles away, in the woods above Maddleskirk Abbey, but the name had obviously meant something in the past, even if its importance was no longer evident.

The charming single-storey stone cottage with its blue-tiled roof and tiny garden was tucked neatly away behind some larger properties at the western end of Aidensfield. This meant visitors and delivery people experienced difficulty in finding it – its tiny size made it even more difficult to locate. A narrow unsurfaced track led to it from the main street and that lane was just wide enough to permit access by a small car. The solitary occupant of Rookery Cottage was himself a small, slightly built man who ran an Austin Mini Traveller in which he transported his two equally tiny Jack Russell terriers. From time to time I noticed him heading for the moors with the excited dogs in the rear, ready for an unrestricted gallop among the bracken and heather, and whenever our paths crossed, he would always wave cheerily from his Mini or, if I was on foot, greet me with a brisk 'Good morning, Constable' but little else.

In the village, all the adults referred to him as Mac, and all respectful children called him Mr Mac; almost everyone used that abbreviated name when chatting to him face-to-face. It seems he did not object, perhaps regarding this relaxed mode of address as friendly and welcoming, a sign of acceptance perhaps? Because he was universally referred to merely as Mac, it was some time before I learned his surname was MacGregor, and even longer before I discovered his Christian name was Stuart. I was never sure whether he had Scottish ancestry because he spoke without a trace of a Scots accent and never made any reference to that country. He did not have a Yorkshire accent either and I suppose his speech could be described as firmly within that range which some consider to be BBC English – that is English supposedly spoken without an accent. In truth, that, in itself, is an accent.

Like his charming little house, Mac was small and very neat. In his mid-fifties, he was only some five feet two inches tall, slimly built and very dapper with a good head of tidy, well-groomed dark-brown hair, a small dark moustache, dark-brown eyes without spectacles and what appeared to be a good set of his own teeth. Even when going about casual activities, like walking his dogs or popping into the pub for a pint, he was immaculately dressed. He always wore a collar and tie and usually sported a pair of smartly pressed cavalry twill trousers with a Harris tweed jacket, even in the height of summer. On more formal occasions, like going to church on Sundays or attending funerals, he would appear in a smart dark-grey suit, white shirt and dark-red tie, immaculate as ever. Not once did I see him with his shirt-sleeves rolled up, or clad in a short-sleeved garment.

I knew that he lived alone – there was no Mrs Mac but I did not know whether that was by choice, or whether he was a widower, and it seemed he did not have children or relations to call on him. Whatever his domestic history, he seemed to prefer a quiet and very private life, not inviting people in for a coffee or alcoholic drinks, although whenever he met anyone in the village street, he was chatty and very friendly. Over time, however, I came to realize he kept people at a distance – he had lots of acquaintances but very few close friends. Even when he popped into the pub for a drink, he arrived alone and went home alone, although he chattered quite cheerily to the regulars when he was there.

In due course, I was presented with an opportunity to visit his neat little house. In the internal mail from Force Headquarters, there was a letter from Department D.1 of the London Metropolitan Police. It asked the local constabulary to check a reference supplied by an applicant who wished to join the Metropolitan Police. D.1 was the department which dealt with recruiting for

17

the Met and, according to their letter, a man called Philip John Westland, a former army sergeant, had made application to become a constable in that force.

His application form had been accompanied by the necessary references, one of which had been supplied by Major Stuart MacGregor. MacGregor, continued the letter, had since retired from military service and was now living at Rookery Cottage, Aidensfield. It seemed that Westland had previously served with Major MacGregor and the letter, currently at Ashfordly Police Station, asked that a constable visit the major to check, that he had in fact supplied the reference for Westland.

Fake references were not uncommon and the police always checked those accompanying any job applications within the service, whether for police recruits or civilian staff.

'Here's a pleasant and simple little task for you, Rhea. No doubt I shall be meeting Major MacGregor before too long; it's nice to know there are people of such standing in Aidensfield. I wonder if he plays golf?'

'He doesn't seem to socialize very much,' I had to tell Blaketon.

'Perhaps he needs a kindred spirit, a man of like personality and standing, someone retired from high office, like I shall be.' Blaketon was chatty that morning as he handed the Metropolitan Police letter to

18

me. 'You will know that I have bought your village shop and post office, Rhea?'

'I had heard, Sergeant,' I acknowledged. 'I hope you can cope with the morning rush of letters...'

'I can cope with any kind of panic, Rhea. Morning rush hour, queues for pensions, advice on overseas postage costs, Christmas mail – you name it and I shall cope! Whatever comes my way will not be all that different from coping with the great British public while serving as a police officer. And I am pleased you have heard about my new career. Knowing about such developments within Aidensfield is the hallmark of a good constable, one who has an ear to the ground and a keen desire to maintain an up-to-date knowledge of events on his patch. A proficient constable needs to know everything that is happening within his area of responsibility, Rhea. I am pleased to note that you know what's going on.'

'I hope you will be happy in Aidensfield.' I was not quite sure what to say in these circumstances.

'I shall be very happy, Rhea, and I trust I shall enjoy my retirement in a crime-free village, one which is devoid of litter, safe from acts of vandalism and well policed by a dedicated and highly professional constable.'

'And I hope all our letters get delivered on

time, that our piles of Christmas cards don't smother you, that your stamps all stick on as surely they should, that you have a queue-free post office and that applicants for dog licences don't bite you,' I grinned. I hoped he would not consider my remarks facetious but I knew he concealed a deep sense of humour which could be exploited on occasions.

'I have a lot to learn and coping with it on a daily basis is the finest way of learning, but I am sure we shall get along very well together in our new roles, Rhea,' he chuckled. 'After all, we've had some good times in the past; I have enjoyed working with you ... but I must not delay your work. You have an important enquiry to complete on behalf of our colleagues in London.'

I left Ashfordly Police Station in the knowledge that I had been formally notified by Blaketon that he was about to become my local postmaster. I wondered if Alf Ventress, young Bellamy and the others had been personally given this news? If so, we'd have to organize some kind of farewell event for Blaketon and perhaps a collection for a retirement gift. That would all be done once we had a firm date for his departure, and I made a mental note to discuss it with Alf Ventress.

In the meantime, though, I had an official reason to call at Rookery Cottage.

Before calling, I rang Mac and made an appointment to see him. He suggested 10.30 the following day and promised coffee and biscuits – 'something to keep out the cold', he said. At the appointed time, and with the necessary correspondence under my arm, I tapped on his clean, white door and was admitted almost immediately.

'The heating's gone off!' were his first words. 'These spring mornings can be quite chilly, but come in, the coffee's nearly ready. That'll warm us up. Black or white?'

'White, no sugar, thanks,' I responded.

As expected, he was immaculately dressed as if for a formal meeting – smart jacket, trousers, shoes, collar and tie, with not a hair out of place – and he ushered me into a minuscule lounge with its two chairs at each end of a highly polished antique mahogany coffee table. Milk, sugar and side plates along with a selection of biscuits were already in place, but the room was as cold as the North Pole. I noticed the fireplace contained paper and kindling topped by pieces of coal, as if ready to be ignited, but for some reason Mac had not put a match to it. He bade me be seated then disappeared into the kitchen to busy himself with the coffee and so I settled down in the chilly room and placed my papers on the table.

He returned within minutes bearing two china cups on saucers and placed them on the table. 'Help yourself to milk,' he invited, pointing to the matching jug. 'So, when you rang, you said it was about a reference I had supplied? There's nothing wrong with it, is there?'

'Oh, no, it's routine,' and I explained our system of checking the authenticity of references relating to posts within the police service. He agreed that it was a wise and necessary precaution. As I was explaining things to him, I produced my copy of the reference he had supplied for Philip John Westland and asked if he had written the reference; I also checked that it was his signature upon it. He had written it, he assured me; it was a genuine document and so, within seconds, our brief but necessary business was concluded.

It was over far too quickly – I had not even begun to enjoy my coffee nor had I had time to learn more about the quiet Stuart MacGregor. He seemed happy to extend his hospitality, bringing in his two terriers – Ben and Nevis – for me to pat and stroke, and chatting about inconsequential things like village matters such as garden fêtes and local dances, and the adverse effect of loud pop music on the ears of young people. He insisted I had a second cup of coffee, once again apologizing for the chilly atmosphere and adding he had called out an engineer to his oil-fired heating boiler; the fellow was expected this afternoon. Mac said he would be in the house all day and that statement made me wonder anew why he did not light his fire.

I was still wondering when I left to go home to write my report which would form the official response to the Metropolitan Police. At least I could get warm at home! Even if the electrically powered night-storage heater in my office had failed, I knew Mary would have a coal fire in the lounge. Truthfully, I was not too chilled because the walk home warmed me through and the early frost had disappeared, but I must admit I continued to wonder why Mac had not lit his fire.

It was particularly puzzling as he'd entertained a visitor. I didn't think he was short of money, nor was he a miser. The general appearance of his house, albeit small, suggested money was not a problem and in all other respects, he had made me most welcome. However, I told myself, the way he lived his life at home was nothing to do with me so I completed my report and would return it to Ashfordly Police Station during my next visit, from where it would find its way via Force Headquarters to the Metropolitan Police Recruiting Department. I hoped the anonymous Mr Westland would have a satisfactory career with them.

With Mac's chilly existence at the back of

my mind, it was a week or two later when my delivery of coal arrived. As I boasted a coal shed of considerable size, I could accommodate a ton or more and after Ken had emptied the last bagful, I went outside to pay him. For a few moments, we chatted about inconsequential things then jokingly, I said, 'You make a better living out of me than you do out of Mac in Rookery Cottage!'

'He never has any coal in the place,' Ken told me. 'Not one piece – except a few bits on the lounge fire which he never lights. The outgoing couple laid that fire as a welcome for him when he moved in – that was ten years ago or more – and he's never put a match to it. It's just like it was all those years ago. He won't have a fire in the house, Nick, not an oil lamp or even a candle. Not a naked flame anywhere.'

'Not even in the depths of winter?'

'Never,' confirmed Ken. 'He relies on his oil-fired central heating.'

'No wonder the house feels cold!' and I told him about Mac's heating problems during my recent visit.

'He's got it fixed, I saw him a couple of days ago. He's a nice chap, Nick. He's not overcareful with his money in spite of his name.'

'So why won't he have a fire in the house? Is he afraid of fire or something?'

'Yes, he is afraid of fire, Nick, well, *afraid is* maybe not the right word. Very respectful might be a better way of putting it because he is a brave man. He's no coward. His wife died in a house fire, so I'm told, long before he came here. He did some kind of brilliant rescue, he saved another woman who was in the house with her at the time but lost his wife. A mate of mine told me; he lives near Lincoln, that's where Mac comes from; that's where the fire was. It happened before he came to live here. In fact, I think it was his wife's death that made him want to live somewhere else and Rookery Cottage happened to be on the market. There was quite a splash about it in the papers at the time. Now, though, he won't risk the same thing happening to himself, he hates the idea of his own house catching fire. So he never buys coal, Nick.'

'Oh, crumbs, I had no idea,' and I was pleased I had not mentioned the absence of a warm fire to him. If the poor fellow had lost his wife in a blaze, I could understand his reluctance.

'Thanks, Ken, thanks for telling me.'

'He doesn't talk about it, Nick, so keep it to yourself. Mac did once apologize because he wasn't buying coal, but that's as far as it went. He never said he was afraid, but I reckon he just wants to make sure he doesn't risk another blaze. He doesn't smoke, he never lights a candle, won't use an oil lamp, not even in his little greenhouse. In fact, I doubt if he's got a box of matches in the place, and he never goes into the pub lounge when the fire's on. He'll use one of the other bar rooms.'

'I'd never noticed that, but it might explain his lack of social contact, Ken,' I mused. 'It seems he doesn't want to visit places where there is a coal fire. And if folks do like to see one blazing away when it's chilly, he won't oblige. Do you think the villagers know the circumstances of his wife's death?'

'I think somebody would have mentioned it if they had known. I've never breathed a word, except to you, and I know you'll be discreet.'

Having been educated into this aspect of Mac's life, I regarded him with a new respect and was determined not to reveal my new-found knowledge to anyone. But fate, with one of its famous twists, was determined to do otherwise.

Some weeks later, Mac was enjoying a late afternoon walk with Ben and Nevis on the edge of the moor beyond the village. It was a route they frequently followed; it carried them through the village, over the beck by the stone bridge and up to the moor with wide views across Aidensfield, the railway station and the surrounding landscape. At

that late stage of the afternoon, the landscape was dotted with lights as houses and
farms prepared for darkness. Cars and other
vehicles were illuminated too, as they went
about their business either in the village or
upon its approach roads.

But among all that blossoming illumin-
ation, Mac noticed a different sort of light:
it was flickering and it came from within a
moorland cottage which was otherwise in
darkness. At first, he thought it was light
and shadow cast by the coal fire, but quickly
realized the effect was far greater than any
domestic fire. He knew that the cottage was
on fire and, judging by the glow from the
window, it seemed to be confined to the
living room-cum-kitchen. In these moorland homes, people lived in their kitchens
which was really a lounge with cooking
facilities, either a coal fire or an oven tucked
into one corner. Mac also knew, by dint of
his regular walks along this route, that it was
the home of an 84-year-old semi-invalid
widow called Ada Pickard. From his
position high on the moors, he realized he
was a considerable distance from Ada's
lonely home and his immediate dilemma
was whether to seek help first, or run to her
house first. He chose the former on the
grounds that if the house really was on fire,
the presence of the Fire Brigade was crucial.
So Mac ran as fast as his legs could carry

him, first to a telephone kiosk on the edge of the village where he gasped out his story during a 999 call, and then to Ada's house.

I know all this because, after the event, I had to obtain a long written statement from him to account for his part in her rescue. But I am leaping ahead at this point. When Mac arrived at Ada's cottage – and he was first on the scene – he could see from the outside that the downstairs interior was well ablaze but there was no sign of Ada. He knew she lived downstairs, her semi-invalidity meant she could not cope with a staircase. She'd have been cooking her tea either on the fire or on the stove ... maybe she'd gone to sleep and the fat of her frying pan had caused the blaze?

But in those desperate moments he cared for none of that kind of speculation, that was for later. He knew the dangers of opening her front door, it would create more draughts which would fuel the flames, but there was no alternative. He had to get into the house, he had to see if she was there and the door was his only point of entry.

Pausing only to drench himself from head to toe from a bucket of cold water outside the door, Mac burst into the house taking the bucket with him, slammed the door shut behind him and began to look for Ada. When he entered the kitchen, her chair, curtains and carpet were ablaze, with flames roaring up the chimney and the tell-tale frying pan lying in the hearth. Her hair and clothes were alight too and she was lying on the mat unable or too frightened to move. Making best use of his limited supply of water, he threw the contents of the bucket over her, rolled her into a large clip rug which was scorched but not burning and began to drag her from the flames, away from danger and out into the cold, dark, night. He could not carry her, she was a heavy old woman and he was a little man, but, in his anxiety, he produced unexpected strength from somewhere and managed to drag her unceremoniously to safety outside of the house. After making sure she was free from flames, he tried to quench the blaze in the house. He had the bucket, there was a trough of water outside and there were taps inside, so he began to throw useless bucketsful into the house, through the window that had smashed in the heat and through the open door whose cavity now meant nothing to those rampant tongues of fire.

As he laboured mightily, the Fire Brigade arrived, rapidly followed by Dr Archie McGee from Elsinby, myself and several villagers who had seen the fire appliance hurtle through the village towards the fierce glow in the sky. Everything seemed to be happening at once as it does on these dramatic occasions, but out of chaos came some kind of order and the house was saved from further damage.

Ada survived although she was badly burnt and had to spend a long time in hospital, after which she was admitted to a nursing home. Later, we learned she had placed a pan of fat on the fire to make herself some chips for tea, but had fallen asleep and the fat had caught fire. Her house was not totally destroyed, but the kitchen area was severely damaged and required complete renovation, a job for Ashfordly Estate who owned the property. But the hero of the moment was Stuart MacGregor. He tried to hide from the Press who wanted to interview him afterwards, but they found him and photographed him and elicited his story, partly from by-standers and partly from the reluctant man himself.

What none of us knew, until a glamorized account of his actions appeared in various local papers, was that Mac was a hero even before attempting to rescue his wife and her friend from that earlier fire. During the war, he had saved the entire crew of an armoured tank from certain death when it had caught fire following an enemy attack. Mac, then a captain in the army, had dragged out the crew, risking his own life to haul them from the blazing vehicle and getting severely burnt himself, oddly enough, his face and head had been unscathed, probably due to a helmet he'd been wearing, but his body had been badly scarred for life. Which, I reasoned, was why he always wore long sleeves and formal attire. But he had been awarded the Military Cross for his bravery during that incident, later being promoted to major.

I had to go back to Rookery Cottage a couple of days after Ada's fire to obtain a long and detailed statement from him. Much to my surprise, the lounge fire was burning as he showed me into the tiny room.

'Things come in threes, Nick,' he smiled. 'I've survived three fires, so I reckon I'll not encounter another. It does make a house nice and warm, doesn't it? A cosy feel, and so comfortable.'

'You're not frightened of your own house catching fire, then?' I smiled.

'I'm not frightened of fire, if that's what you were thinking. But I have great respect for it and I never tempt fate. But things do come in threes, Constable, and my three fire events have come and gone. If a fire does happen again, in this house, I shall cope,' he said. 'But look, I don't want a fuss making over this, I just did what anyone would have done.'

'Someone else might have panicked;

someone else might have thought it was a bonfire in the darkness and done nothing; someone else might have made the blaze worse, someone else might not have done things in the right sequence ... you did all the right things, Mac, so your contribution was rather special – and most important so far as Ada was concerned. So come on, talk to me. I need the full and factual story.'

'How about a glass of whisky to warm us up as I talk?' he smiled.

'I don't normally drink on duty, but I think I can make an exception on this occasion,' I said, realizing you never knew who or what was behind closed doors.

Chapter 2

One of the most intriguing houses in Aidensfield was the one known as Kirkside. It had been given this name because it stood in its own walled grounds very close to All Saints Anglican Parish Church. It was a handsome house of considerable size and stature, and one could have been forgiven for thinking it had been a former vicarage but that was not the case. It had never been the residence of any Aidensfield vicars; indeed, the owners were Catholics and had been for generations. Nonetheless, it boasted the very distinctive appearance of an imposing Victorian vicarage and one story was that the gentleman who had commissioned its construction around 1860 – a man called Groves – had always wanted to live in a house which was comparable in stature, size and appearance to the home of the local reverend Anglican gentleman. As a Catholic layman, Mr Groves had felt he was equal to any Protestant minister under whatever guise he appeared. As a consequence, Kirkside had materialized in all its splendour right next door to the church. It was an extremely spacious and beautifully proportioned house of local stone with a blue slate roof and lots of windows enjoying far-reaching views of the dale. It was surrounded by lawned grounds full of shrubs, trees and soft fruit and there was also a vegetable patch. Internally, it boasted seven bedrooms, a massive lounge, morning-room, dining-room, kitchen, wine cellar and sundry other rooms, one with a piscina. All were served by a grand oak-panelled entrance hall containing a gallery landing above a wide and elegant sweeping staircase. None of it would have looked out of place in a cardinal's residence, an Anglican archbishop's palace or even a royal household.

The problem with this wonderful place,

however, was that the present owner, unlike his illustrious and wealthy ancestors, could not afford to maintain it. In spite of its undoubted style and evident past splendour, it was always shabby. There was a sad and perpetual air of dusty neglect about both the house and its once-pleasing grounds. The windows never looked clean, the curtains looked dirty, the external woodwork was always in need of fresh coats of paint and the gutters around the roof needed to be cleared of weeds and leaves which had gathered over the years. The forecourt and paths around the house were in dire need of weeding too, while the large and once fine garden was overgrown and neglected. Much as I would have longed to own such a place, I realized that my very modest police salary would never allow me such a privilege, and it was equally clear that the present occupant of Kirkside had neither the money, the time nor even the inclination to lavish the necessary care upon it.

Like so many of the village households, this was one into which I would love to have been invited. In the early stages of my posting to Aidensfield, there hadn't been any reason to visit the family or their house, but in due course, I learned that the owner/occupier was called Trevor Groves. He was a tall, lithe but rather quiet man approaching forty with thinning light-brown hair, heavy-rimmed spectacles and a somewhat pale complexion. The house had been built by Trevor's great-grandfather and inherited by the eldest son ever since – the family had been wealthy furniture store owners until the effects of the Depression then World War II had resulted in closure of his business.

In spite of his troubles, Trevor's father had clung on to the house in the face of tremendous odds and with very little money; upon his death he'd left it to Trevor albeit with no cash to maintain it. For some reason, in spite of inheriting such a fine property, Trevor seldom looked happy or fulfilled; he looked as if he bore the worries of the world upon his slender shoulders. I wondered if he was suffering at work, or facing some financial or personal crisis. Certainly, the air of neglect which surrounded the house did seem to have affected Trevor.

By contrast, his wife, Alison, was chubby and cheerful with a ponytail of light-brown hair which complemented a round and happy face. Shorter and a couple of years younger than her husband, she had never worked since producing her family. In spite of Trevor's perpetual gloom, she managed to look cheerful most of the time, but I think her husband's general demeanour was starting to affect her. There were times she looked jaded and weary, as if a good holiday or even an evening out might revive her spirits. They had three children, two boys called James and John who were fourteen and twelve respectively and a ten-year-old girl called Judith, all of whom regularly attended Aidensfield's Catholic Church of St Aidan. That's how, over the months, I gradually became better acquainted with the family.

Trevor's permanent solemnity did not appear to affect the children; they were a very happy trio of youngsters who enjoyed living in the ample space of their rambling home. I don't think they worried that the family car was a battered twelve-year-old Ford or that Mum and Dad seemed to be existing on a pittance.

When Trevor went off to work in the car, Alison and the children used bicycles to travel the countryside and the cheerful cycling Groves were a familiar sight in the lanes and byways of the district. Trevor joined their cycling activities at weekends when the family would ride out to the moors for a picnic or merely tour the villages and market towns as a form of exercise or recreation. That seemed to cheer him up, but they never took long holidays; if Trevor did take an extended period off work, it resulted in more cycle trips and he took the children to see places of historic interest such as Rievaulx Abbey, Byland Abbey, Castle Howard, the Cawthorne Camps and Pickering Castle.

On some occasions, Trevor would use his car for trips deep into the moors and dales so that he could transport an easel, paint and brushes from which he produced well-executed watercolours of the better known places around the North York Moors. I believe he sold his work to people who appreciated it and, hearing him talk among friends, I wondered whether he yearned for the life of a freelance artist. As I came to know more about him, Trevor reminded me of a former colleague called Alan Knight. Alan, a policeman for twelve years, was never happy in his work, detesting the shift system and the ponderous man-management style of mid-ranking supervisory police officers. Like Trevor, Alan was a very talented artist who was capable of producing desirable seascapes and highly attractive scenes of ships in full sail. Much to everyone's surprise – and admiration – PC Knight threw up his secure job, complete with a free police house, to pursue his ambition to become a full-time artist. And so he did achieve considerable success through much hard work.

Some time ago, Alan and I had met in a pub and he'd told me how he'd done it ... so,

I asked myself, if Alan could take that kind of giant step, why could not Trevor? After all, Trevor had a house of his own. Surely that was a bonus? Trevor did not have the burden of a free police house which would have to be vacated upon departure from the service, neither was he paying rent.

With my limited knowledge of art, but knowing what the public would buy, I thought Trevor had the necessary talent, but earning a living from art, especially with the responsibility of a growing family, is fraught with danger no matter how talented the individual. In spite of Alan Knight's success, I felt that living the precarious life of a full-time artist would make retention of the big old house even more difficult. It wasn't impossible, though.

For all their very evident financial hardship, the Groves were a likeable, respected, well-rounded, polite and very knowledge-able family. On balance, I think they were very content in spite of financial hardship and certainly, Trevor enjoyed his leisure time on the moors with his family.

As time went by, Mary became more friendly with Alison, Trevor's wife, and con-sequently I saw more of him, coming to know him a little better with each passing month. During that time, I gained the impression that his painting was becoming more important than his job. Certainly, it was more rewarding from the point of view of personal satisfaction. He worked hard in the little spare time he had, and from time to time I did see his work on sale in the locality, sometimes in small galleries and on occasions in shops and even restaurants.

He even painted a very atmospheric picture of the Virgin Mary at the feet of Jesus during the crucifixion and gave this to the village's Catholic Church to mark the hundredth anniversary of its construction. His landscapes were now selling very quickly and the extra income helped the Groves to pay some important bills whose totals increased in direct proportion to the growth of their children. Clearly, though, Trevor's time spent painting was extremely limited, due partially to his work and partially to his never-ending domestic commitments. As I observed his behaviour over the months, I began to wonder whether he might throw up his job for the uncertain life of a professional artist.

Trevor worked at a small engineering factory on the outskirts of York. Each day, he drove the twenty-two miles or so to work, leaving Aidensfield around seven in the morning and returning shortly after six each evening. The factory specialized in making components for motor vehicles and seemed to produce everything from wheel discs to windscreen wipers by way of petrol filler caps and metal door fittings. Trevor's responsibility involved quality control; I was never quite sure what that involved, except that it was not a very senior post and he was not one of the bosses even though he could boast some managerial skills. I do know that he worked for a rather modest salary and that, on occasions, he seemed rather frustrated with his professional duties. On one occasion, he told me that he'd rather be out on the moors painting his watercolours than coping with the vagaries of bosses and workers alike as they churned out a never-ending supply of metal bits and pieces for motor cars.

As my knowledge of him increased, I realized he was unhappy working with other people and it was increasingly evident that he was growing very dissatisfied with his rather dull and routine job. What had been a secure means of supporting his family now lacked that vital spark of interest; the older he got, the more he wanted to do something more meaningful with his life. I realized – and I think he did too – that he'd rather be working alone, as his own master, so that he might develop his personal skills and his undoubted artistic ability. Those who knew Trevor felt the same as I – that he was a proverbial square peg in a round hole, working at a job he did not relish, one which did not seem to fulfil him and one which he did not enjoy. Again, I was reminded of Alan Knight and this connection was reinforced whenever I talked to Trevor. Usually, that was after Mass when some of us popped into the local pub for a pint before lunch.

Most of us advised Trevor that he should be doing something more creative, something to exercise his talents even if it meant less money and no security. It would be better than suffering a boring, routine job even if that job did carry a regular wage which serviced the household bills. I did wonder, though, whether the fact that Trevor lived in such a large house was the root cause of his dissatisfaction. Even without a mortgage, maintaining such a mansion must stretch his limited finances and that must create stress within himself and ultimately his family. Merely heating the place in winter must have cost a fortune and there was always the price of petrol and never-ending car maintenance to be funded in order to get to work. A daily forty-five mile round trip would not come cheap.

I felt that Trevor was paddling like fury merely to stand still. Unremitting financial demands were bound to cause anguish while putting him constantly under pressure, and instead of progressing along some kind of career ladder, he would be doing all in his power merely to maintain the famous status quo. Unpopular though the decision

41

was, I do know he and Alison had discussed selling the house to move into something smaller; he had mentioned this several times during one of our chats in the pub over a pint, but I knew his heart was not in that solution. He did not really want to leave Kirkside or Aidensfield. However, it was nothing to do with me, as I had told myself on frequent occasions. The domestic lives of others were not my concern!

Then, out of the blue, came an invitation to Kirkside. It was Trevor's birthday, his fortieth, and therefore worthy of celebration, and Alison had arranged a buffet supper for some of his friends. Mary and I were invited; the party was to be in Kirkside, making full use of its splendid rooms and thus I would enter its imposing portals for the first time. The Groves were not party people – most of their friends had young families anyway which meant it was never easy to arrange a date which suited everyone, so this was clearly a very special occasion.

On the night of the event, we had arranged for Mrs Quarry, our baby-sitter, to look after our own four children and, feeling very cheerful at the prospect of a night out, we walked down the hill into the village and along the street to Kirkside. Although it was a chilly evening, we enjoyed the walk.

Kirkside stood behind a very high stone

wall which fronted the street. There were two entrances in that wall, each leading to the gravelled forecourt behind it, and thus a one-way traffic system could be implemented! But we were walking, therefore car-parking was not a problem. The front door, a sturdy oak structure with iron studs and massive hinges like those of a castle keep, was located beneath a pediment supported by a pair of Tuscan pillars. A most imposing entrance. A temporary sign outside said, 'Walk In, Don't Knock!' and so we obeyed. As we entered, clutching our present for Trevor (a music token as we'd heard he liked the classics), I was staggered by the adornment on the interior wall immediately to our left. That wall, a huge broad expanse which rose to the height of two floors and almost the width of two substantial rooms, was decorated with a colossal brightly coloured mural. My first impression was a broad canvas of rich dark colours, deep reds and warm greens, but as my eyes grew accustomed to it, I saw it was a mythical scene full of human figures, male and female, which showed some apparently airborne upon wings like angels. Others were engaged in a variety of activities which required some detailed study and in the middle background was what appeared to be an area of barren landscape surrounded by the pale blue ocean.

43

It was the kind of huge picture that requires the viewer to stand back at a great distance in order to appreciate it and to study the detailed content, and I wondered if such a view could be obtained from the wonderful staircase which climbed to the first floor over to my right. Then our hosts appeared through another door to welcome us and after discarding our coats in a cloakroom, we were ushered into a bright and spacious room full of people – the lounge – and handed a glass of wine.

Next, we were introduced to those who had already arrived. I estimated there were about fifty people at the party, including the Groves' own children who were helping dispense drinks and canapés. Beyond doubt, the house was large enough to accommodate everyone with ease; supper was laid out on two long tables in the adjoining dining-room and when everyone was present, we would eventually be invited to help ourselves.

It was a most enjoyable occasion and we met people from Trevor's place of work – workers like himself, he told us, and not the bosses – and we also met some of his relations while chatting to other guests from Aidensfield and nearby villages. Then, around nine o'clock, Trevor stood upon a stool and called for our attention. Having persuaded us to become silent, he thanked us for coming and for our presents, thanked Alison for organizing the party, told us that supper was next door and that we had to help ourselves both to food and more drinks. But he also said he had something else to tell us, some family news.

'I wanted you all to know at the same time,' he said; adding swiftly, 'We're moving. Alison and I have talked about it for a long time – and discussed it with the children I might add – and it's not been an easy decision, but we think we should be closer to my work, so we're going to put Kirkside on the market. We've found a nice semi-detached house in one of the York suburbs and we shall be putting in an offer. I know it means leaving something dear to us, something that is a part of our family – Kirkside I mean – but the new house will be handy for work and the shops, and close to schools for the children and Alison might get a job...'

'But you can't!' someone called. It was one of his relations, because he added, 'You can't leave Kirkside, Trevor! It's your family home! It was built for you ... you can't abandon it!'

'It was my great-grandparents' house, then my grandparents' and then my parents', and now it has come down to me as my inheritance. But it's too big and expensive for a modern family, and far too costly to heat; it needs someone with more money than I have but I won't go into the boring details. Quite simply, I can't afford to maintain the house in the manner in which it ought to be kept,' he smiled. 'It needs a loving owner with lots of money and more time than I have! I know it is a break with family tradition, but time cannot stand still and we have to accept progress, whether or not we like it. Anyway, we thought you, as our friends, should be the first to know about our decision.'

It was quite evident from the shocked response of the gathering that no one wanted the Groves to leave Kirkside and an uneasy silence fell upon the assembly, but that was speedily broken by Alison who called loudly, 'Come on everyone, this is a party, not a wake! Food's in the dining-room, help yourselves. Get a drink as well, and then I'll propose a toast to Trevor, and to our new and exciting future as townies. James, John, Judith, make sure everyone has a full glass...'

Trevor's news provided a lively debating point for the rest of the evening with some us thinking he had made the right choice, believing he had no alternative if he wanted to live a quiet and contented life made easier by sufficient money for domestic essentials.

According to the townies present at the

party, life in a smaller house in the suburbs might solve all his problems; he'd be handy for the shops and for work and there was the works canteen for cheap meals and evening entertainment and he wouldn't need to run a car. But those of us accustomed to a country style of life felt he was making a mistake. He'd miss the open spaces, the freedom of the moors and dales, village life, the opportunity to practise his art in the open air – and he'd miss the house itself, in spite of all the problems it was now giving him and Alison. Somehow, I couldn't envisage Trevor settling down to a dull factory job while living in the blandness of suburbia and falling into the trap of trying to keep up with the neighbours. Although I could understand his motives, I thought he was making a grave error, one born out of financial considerations rather than a true desire to be nearer work or close to the shops. Trevor was an individual and an artist, not a factory worker or a suburbanite; he'd be miserable if he was closer to the job he disliked. As a countryman, he'd be miserable living in a town, too – and so the discussions went on, sometimes between ourselves and Trevor or Alison, and sometimes among the other guests.

Then, as one invariably does at these events, I needed to attend the toilet and so I excused myself and made my way to the cloakroom. Leaving the crush of people, it meant a trek through that wonderful hall with its amazing mural and I made a resolution that I would stop and examine it in detail on my return journey. I could do so in peace while everyone was partying. And so I did. I stood as far away from it as I could, even climbing halfway up the flight of stairs to gain a wider view.

Then Trevor emerged from the party, also *en route* to the cloakroom and saw me. He stopped to see what was creating such interest in me.

'I'm admiring the mural.' I descended the stairs to talk to him. 'Who painted it?'

'I did.' He grinned almost mischievously. 'I didn't know what to do with that huge expanse of undecorated wall so rather than cover it with emulsion, I did that. It took a long time, Nick, but it's covered up a lot of dodgy plasterwork and a few screw holes, and it was cheaper than buying wallpaper.'

'I think it's brilliant, a real work of art. So what's going to happen to it when you move house? Is it on a board of some kind? Can you take it with you?'

He laughed. 'No way! It's painted directly on to the wall, and I can't take the wall with me. Besides, there's no way a thing of that size would fit into a semi, not even as a floor covering! And don't suppose any buyer of this house would want it, so I'll probably cover it up – with emulsion! Or wallpaper!'

'I'd be trying to find a way of preserving it.' I could not imagine anyone putting such an amount of expert work in a project of this kind and then destroying it. 'It looks like something from the roof of the Sistine Chapel.'

'I got the idea from Tintoretto's *The Ascension,*' he told me. 'That's in Venice, I think, not Rome. This is not a copy of that work, but it gave me the idea. I call this *"The Council of Ten"*, although you'll see there are seventeen faces in the picture.'

'That's sounds distinctly puzzling to a simple mortal like me!'

'The Council of Ten was a group in the old Venetian republic,' he told me. 'They had unlimited powers – not a very good thing for good government – and there were ten of them. Later, they expanded to include seventeen members, but they still called themselves the Council of Ten; they disappeared with the fall of the republic in 1797,' he added.

'So there are seventeen faces in the mural?' I proffered that piece of wisdom to him. 'I haven't counted them.'

'Right!' he grinned. 'Seventeen faces beaming down from my wall.'

'So,' – my mind was still searching for the reason why he would use seventeen faces from an obscure Venetian government and

49

reproduce them as if they were performing various activities on the wall of his house – 'why select those people? Is there some kind of link between this painting and that ancient group? Or a link between this house and the Council of Ten?'

'Oh, no, not at all, nothing like that.' He was enjoying himself now, 'But there are seventeen bosses at work, with differing responsibilities, and they're all there, in this mural. Disguised, I might add, they'll never recognize themselves, but they're all there, from the managing director downwards.'

'Your way of hitting back at them for some reason?'

'Absolutely right, Nick, they're like that Council of Ten, too powerful by far, too inefficient, too insular, far too ignorant of the needs of the work-force, too wrapped up in their own elevated world ... it's not good for the company, Nick ... it makes me so frustrated...'

'None of them are here, are they? At your party?'

'Oh, no, I didn't invite them, the people from work who are here are some of my shop-floor colleagues.'

'They won't recognize the bosses on your wall then?'

'No chance. If I've depicted a man, say in the adultery section...'

'Adultery section?' I puzzled again.

'Oh, yes, I realized that each of my bosses has either broken one of the Ten Commandments or is guilty of one of the seven deadly sins, gluttony, sloth, lust, envy and so on, and there's "Thou shalt not steal; Thou shalt not covet thy neighbour's wife; Thou shalt not bear false witness against thy neighbour", and so on, so I've incorporated all those sins in this picture, with the face of the person who's doing such wrongs, but you'll have to hunt pretty hard to find them all...'

'Ten Commandments, seven deadly sins.' I could see how his mind was working now. 'That's seventeen in all. Seventeen people, seventeen sins, seventeen members of the Council of Ten ... very good, Trevor. But if they do happen to recognize themselves...'

'They won't. If a man has been guilty of, say, stealing parts from work for his own car, I've shown him as a woman shoplifting. I've disguised all their features, but I know who they are!'

'It's a clever piece of work.' I was staggered by its implications and range of meanings. Would anyone, apart from its creator, be able to interpret this mural?

'I enjoyed doing it,' he smiled. 'It kept me sane, trying to cope with a batch of bad bosses.'

'And you're going to give all this up to be closer to them!' I said. 'I can't imagine you wanting to live so close to such a bunch of bad bosses!'

'There's no option.' He shrugged his shoulders with a show of acceptance of the inevitable. 'We can't afford to stay here.'

'But in York, Trevor, you'll be saddled with a mortgage, a bigger one than you have here, I guess...'

'I've no mortgage here; Dad left the house to me, it was paid for. No outstanding debts. The snag was he left no money to maintain it, he had none, it all went on the house. That's why we went to the local schools, not some smart public school and, I suppose, that's why I'm in a dead-end job instead of some high flying personal career. But that's the way things were. When Dad went, there was just the house, nothing else, no money; that was my legacy. Like me, he could barely keep it afloat either but he struggled along until he died. Now it's my turn. I'm struggling like he was, but I don't want to carry on. I want some free time with a little cash in my pocket for Alison and the youngsters.'

'And you're going to give this up to achieve that? Shame on you, Trevor! There's no mortgage either! That's heaven, you know! Even if you sell this place, you'll need a mortgage to buy a suitable house in York and I can't see you're going to be all that better off, what with paying higher rates and so on.'

'We should make a useful amount when we sell this place. No one really wants to buy big houses right now, not with a Labour Government in power and with their record of increasing taxes, so it won't bring a very big sum, but I reckon it'll pay for a good house in York, with a bit spare for investment, and a new car. We'll have to take out a small mortgage that's based on the valuation of both properties, and it allows a small amount to be invested for security, but at least we'll have more than enough for a deposit, more than enough to buy a smart car and enough to put aside for investment.'

'And your job will pay the housekeeping expenses, food, clothes, that sort of thing, rates and electricity bills.'

'Right.'

'So you'll still have no cash to spend, not a lot anyway. Not when you've paid the bills for running the car, the house, clothing the children and so on.'

'Well, you don't expect to have a lot of money to spare when you've a house and a family and a car to run.'

'Have you worked out what it costs to run a car to work in York, from here?' I smiled. 'And you've no mortgage here. I'll bet you'll not be any better off, moving to York, and you'll be tied even more tightly to a job you don't want! Look at it another way, Trevor:

53

imagine not working in York. Imagine working from home. Imagine packing in your awful job to do something you really want to do – to become an artist. You could raise money on this house if you have to, it's a wonderful asset in its own right. A mortgage on this house would allow you to put some of the cash away to provide capital and an income ... you needn't spend all your life travelling to work, you needn't be away from home for nine or ten hours every day...' And now I was thinking about Alan Knight and what he had told me. 'You could make prints of this mural and sell them, keeping the mural. The mural is your security, part of your security. You could paint lots of your landscape pictures and make prints of them and sell the prints, keeping some of the originals as further security, and you could use part of the house as a gallery to display them and you could teach art once or twice a week...'

'We did talk about doing that, Alison even said she could get a part-time job.'

'Good for her. That's exactly the kind of support you need. But you must be sure not to spend time dealing with customers and viewers,' I said, basing my expertise upon the experiences of Alan Knight. 'You'd have to be creative and get out into the moors to paint while Alison runs the office, sees to visitors and potential buyers, answers the

54

telephone and so on. There'd be no dreadful bosses to cope with and think of the tax benefits of being self-employed – even under Labour!'

'It all sounds very tempting; we did talk about it, a lot,' he said, 'but I have no capital to carry me over the first hurdle or two. If I had enough to get me started, to keep me even for six months, I think I could manage to earn enough to provide a living as good as the one I've got, perhaps with a bit of teaching, night-school work and so forth thrown in. And I do have a stockpile of pictures which I've done over the years.'

'And don't forget you've got the Council of Ten,' I laughed. 'Have it photographed, Trevor, make reproductions of it and sell them locally and to a wider audience. This is a classic picture! Instead of covering it up with emulsion when you move to York, stay here and sell the same picture time and time again – that's part of your capital, surely? Your raw material.'

'You sound very convincing,' he said. 'Others have said exactly the same thing. Even my family. And you're saying exactly what's been going through my mind for weeks and weeks.'

'A friend of mine did exactly that,' I said. 'I know nothing about the world of art or business, but he did exactly what you want to do. Alan Knight, he used to be a policeman and was fed up of shift work. He gave it up to be an artist. Why not talk to him? Give him my regards and arrange a chat.'

'I know him,' Trevor smiled. 'Well, I know of him to be more precise, he does seascapes, doesn't he? Of the North Sea? And ships in full sail?'

'That's him. He had no house, no capital, nothing, but he had a supportive wife, a talent for hard work and enterprise, and guts. Guts was the thing that persuaded him to pack in the police force and launch himself into the world of freelance painting. And he's doing very well.' And I told him how to contact Alan if he felt it necessary.

'Thanks, Nick,' he said. 'I'll think about it. If I did leave work to go it alone, and if things went wrong, I could always clean windows. Starting with my own! Now I must dash or I'll burst...'

As he vanished into the toilet, Alison appeared in the doorway as I was heading back into the party room. 'Have you seen Trevor?' she asked. 'We've been looking everywhere for him, I want to make a toast to our future.'

'He'll be back soon,' I said. 'We've just had a council meeting.'

'Council meeting?' she frowned.

'The Council of Ten.' I knew she would understand. 'Except there was just the two of us.'

'You think he should stay, don't you, Nick? And risk every thing as an artist?'

'You could always take in bed-and-breakfast if things went wrong!' I told her. 'With a house of this size, you've always got the potential to earn something. He won't be happy in suburbia, Alison! That's just not his life-style. Factory work, semi-detached houses, streets, nosy neighbours, that sort of thing. It's not him, Alison.'

'I know that, you know that and he knows that, but he worries about security...'

'He could get killed in a traffic accident driving to work,' I said. 'Or he could be made redundant. Or there could be a take-over and he could lose his job. Even in a supposedly secure job, nothing is absolute. His talent is his security, Alison, and he's got a massive talent, that mural says so.'

· 'There's nothing we can do with it!' she said. 'It's painted on plaster, it's part of the wall. What can we do with a painting like that?'

'I've put some ideas into his head,' I said, and then I saw Trevor heading back into the party. 'He'll tell you, I'm sure.'

I could see by the expression on Trevor's face that he had already been mulling over my words and I didn't think he needed much of a push to launch himself into a new career away from the factory which was clearly sapping his self-esteem. I guessed he was paying much of his salary just to drive to work and back. What few luxuries they did enjoy already came from his painting; if he spent all day painting, surely he could earn more? Clearly, the idea of changing the direction of his life had been going through his mind anyway; my chat, which had reinforced what he'd already been told, might have provided the extra impetus that he needed and I felt sure that Alison would be totally supportive whatever he chose to do.

But as people were preparing to toast him on his fortieth birthday, Trevor was hauling a dining-chair into the middle of the room and clambering upon it, with a glass of wine in his hands.

'I'd like you all to drink a toast to our future, me and Alison, and the children. And this house,' he said. 'I've decided not to leave. I made up my mind just now. So it's a toast to the Council of Ten,' he grinned, winking at me. I knew what he meant.

And a week later, he told me he'd resigned from his job in York, and he and Alison were planning his first exhibition of landscapes which he'd done and saved over the past few years. And among them, he said, would be photographic prints of his astonishing mural. He gave one to Mary and I – autographed, of course. He thanked me for providing the little push he needed, but I said it was nothing to do with me – he'd had the courage to make that decision. I just talked about it. And guess what? I really did envy him.

I found myself wishing I could have done the same, except that I always wanted to be a writer. But would I have the courage to throw up my regular job? Perhaps, one day, I'd talk to Trevor about it because Trevor is now a very successful artist. And that wonderful oft-reproduced mural can still be seen on the wall in Kirkside House.

Another intriguing house was situated on the moors a long way from Aidensfield. It was neatly tucked into a fold in the hills above Gelderslack and I had never been to it because it was not a working farm, nor had its owner or occupant given any reason for me to call. On occasions, however, I had patrolled the lofty moorland road which passed the entrance to this house – called White Ghyll Head and had sometimes seen smoke rising from its chimneys. For many months, my sole association with this place was wispy smoke rising from its two sturdy stone chimney stacks. The rest of the house was hidden from view. By dint of keeping my eyes and ears open, I discovered it was owned by a businessman called Robert Scholes, a haulage contractor on a big scale who lived in Bradford in the West Riding of

Yorkshire. Rumour said he operated over 300 vehicles both in this country and on the Continent, working at everything from heavy haulage to cattle transport via food deliveries and furniture removals. He and members of his family came to White Ghyll Head for the occasional weekend during the year, and for longer periods in the spring, summer and autumn. Between his visits, Mr Scholes allowed friends to use it for holiday breaks, but it was not available to the general public.

His desire for privacy was reinforced by a large notice near the main gate which said, 'White Ghyll Head. Private Property. Keep Out. No hawkers or pedlars; no representatives without an appointment'.

The house was known as White Ghyll Head because it occupied a site very close to the source of a lovely moorland stream called White Ghyll. Hereabouts, streams were variously known as becks or gills, although the name ghyll and even slack were sometimes used for small waterways. The source of White Ghyll was a patch of soggy marshland, rich with cottongrass which was formerly used for stuffing pillows and cushions. It was also the haunt of the skylark and the summertime playground for the curlew. The moorland bog, some two acres in extent, drained into a narrow gulley behind the house and from there its small outlet wove an erratic way through the heather and bracken to eventually tumble over a sheer cliff to form the spectacular White Ghyll Force, a famous local waterfall set deep in a rocky cove. A deep pool, popular with kingfishers and dragonflies, had been formed by the falling water and from there the beck flowed into the lower section of Gelderslack Dale before joining the River Rye. There were no public footpaths in the area, although the local landowners, including Scholes, did not object to the local people walking along the route of the beck – but their permitted route stopped well short of the remote house. For me, the house was intriguing because I had never stepped foot across its threshold, but in fact it became even more interesting due to a strange case of what might be called reverse housebreaking!

It happened like this. One Saturday morning, around half past ten, I received a telephone call from Mr Scholes. 'Can you come to White Ghyll, Constable?' he asked in a polite voice with a strong West Riding accent. 'We've just arrived for a family weekend and find we've had visitors.'

'Visitors?' I knew my voice contained a question.

'A break-in,' he said. 'Burglars.'

'What's been taken?' I asked immediately in case it was necessary to issue to our mobile patrols quickly with a description of the missing property.

'Nothing of mine so far as I can tell,' he said. 'He's left a note though, saying he's sorry for taking the post. We've had no letters sent here – I haven't given this address to anyone outside the family – but nothing else seems to be missing. Whether he has taken any letters is something I may never know, and if the mail was addressed to the previous owner, then it's nothing to do with me anyway. But you'd think the Post Office would have been asked to redirect the previous owner's mail and if this burglar had asked if he could come and pick up his letters, I'd have been more than willing. Not that we're here all that often though. Anyway, the point is we've had an intruder, Constable, and it's all very baffling. I thought you should know.'

'All right, Mr Scholes, I'll come straight away,' I assured him. 'It'll take me half an hour to get there.'

'I'll have the coffee pot on,' he assured me.

It was a fine, dry but rather chilly Friday morning but a bonus was that the views from the heights of the North York Moors were crystal clear beneath a cloudless sky. It was possible to see for miles; one view opened across to the North Sea which appeared Mediterranean blue in the morning sun, and another extended through a gap to the high Pennines and Yorkshire Dales, some seventy miles to the west. It was a spectacular run and I enjoyed it. Eventually I was chugging in my little van down the unmade lane to White Ghyll Head, having passed the familiar privacy signs and soon the drive dipped into a moorland hollow. Deep in that hollow stood White Ghyll Head and I could see the marshy area behind it with the waters of the beck flowing from it like a silver ribbon in the morning light. The house was built of local dark-grey chunky stone with a roof of matching stone tiles; it looked as if it was sinking into the ground, so low and long did it appear in its setting, and it seemed there was no view from the building. It was one of the traditional longhouses of the moorland regions; in those houses, all the rooms were situated in a straight line and linked by a corridor which ran the length of the ground floor along the northern wall.

At the east end of the house, the building continued along the same line to form the cattle byre. One could walk directly from the cattle byre into the house, the idea being that in winter, when the cattle spent their time indoors, the heat they produced would help to warm the domestic part of the building. The bedrooms would be to the same plan, each opening on to a long corridor which ran the length of the house.

Probably, there would be two staircases.

Such houses, when used as working farms, employed several labourers who 'lived in', being resident at one end of the building while the owners occupied the other. Some of those labourers, or maids, might live over the cattle byre or stables, and in winter, their quarters would be cosy and warm. In such houses, larger windows faced south and allowed the light and sunshine to enter all the main rooms, upstairs and down. At intervals along the roof of this house were the chimneys, some of which could be seen from the moor road, and I saw that a few tiny windows had been let into the north wall, the one I approached upon my arrival. Each wall was over two feet thick and the windows visible to me upon my approach were all very small, little more than two feet deep and eighteen inches wide, some on the ground floor and some upstairs, all with a northern prospect. The idea was to keep the heat inside the house – views of the surrounding splendour from such remote houses, or a huge influx of sunshine and light, were not considerations. Shelter and warmth were more important than views and light.

As I absorbed these snippets of information, I noticed there were two cars on the rough stone forecourt outside the house, a smart new Rover 2000 and a more elderly

Ford Consul. I parked behind them, booked off the air and went to the solid oak door. It sported a large black cast-iron knocker, but even as I raised my hand to use it, the door was opened and a large, smiling man said, 'I saw you coming down the track. You must be PC Rhea. Come in.'

He introduced himself as Robert Scholes, then shouted through to the kitchen for his wife to make the coffee now that the constable had arrived.

Meanwhile, he said, he would show me where the intruder had entered. I referred to the person as 'intruder,' not 'burglar' because at that time, a burglar was a person who broke into a dwelling house only during the night hours, i.e. between 9 p.m. and 6 a.m. To break into a house at any other time was known as housebreaking. Unless it could be proved beyond doubt that the break-in had occurred between 9 p.m. and 6 a.m. then such crimes were recorded as housebreaking and the villain of the piece was known as a housebreaker. This terminology changed with the Theft Act of 1968, when all crimes which involved breaking into properties such as shops, garages, houses, churches, etc., became classified as burglary which in turn meant that all such villains have since been described as burglars.

Scholes led me along the passage towards

the former cow byre. The passage ran the full length of the house but in this case, I noticed with some curiosity, it followed the line of the southern facing wall, not the north. And there was not one window in that southern wall. I didn't mention it at this early point because Scholes was striding along the passage at a fairly rapid rate, then he halted at a thick wooden door, painted black. It was secured by only an old-fashioned sneck.

'He got in through here,' he said.

'There's no lock,' I noticed. 'And no internal bolts.'

'No, we never lock the house,' he said. 'There's never been a need. Not until now that is.'

'So how do you know he came in this way?' I puzzled.

'It was standing open when we arrived. We've only just come this morning, ready for the weekend, me and the wife, and my son and his wife.'

'So he didn't smash his way in?'

'No, he just lifted the sneck and walked in. I hope I haven't disturbed any fingerprints or anything by closing the door.'

'I wouldn't think there's much chance of useable fingerprints on something as small as a sneck. But in legal terms, opening a closed door is termed "breaking and entering", so we do have a break-in even if there's no damage.' I was thinking of the right classification for this crime. 'But for the crime of housebreaking to be complete, our villain must have either stolen something, or intended to steal something when he entered. So is this an outer door?' was my next question.

'No,' he said. 'It leads into the cow byre. The byre door leads outside. We're hoping to convert the byre into living accommodation, we haven't had the place many months, so it's pretty much in its original state. We're coming here whenever we've a free weekend so our plans aren't anything like firm at the moment.'

'Right. So the byre door? The outer door? Is that locked?' was my next question.

'No.' He shook his head. 'As I said, we never lock any doors.'

'Show me the byre door,' was my next request.

He led me through the former cow byre which was still fitted with skelbeasts, the local name given to wooden partitions between the stalls.

Tethering chains hung from walls at the head of each stall, and in each there was a wooden trough for cattle food; the floor was cemented and lined with grooves to help swill away the inevitable mess. There were two-dozen stalls, I noted, but all the windows were in the north wall. At the far end was a large wooden double door, now closed. We tramped through the clean byre and he led me to the door. 'He got in through this one,' said Scholes.

'Without smashing his way in?' I wanted confirmation of this.

'Not a mark on it,' he confirmed. 'But this one was shut when I looked this morning. If he hadn't left that inner door ajar, I'd have never known he'd been in the place. Except for that note he left.'

'No evidence of a break-in then?' I noted. 'No forced entry? No broken woodwork, windows, internal damage to cupboards or cabinets?'

'No. Nothing,' he said.

'And can you be absolutely sure he's taken nothing of yours?' I put to him.

'That's the funny thing about all this. We've done a check of our belongings and so far as we can see, nothing's been taken. I wouldn't know anything about that post he mentions though. It comes through the front door but the only stuff we've had is circulars. There's not many belongings of ours he could have taken, to be honest. We left behind some cans of soup or beans, a few bits of crockery and cutlery if he'd wanted those, a battered old radio, an old TV set, a few ancient chairs ... but all that stuff is still here. So far as I can say, nothing's been taken, Constable. We bring most of the other stuff like bedding, towels and fresh food each time we come.'

'So how can you be sure you didn't leave that door open last time you were here, or that the wind or something didn't blow it open?'

'Well, I can't be a hundred per cent sure, but he left that note I told you about. It's in the kitchen, I'll show you. If it hadn't been for that, I'd have said we'd left the door ajar.'

'Before I see the note, I'd like a look around the outside of the house, and at the other side of this door. If it's not broken or damaged, and if he's not smashed any windows to gain entry, it's pointless calling in our Scenes of Crime team.'

I lifted the sneck of the byre door and it opened onto a large, stony area, now dry. In addition to signs of a break-in, I was seeking tyre marks or footprints, or anything that might have been left or abandoned by the intruder, but there was nothing. Chummy had evidently arrived on a dry day when the earthern portions were firm because there was no evidence of his presence. 'So he came through here, crossed the length of the byre and let himself into the house through the inner door. And out the same way, you think?'

'It's hard to tell; he could have gone out through the main door, the one you came through when you arrived. That's the one with the letter box in it. That's never locked either.'

'I'd better have a look around the rest of the exterior,' I said. 'Just to clear my own mind about any marks or evidence he might have left.'

'I'll come with you.'

Using the cow byre door as our exit, I led the way to the exterior and found it was possible to walk around the entire house on paths with a rock-like stony base, but there was no sign of a vehicle tyre mark or footprints. But not even my own footprints showed on this tough surface, nor did the tyre marks of the vehicles now present. I also checked all the outbuildings, in case he was sleeping rough or had abandoned anything. The outcome was that I found absolutely nothing which might be associated with the intruder.

'From what I have seen so far, I can't justify calling out our Scenes of Crime team; there's no real evidence that a crime has been committed, but let's have a look at that note he left.'

'Follow me, the coffee should be ready now.'

He took me into the kitchen where Mrs Scholes had prepared five mugs of coffee. She was a smart-looking woman, busty and well built with blonde hair, and I reckoned she'd be in her early fifties.

70

'That note, Eunice, where is it?'

'On the mantelpiece,' she pointed.

'And Alan and Julie?'

'Upstairs, unpacking and making the beds. They'll be down in a minute, they said. Sit down, I'll see to your coffee.'

As we settled at the large pine table, she removed a piece of paper from the mantelpiece. 'It's our own paper, Constable, from a notebook we leave in the kitchen so we can jot down reminders of things to bring next time, shopping and so on.'

Written in pencil – probably with a pencil which was lying on a kitchen shelf – were the words: *Sorry I took the post. No harm done I hope.* And that was all. No date, no signature, no explanation, nothing.

'I'll speak to the postman to see if he's delivered anything recently, but it's all very baffling,' I had to admit. 'As things stand, this is not a case of housebreaking. If the man has entered your house to remove his own mail, I can see nothing criminal in that. Certainly, there's a civil trespass but that doesn't make it a criminal case.'

'So what do you propose to do?' asked Scholes.

'There's not a lot I can do,' I had to admit. 'I'll report to my sergeant and I'll ensure the incident is logged into our system so that if something similar happens again, we can compare notes. And I'll have words with the

71

postman to ascertain what's been delivered here since your last visit.'

'Fair enough, I understand. But you will try to find out what's behind all this, won't you? For our peace of mind. I mean, Constable, if there is some nutter living on these moors who's in the habit of going into people's houses and nicking the mail, I think we should know.'

'I agree, and I'll do my best to find out just what's been going on. And I'll speak to the post office investigation branch. But surely this is a case for locking your doors?' I smiled.

'All right, point taken. But you will let me know the outcome.' He sounded happy with my decision. 'And for my part, I'll get locks for all these doors, I promise you that!'

'Coffee,' said Mrs Scholes, placing five mugs and a plate of chocolate biscuits on the table. Then she went through a door into another part of the house and shouted upstairs, 'Alan, Julie. Coffee!'

'Julie's my daughter, Alan's her husband, they live in Castleford,' Scholes explained. I heard a shouted response and then the clatter of feet on a wooden staircase in the adjoining room, after which a couple appeared. Julie was a younger version of her mother, in her mid-thirties I guessed, and Alan was a sturdy man with short-cropped fair hair who looked as if he could handle himself in a rough house.

After the introductions we all sat down to enjoy our coffee. We discussed the peculiar incident, with me explaining the law on burglaries and housebreakings to the new arrivals, adding that I knew of no local wanderers or mentally ill people who might come into the house during their absence. I did assure them I'd make enquiries locally, however, and we concluded that this incident was something of a mystery.

And then, during a lull in the conversation, Alan said to his father-in-law,

'Where did you find that beautiful piece of timber, Bob?'

'What timber?' he puzzled.

'Lying near the fireplace next door. It's quite a length, six feet high, four inches square. Like a beam. A nice-looking bit of old wood, antique I'd say, with some curious carvings on it. I thought you must have found it in the outbuildings and thought it suitable for something in the house. It's not scrap, that's for sure.'

'Not me, I know nothing about it. Has it fallen from the roof?'

'I can't see any sign of that but it is lying on the floor as if it has fallen.'

'We haven't unpacked the car yet. I haven't been upstairs so I haven't noticed it,' Bob said.

'You checked upstairs for the intruder, to

make sure he hadn't taken anything?' I asked. My thoughts were still dwelling on the intruder; he could be hiding in the house and I should have searched upstairs.

'I checked,' said Alan. 'We got here before Mum and Dad, nothing's gone. And he's not in any of the rooms or hiding in the wardrobes, I checked them all – and the loft!' he grinned, as if reading my thoughts and I wondered what he might have done to the intruder if they'd met. 'Anyway, I'll get this piece of timber to show you.'

He left the table and soon reappeared with the piece of old wood. It was a length of very dark oak, polished with age and smooth in places due to regular handling and cleaning. It was taller than me – six feet or so. And, as he turned it around, I noticed the intricate carving on what I now realized was the top; clearly the pillar was meant to stand upright with the carved portion on display. The elaborate carvings were on what seemed to be the face and two sides of the post; I could discern crosses, good luck symbols and etchings of what appeared to be signs of the zodiac. There was a date too – 1665, fairly recognizable amidst the surrounding carvings.

'I've never seen that bit of wood before!' said Bob. 'What is it? Where's it come from?'

'It's a witch post,' I told them. 'There are lots in the older houses in the village where

I grew up. They used to be very common on these moors during the seventeenth century. Their purpose is to keep witches away, but in practical terms, they also supported the smoke-hood...'

'Smoke-hood?'

'It was over the fireplace,' I told them. 'Posts like this were part of the inglenook ... the cross and other carved charms were thought to ward off witches. That's why they were built into the house. They're found only around the North York Moors.' I aired my knowledge of the beliefs which were so prevalent in my home village a couple of centuries earlier. 'Although they are not generally known outside the North York Moors, one did exist at Rawtenstall in Lancashire but no one knows why it appeared so far from the moors. Some witch posts from our local cottages have been placed in the Pitt-Rivers Museum at Oxford, some are still in their original settings and some are in local museums.'

'Well, what am I supposed to do with it? There aren't any witches around now, are there?'

'No, these posts have frightened them all off!' I laughed, before adding, 'Mr and Mrs Scholes, whatever you decide, you are the proud owners of a very unique object – a genuine witch post. Has it come from your fireplace?'

'Let's have a look. As I said, I can't say I've noticed it before,' he said without finishing his coffee. 'It must have worked loose and fallen out.'

Moving as rapidly as he'd done earlier, he left the table and led us all into the small, dark room which led eventually to the staircase. With a heavily beamed and very low ceiling, the room had a stone-flagged floor covered with clip rugs and a cast-iron range complete with oven, hot-water boiler and moveable hooks from which to dangle kettles and other cooking utensils. The fireplace was in a recess formed by the wall on the left, and a partition on the right. The corridor of the house ran to the far side of that partition, leading to the staircase. But the front of the partition was bare – and that is where the witch post would have stood.

'It was lying in front of the fireplace,' said Alan. 'Just as if somebody had placed it there.'

'It's come from here.' I showed marks on the partition where it had once rested. 'The slot at the top would fit into this groove, and the base would be set in stone at floor level. It's been forced away from here, by the look of things, but not recently. There's a spider's web in the groove ... so it was taken out a long time ago.'

'Let's see if it fits,' said Bob. Carefully, he inched the tall, heavy post into position and it fitted like a glove. 'Well, I'll be damned. It's perfect ... but this is the first time I've seen it. So where's it been until now? And where's it come from? It hasn't been in this house since we bought the place, I'm sure of that.'

'Maybe your "burglar" brought it back!' I laughed, and the moment I said it, I realized that was precisely what could have happened. 'Yes,' I said. 'I think that's it ... this is the post referred to in that letter! Not mail, but a post, this post! He's brought it back for you!'

'Brought it back?' laughed Bob. 'But the letter says he took it...'

'Perhaps he took it a long time ago, when the house was deserted, and he's had a twinge of conscience because someone's living here, so he's brought it back to its rightful place. He said he was sorry he took the post ... now he's rectified his error!'

'But who would do that? I can't believe anyone would do that!'

'We might never know who or why he did it, or even whether that is what happened,' I smiled. 'But can you think of a better solution?'

'No,' he said after a moment's thought. 'No, mebbe you're right, Constable. But it's no crime to break in and return stolen property, is it?'

'It's not a criminal matter,' I said. 'Civil

trespass perhaps, but not a crime. And if the house had been abandoned all those years ago, it will be difficult to trace the owner of the post at that time. So, I think I can write this off as "no crime" – and you are the proud owners of a witch post.'

'I think it should go to a local museum,' said Eunice. 'I'm not sure I want that sort of thing in the house!'

'There's a new folk museum at Hutton-le-Hole,' I said. 'They'd welcome something as unique as this witch post.'

'I'll think about it,' agreed Bob. 'But it does say something about this house – the chap who had it built, according to what I have been able to find out, seems to have been a peculiar character. There are no windows facing south, not one, and it seems he regarded love of the sun as something pagan. He was from one of those small religious sects ... so I wonder if he had the witch post installed?'

'It strikes me you've a lot of research to do,' I said. 'Well, I must be off. I'm pleased your stolen post has been returned.'

'At least the house will be free from witches,' grinned Robert Scholes.

'And you will get locks fitted to your doors?' I reminded him.

'Is that because you want to stop people returning my property to where it belongs?' he chuckled.

Chapter 3

'If there's one thing that promises me great pleasure during my retirement,' said Sergeant Blaketon during a relaxed moment in Ashfordly Police Station, 'it is the fact that my working days will no longer be blighted by the activities of that man Greengrass.'

'He'll never be far away, Sergeant,' I smiled, 'not if you're going to run Aidensfield Post Office.'

We were all enjoying something that was supposed to be a cup of coffee. It had been prepared by Alf Ventress and looked like a mixture of beef gravy, sewing machine oil and lemon barley water. Nonetheless, it was wet and warm and enabled us to have a few moments of informal chatter with Sergeant Blaketon. Certainly, he did seem more chatty and amiable than usual – no doubt his impending departure from the responsibilities of office was making him more relaxed.

'Talking of Greengrass.' PC Ventress appeared from the cell passage where he had brewed our coffee and he was carrying his own chipped mug full of the curious brew. 'I hear he's started giving driving lessons.'

'Driving lessons! You mean that man's teaching other people how to drive cars?' Blaketon almost exploded and managed to spill some of the coffee down his uniform. He made no effort to wipe it off and I wondered if it would rot the cloth in due course, but as he was soon retiring, that might not bother him. 'You can't be serious, Ventress?'

'Well, I must admit I find it a bit strange, but ever since Mrs Ventress came out of hospital–'

'Hospital?' Blaketon echoed our surprise. 'I had no idea she's been in hospital! Nothing serious, I hope.'

'Oh, I don't think it was anything of major concern, Sergeant, but to be honest I don't really know what it was all about. She said she'd had everything taken out. She's just about back to normal now, but it was all very embarrassing because it was something to do with womens' problems and I'm not very knowledgeable about such things. I found it most difficult, talking to her about it, and I never did find out what was really the matter. I find the anatomy of women to be a very peculiar subject, Sarge, something a simple chap like me really needs to know nothing about. Anyway, now she's fit and well, whatever it was that she had out seems to have given her a new lease of life because she said something about studying self-defence, climbing Helvellyn, learning to ski and taking driving lessons.'

'They call it the mid-life crisis, Ventress, when women start wanting to leave the family home and do strange things like driving cars or running businesses. Some people call it "that time of life", I am told. That time of life does affect women in different ways, I know it made my wife very irritable. But Mrs Ventress is not taking driving lessons with Greengrass, surely?' I could see that Blaketon's mind had rapidly switched back to police work. 'If she is, there must be something to stop him, he's a risk to the public at all times and if he's going to teach others his doubtful skills, it'll mean there'll be dozens of dangerous drivers on the roads.'

'How did Mrs Ventress know about Greengrass's driving school?' I asked Alf. 'I didn't know anything about it.'

'She'd been to see a friend in Aidensfield, only yesterday it was, Nick, and she spotted a notice in the post office window,' responded Alf. 'It said, "L-passo. The Greengrass School of Motoring. Comprehensive tuition. Satisfaction guaranteed. Own car or pupil's car. Very reasonable charges. Get started without getting choked. Crash courses extra".'

'Aidensfield Post Office?' I could see Blaketon's face going a deep crimson now.

'You mean he's actually advertising in my post office, for something as dubious as one of his enterprises! You'll have to stop him, Rhea. I never thought I'd have to face that man in my retirement, so get him stopped. And Ventress, why don't *you* teach Mrs Ventress to drive? It'll be cheaper and safer.'

'Oh, she'd never take any notice of what I told her, Sarge. If I said turn right she'd turn left, and if I said stop she'd go faster, and if I suggested she operate the windscreen wipers she'd ask why. She wants to know the far end of everything and thinks the choke is a useful knob to hang her handbag on. We'd fight all the time, she'd drive me crackers. No, Sarge, it would never work. I'd prefer it if she went to Greengrass for that sort of thing. I'll be happy letting her drive *him* crackers.'

'But Greengrass ... why Greengrass? Aren't there other driving instructors?'

'Well, his prices are reasonable, he does supply the vehicle for the lessons which means she won't be likely to crash my car, and she does go to Aidensfield to see her friend on a regular basis, so she could include a driving lesson while she's there.'

'She's clearly thought it all through, Ventress.'

'She has, Sarge, and after all, any fool can teach someone else to drive.'

'Except you can't teach Mrs Ventress?'

'No, Sarge, I'm not as foolish as that. To be honest, I thought if she took lessons with Greengrass, she'd get nowhere fast and in the due course of time she might get fed up with the whole idea and give it up. With a bit of luck, it might put her off driving for ever.'

'Good reasoning, Ventress. Keep death off the road, eh? Well, whatever the reasons behind Mrs Ventress having lessons with Greengrass, it sounds like a very dubious enterprise to me. You'd better check it out, Rhea, see if he's properly insured, that his car is roadworthy and all that.'

At that time, anyone could teach another person to drive a motor vehicle on the road provided the teacher held a valid driving licence for the class of vehicle involved and that he or she had held that licence for at least two years without having been disqualified. Towards the end of the 1960s, however, persons who were paid to teach others to drive had themselves to take a test of competence and, if they passed, they were registered; they could then use the title Ministry of Transport Approved Driving Instructor. After that time, it was illegal to charge for driving lessons unless the instructor was registered, although this did not affect 'L' drivers being taught by friends and family without payment. Greengrass's scheme therefore pre-empted that change in the law and he was then quite within his rights to offer driving lessons for payment.

As I left Ashfordly Police Station that morning, I felt there was little I could do to prevent him offering his services as a driving instructor, provided, of course, he was adequately insured. If I was to satisfy Blaketon's orders, though, I would have to wait until I encountered Greengrass on the road with one of his pupils at the wheel – with 'L' plates displayed – then ask to see the pupil's driving documents – road tax, driving licence and certificate of insurance, and likewise, Greengrass's documents. I did feel, though, that it was unfair to stop a vehicle being driven in a perfectly satis-factory manner by a learner driver. Being stopped by the police was harrowing at any time and I had no wish to be oppressive to someone on the threshold of their driving career, so I thought I would visit Greengrass at his ranch, just to explore the legality of his latest scheme. This was one house I knew well, and when I arrived I found him cleaning a vehicle – an old fire engine.

'Morning, Claude,' I greeted him, as I parked my little van among the pile of scrap metal in his yard.

'It wasn't me and I never saw a thing,' he muttered. 'Whatever it is, Constable, it's not my fault, I didn't do it and I know nowt about it.'

That response was quite normal so I

ignored it, asking, 'So what's all this about you giving driving lessons, Claude?'

'Why shouldn't I give driving lessons? I give value for money, Constable. There's not many folks can remain as calm as me in a crisis – ideal for somebody who's teaching driving – and I do know my nearside from my offside, my choke from my reverse gear and I might even distinguish an alternator from a distributor cap.'

'Eyesight in good order, is it?'

'I can spot a copper a mile off, if that's what you're getting at, and I can read a number plate at twenty-five yards. And I know the colours of traffic lights, in the correct sequence. So what's this? The third degree or something?'

'Sergeant Blaketon–'

'I might have known he was behind this! He has no time for enterprise and initiative, hasn't that man. Too rule-bound, he is. He dislikes us entrepreneurs, businessmen serving the local community, caring folk who are prepared to offer their skills and services for the benefit of others. It's professional jealousy.'

'He'd heard you had started a driving school and asked me to give you any suitable advice you might need,' I said, tongue in cheek.

'Suitable advice? From Blaketon? Like "don't"! Is that what you mean?' he grinned. 'That's the advice he'd give me. But in case you're worried, I am insured, all my vehicles are insured for business purposes and unnamed drivers, my driving licence is valid for all groups of vehicles and if I give a lesson in a pupil's car instead of my own, I shall check that their insurance covers us. Right? I am a professional, Constable, in spite of what you and Blaketon might think.'

'So which of your splendid fleet will you be using for lessons?' I asked.

'It depends,' he said. 'I mean, if a chap wants to drive a three-ton truck, it's no good teaching him to drive a car, is it? So I'll use the truck. It's best he learns with the real thing. And I have a three-wheeler for folks who want to drive one of them, and a car and a van. I could even lay hands on a bus if necessary.'

'I thought most of your vehicles were off the road, Claude,' I commented. 'Scrap, in other words.'

'Awaiting repairs, Constable. When my driving school hits the big time, I'll have enough money to get all them vehicles put in first-class working order as well as running a fleet of different vehicles for specialist lessons. I'm on to a good thing here; motoring is the leisure facility of the future, Constable, and it's us wide-awake entrepreneurs who are getting our feet in the door very early on, in a manner of speaking.'

'Right, well, I felt you should know of Blaketon's official interest in your new enterprise – and my official constabulary interest too, I might add – but I wish you all the best, Claude. I'm not one for preventing people earning a living by skill and enterprise. So long as your documents are in order and you make sure your pupils obey the rules of the road as they learn their craft, there should be no problem.'

I did not demand production of his driving documents at that time, chiefly because I had not seen him driving on the road under his new guise, but I felt my visit had alerted him sufficiently to ensure that all the necessary papers would be in order. Likewise, I decided not to mention Mrs Ventress at this stage, but I would keep an eye open for Claude on the road with one or more of his pupils – merely as a matter of passing constabulary interest! I left him, knowing that he would have regarded my visit as not unexpected.

It was a few days later, as I was on foot in Aidensfield main street, when I noticed Claude drive past with a pupil at the wheel.

It was a young man whom I recognized as David Stockwell and he was driving Claude's old fire engine with 'L' plates fore and aft. I couldn't imagine anyone wishing to learn to drive a fire engine (other than a member of the fire service, of course – and they taught their own staff) but decided there was no reason for me to interfere at this stage. The vehicle did seem to be going very well even if it was producing a lot of smoke and David, in his early twenties, seemed fully in command. Claude had the audacity to give me a cheery wave as he passed out of my sight. At least, I think it was a wave.

It was later the same day when I spotted Claude's fire engine emerging from a farm entrance, still bearing its 'L' plates and with David still at the wheel. In my view, it seemed a rather long driving lesson – it must have been four hours after I'd first seen the pair of them in Aidensfield main street. Again, though, things seemed to be progressing very smoothly and I did not interfere. Then, even later that day, I saw the same fire engine parked outside a house in the village, with David sitting in the driving seat alongside Claude's dog, Alfred, but with Claude himself nowhere to be seen. I thought this was my opportunity to find out what Claude was up to.

'Hello, David,' I greeted the lad as I approached the driver's window. 'Having a lesson, are you?'

David Stockwell, a pleasant and rather simple soul whose father was a retired farm labourer, was not the brightest of young men but he had managed to earn a few pounds by offering his services to local people for tasks such as clipping hedges, mending fences, clearing ditches, cleaning cars, washing windows and other odd jobs.

'Mr Greengrass is very good to me; he said he'd teach me all I needed to know about driving, Mr Rhea.'

'So where is he?'

'Delivering eggs, Mr Rhea. At this house. He showed me his round this morning. He buys his eggs at Moorside Farm, you see, then goes around Aidensfield, Elsinby, Thackerston and Briggsby selling them. He's a very busy man, Mr Rhea.'

'And he's teaching you to drive?'

'Oh, yes, he's a very good teacher, Mr Rhea.'

'In a fire engine?'

'Yes, well, he said I should learn to drive something big right from the start, then I could cope with anything, especially something smaller like a van or a car, and he said if I learned to reverse it along farm tracks and into barns and through gates and things, then I could cope anywhere. I'm quite good at driving along farm tracks, Mr Rhea, in this fire engine.'

'So you are driving him around his customers today?'

'Yes, Mr Rhea, I am, and I'm learning a lot

while I do it.'

'Is he paying you or are you paying him?' was my next question.

'Oh, I'm paying him, Mr Rhea, or I should say my dad is because it's a lesson, you see. A driving lesson.'

'So he gets a free driver for the day... I hope he gives your mum a dozen eggs when all this is over.'

'Mr Greengrass did say he might think of giving me a job if I do well, you know. He said if I learn to drive him on his rounds I would soon get to know my way around his customers then I could become a great help to him, and I want to be a great help to somebody, Mr Rhea, so it's important I drive as much as I can, isn't it?'

Before I could think of a suitable answer, I heard the familiar voice saying, 'What's all this then? Police harassment? Or do you want to buy a dozen eggs, Constable? Fresh from the farm.'

'Not today, Claude,' I said. 'David's been telling me about his driving lessons.'

'Has he now? I hope he's not given away any of my trade secrets, like how he's learned to double-declutch and reverse into dark places and other technical details.'

'No, Mr Greengrass, I've been very careful what I've told folks, like you said.'

'You've hit on a winner here, Claude,' I said. 'David's paying you for lessons while

90

he's working for you...'

'Well, it's a kind of paid apprenticeship, like lawyers and accountants do, and if the lad does well, I'll consider giving him full-time work. David knows that. He can recognize an opportunity and he needs a steady job, don't you, David?'

'Yes, Mr Greengrass, and there's not a lot of jobs around here unless you are a passed driver, you see, Mr Rhea. Learning to drive will be the key to everything, that's what Mr Greengrass told me.'

'I hear Mrs Ventress is one of your pupils, Claude,' was my next sentence.

'It shows just how good a reputation I've got, if the local constabulary supports me and trusts me with their wives,' beamed Claude.

'Will she be collecting and delivering eggs in a fire engine, or might you give her the job of driving that old ambulance of yours and running people into Ashfordly market?'

'Look, David is special, he's a potential high-flyer like me. Mrs Ventress only wants to drive so she can take herself off to Scarborough for shopping trips, so she'll be learning in my car. When I get this enterprise off the ground, I'll have a car with dual controls, Constable. Think of that. Dual-controlled driving tuition... I'll be ahead of the field then. L-Passo Ltd. That'll be me.'

'Has this fire engine dual controls, Mr Greengrass?' asked David.

'No, it can only put one fire out at a time, David. But I can't stand around all day talking when we've customers waiting, so, Constable, if you're not going to arrest me and David for something, we'd best be getting along.'

'I wonder if the tax man would be interested in the way you're conducting your driving lessons?' I smiled.

'Look, you look after your business and I'll look after mine,' he snapped, as he headed for the passenger seat. 'Come on, David, start her up. It's Mrs Rawcliffe next at Ash Tree House. Two dozen white eggs, two dozen brown ones, a dozen bantam eggs and half a dozen duck eggs, a regular order.'

'Right you are, Mr Greengrass,' and the massive old fire engine thundered into life as Claude clambered to sit beside his eager pupil. David looked thrilled with his new skills and I hoped he would never become disillusioned with his blossoming career.

He seemed like a schoolboy train enthusiast driving a proper railway engine for the first time and pipped the horn as he chugged towards Mrs Rawcliffe's fine house at the other end of Aidensfield. David was in his seventh heaven, but I wondered what Mrs Rawcliffe would think about a fire engine delivering her eggs. I had heard, though, some time earlier, that Claude had once borrowed Bernie Scripps's hearse to deliver his eggs. I just hoped he never gave driving lessons in it.

Much to my surprise, and to that of Sergeant Blaketon, Claude Jeremiah Greengrass seemed to be a success with his driving school. He managed to run a smart Vauxhall saloon for most of his lessons and he got several of his pupils through their driving test, not always at their first attempt, but he did succeed within two or three return visits. Even Mrs Ventress seemed to enjoy her lessons with Claude, although she lacked the confidence to submit herself to a driving test. All in good time, we were told; when she was ready, she would apply for her test. Then things went wrong.

One of the main junctions in Ashfordly was altered at the end of the High Street. It was always extremely busy with through-traffic from Harrowby heading towards Brantsford and the coast, while traffic from Brantsford and the coast rushed in the opposite direction. Both these busy routes used the same stretch of road which crossed the end of Ashfordly main street. The main street formed the junction with that busy main road, but because there were no traffic lights it meant that vehicles in the town centre could not easily or safely join that hurried and heavy flow during peak periods.

The result was that a back-log of traffic jammed the High Street at peak periods. Those included the morning and evening rushes in addition to weekend traffic heading to and from the coast. There were times when Ashfordly was blocked solid with traffic waiting to join the busy Harrowby-Brantsford road and when a police officer saw this, he would leap into the middle of the junction and perform a spell of traffic duty in an attempt to get things moving. Standing at that point was one of our regular chores, especially at busy weekends during the summer months and we were always instructed to be available in the event of a traffic hold-up.

Then the authorities decided to rectify the matter by building a roundabout. The installation of traffic lights had been discussed but it was felt that a roundabout would be more aesthetically pleasing and just as efficient, and thus the construction of a roundabout was agreed. This meant widening the approaches to it, especially from the High Street, thus providing two lanes of traffic out of Ashfordly, one turning to the left to Harrowby and the other turning right to Brantsford and beyond. It all sounded very simple and, in fact, when the roundabout was completed, the system did appear to function very satisfactorily.

If there was a local problem, it was

educating local drivers into the idea of using two lanes leading out of Ashfordly as they approached the roundabout. For years, they had been accustomed to just a single lane entering this notorious junction, taking their chance with oncoming traffic as they darted out. Now, they had to contend with a roundabout *and* two lanes of traffic on the approaches to it.

One Sunday I chanced to be on duty in the town centre and for a few moments was watching traffic entering and leaving the newly designed junction. It was a busy morning with non-stop traffic moving in both directions along the main road. Even with the new roundabout, Ashfordly traffic was having to wait a few minutes and I did wonder whether I needed to perform a short spell of traffic duty. Then in the distance, I noticed Greengrass's familiar red Vauxhall heading along the Ashfordly main street with 'L' plates displayed and a lady driver at the controls. As she approached the point where she had to decide whether to take the left or right lane I could see Greengrass, in tutorial mode, indicating she should take the left lane because he wanted her to turn left and head along the Harrowby road. While she was dithering, two cars came swiftly alongside, on her left, and slowed as they approached the roundabout. Other cars followed immediately behind, thus making quite a long queue waiting to enter the Harrowby road. Her lane was deserted apart from the Greengrass car but, because she could not cross to the left, she was obliged to continue moving towards the roundabout in the right-hand lane.

Then Greengrass noticed there was a large gap between two of the waiting cars on his left. I could see him gesturing for her to move into the gap before it was closed – not an easy task for a learner driver. I think he must have taken hold of the steering wheel because, with striking suddenness, his Vauxhall switched lanes and the car managed to squeeze into the gap. There was a good deal of horn-tooting with Greengrass responding with hand gestures of his very own, but at least the Vauxhall was in the correct lane and position to drive forward when the traffic moved.

It was a remarkable piece of driving by a learner. Almost immediately, there was a gap in the Brantsford-Harrowby traffic, and the Ashfordly queue began to move, but suddenly, Greengrass's car shot into the air as if it had been lifted by a jack at one side; it was stranded and had almost tipped on to its side. I could see its underparts from my position. The other cars stopped immediately. There was a great deal of tooting as I ran across to find out what the problem was, and when I arrived, the driver of the car in front of Greengrass's was shouting and gesticulating wildly as the driver of the car to the rear was doing likewise. In the middle of it all, Greengrass was shouting and gesticulating at them both, having somehow scrambled from the uplifted passenger seat. The woman, in the meantime, was weeping in her steeply sloping seat and hanging on to the steering wheel because she could not get out; her door was too close to the road. All other traffic had come to a standstill.

'Let's all calm down,' were my first words. 'What's happened?'

'This idiot made this lady drive her car between ours,' the man, the driver of the first car, was struggling to retain his temper in the presence of a uniformed police officer. 'I never saw him behind or I wouldn't have set off, but look, Constable, I'm towing my mate. This clown told his pupil to drive into the gap ... she drove across our tow rope and when I set off, the rope tightened and rose into the air and tipped her car on to its side.'

'How was I to know there was a tow rope there!' snapped Greengrass. 'Aren't tow ropes supposed to be marked? I just saw a gap and we needed to get into it...'

'It is marked!' the man bellowed. 'There's a piece of red ribbon tied around it in the middle! You must be blind or daft or both!'

'Gerroff, you can't talk to me like that...'

'Quiet, all of you! Let's all calm down and see if we can sort this out,' I said, as the hooting and tooting intensified around us.

The leading car was parked with its brakes on, while the second car had not moved. It had its brakes on. The tow rope between them was now taut and it had risen from the ground like a tightrope-walker's rope, lifting the nearside of Greengrass's car clear of the road to a height of about eighteen inches. It was suspended partially on the tough rope, but its offside wheels were still on the road. The car had not tipped completely over and so far as I could see, there was no damage and no risk – and no one had been injured.

'I tried to warn you,' the second driver was saying. 'I waved at this chap in the passenger seat and pointed at the rope but he just kept that woman coming...'

'If you reverse gently,' I said to the lead driver, 'the Vauxhall should gradually be lowered back to the road; I can't see any damage so it should be able to drive off the rope. Then we can all go home.'

We did that. With tremendous skill, the driver of the first car eased his vehicle very gently backwards to release the tension on the tow rope and so Claude's Vauxhall was slowly eased back to earth, with his pupil still hanging on to the steering wheel. Once the car was on the level, however, she opened the door and fled. I saw her vanish along a side street in a flood of tears.

Claude then had the job of manoeuvring his car from between the others, but when I looked at them all, there was not a scrap of damage to any. From a road traffic point of view, I did not think this could be classified as a reportable road accident and so I suggested the tow cars continue their journey while Claude moved his car to a convenient parking spot and then went to hunt for his pupil.

'How was I to know there was a tow rope there?' he muttered, as he began his hunt. 'Isn't there some rule about tow ropes being highly visible or something?'

'A tow rope shouldn't exceed fifteen feet in length,' I said. 'I don't think this one was as long as that, but a tow rope more than five feet long does have to be easily seen – and there was a red ribbon tied around this one, in the middle. Those lads did all that they should. Maybe you should have your eyes tested, Claude?'

'Me? There's nowt wrong with my eyesight! You're taking this too lightly, Constable, if you don't mind me saying so. I could have been killed!' he muttered. 'It could have thrown my car right over on to the roof with me underneath it if I'd been thrown out!'

'It was nothing,' I said. 'Nobody was hurt,

no damage was done. You'll laugh about it next week.'

'Laugh? This is no laughing matter, I can tell you. I'm going to give up giving driving lessons after this. And that woman hasn't paid.'

'She did really well to manoeuvre the car into that gap, Claude, it was a masterly piece of driving. It's just a pity there was something else in the way – like a tow rope. It's a good job it wasn't a mobile crane.'

'You're going to have fun with this, aren't you, Constable Rhea? You think it's one huge joke!'

'I'll have to make a note of the incident in my pocket book,' I said. 'It will form part of the road-traffic history of Aidensfield – I'll report it as the car that hitched a lift!'

'Give over,' he groaned. 'Now where can that woman have gone?'

'For a stiff gin and tonic I should think, Claude. And I think you should pay for it.'

'Me pay for a drink? Now you are joking, Constable!'

And as everything started to return to normal, Sergeant Blaketon arrived on the scene, looking rather agitated. 'Rhea,' he bellowed. 'I don't know what's going on, and I don't know what you are doing about it, but traffic's tailed back right to the bridge and halfway up the hill at the other side of it. People are getting angry and you've no idea what some of them called me! Shouldn't you be getting things sorted out?'

'Well, Sergeant Blaketon, it was like this. Claude Jeremiah's pupil–'

'If it's anything to do with Greengrass and his driving school, I don't want to know, Rhea. Just get this traffic moving, will you?'

'Yes, Sergeant.'

This was not the only traffic problem created by Claude Jeremiah Greengrass.

The other was associated with a goat and such was that animal's involvement with motorists in Aidensfield that it led to the reported fulfilment of a piece of local folklore. Perhaps to clarify matters, it would be wise to first mention that folklore.

High in the moors between Aidensfield and Elsinby there is a large and very dense coniferous forest and for centuries, Elsinby Forest has been the home of a herd of magnificent red deer. It is one of the few herds of red deer living wild outside Scotland and folklore says that if ever a white calf is born within the herd, then it heralds the death of a prominent person in the district. Within the last two centuries, only two white calves have been known and on each occasion, the prophecy was fulfilled.

However, there is a little more to that tale – the White Calf of Elsinby is said to leave the herd and come down from the moors to visit the graveyard of the parish church, there to stand beside one of the graves. Whichever grave it decides to visit means that the living descendant of the family in question will die tragically before the next full moon. In both recorded cases, this has happened; in 1756, the White Calf of Elsinby was seen close to the grave of a man called Thomas Blackburn and within the month, Reuben Blackburn, a descendant, had died by being thrown off his bolting horse. Again, in 1877, a white calf appeared within the herd and it came to Elsinby churchyard to stand close to the grave of Adelaide Bowers. Within the month, Joseph Bowers, a direct descendant, had died by drowning. Since that time, almost a century ago, no white calf had been sighted within the herd and certainly, none had been known to visit the graves in Elsinby church-yard.

It was against this background that, for some unaccountable reason, Claude Jeremiah Greengrass acquired a splendid white billy goat. I am not quite sure of its origins or how he came to own it, but it was a handsome beast with a splendid pair of horns, a cross-bred with characteristics of the Bagot, the British Saanen and the English goat. I do not know what possessed Claude to acquire this animal because none of his previous goat-keeping ventures had been a success. My first intimation of this development occurred during a telephone call from Sergeant Blaketon.

'Rhea,' he said, 'get yourself over to see Greengrass and instruct him to keep his goat under control. Tell him that if he doesn't, I will personally report him and will seek a court order to have the thing declared dangerous and kept under control, or alternatively destroyed.'

'I thought that procedure was for dogs, Sergeant,' I said in all innocence.

'Dogs, goats, hens, sheep – you can't let these things loose on the highway to the danger of the public, Rhea, and I don't care if there is no law to say so. Common sense says so, and I conduct my life by common sense, Rhea. So get yourself over to the Greengrass establishment, and lay the law down. Make him understand.'

'What's happened, Sergeant?' I thought it best to know what lay behind this latest order from on high.

'Greengrass's goat is attacking motor cars, Rhea. For some reason, it likes butting headlights and smashing the glass. I've had a chap in only this morning, not very pleased I might add, to say Greengrass's white billy goat had charged at his car and smashed the headlights. He reckons he's not the first.'

'Malicious damage by goat,' I said. 'I've

had no other reports.'

'You will if you don't do something about it, Rhea. And you can't prosecute a goat for committing malicious damage so I have suggested the aggrieved person sends a bill to Greengrass. In the meantime, he'd better keep the goat under control, otherwise he's going to be faced with more bills.'

But even as I replaced the telephone, there was a loud knocking upon the door of my office and when I opened it, Rudolph Burley, the auctioneer who lived in Aidensfield, was standing there with a bright red face bearing an expression of deep anger.

'Nick,' he said. 'I want Greengrass prosecuted for keeping a dangerous wild animal, or for failing to keep a goat under control, or not having a savage animal safely tethered, or for allowing livestock to stray on the highway or whatever else you can think of.'

'Why? What's happened?' I asked.

'That goat of his has rammed my car headlights. There I was, parked outside Armitage Cottage assessing it for a future sale, when wham! This white billy goat took a running jump at both my headlights with his head down and horns like lances and he's smashed both of them, glass, bulbs and reflectors, the lot.'

'You'll send Greengrass a bill?' I asked.

'I'll deliver it personally, and if he doesn't

pay, I'll smash his headlights and see how he likes that!'

'You can't take the law into your own hands, Rudolph,' I advised him. 'But, yes, I will talk to Greengrass.'

'Talk to him? What good will that do?'

'I hope it'll persuade him to take care of his goat. As a matter of fact, this is the second complaint I've had in about as many minutes, so I've plenty of ammunition to fire at him.'

'Same goat, is it?'

'Same goat, and headlights again. It seems it has a dislike of headlights,' I said. 'But leave it with me, Rudolph. I'll have words with Claude. But it's hardly a police matter, more of a civil dispute, I'd say. So make sure you send him your bill for the damage.'

When I called on Claude, he said he had no idea his goat had escaped from the confines of his smallholding, nor did he know about its propensity for head-butting motor car headlights.

'I've only just got him,' Claude told me. 'A mate of mine dropped dead and his widow gave me this goat; it was his, you see. Billy they call him. How was I to know he's a ram-raider?'

'Well, just make sure he doesn't get out again, otherwise you're going to be faced with a lot of bills from irate motorists.'

'You're not going to prosecute me, then?

For keeping an unruly goat or summat?'

'There's no such offence known to criminal law, Claude, but the civil law is just as fierce when it comes to nuisances. If that animal keeps up his head-butting jaunts, you're going to be faced with some big bills and even civil court action.'

'Right, thanks for the warning, I'll make sure he's locked up.'

In spite of Claude's promises, Billy managed to escape several more times, and on each outing he head-butted the nearest motor-car headlights. Fortunately, all the cars were stationary at the time, otherwise I would have had to classify the incidents as reportable accidents, a goat being the equivalent of a dog or cow so far as road traffic accidents were concerned. I think the goat must have heard the sound of the cars near his run because all were very close to Claude's home; it seemed the noise of the cars triggered this overpowering desire to smash their headlights. On each occasion, I was approached by the aggrieved driver, but all I could do was to suggest they invoiced Claude for the cost of the repairs.

In all cases, I rang Claude to say it had happened again and eventually he said, 'That's it. I'm getting rid of Billy. He needs to live somewhere where there are no cars!'

Then the head-butting stopped as suddenly as it had started. I was expecting calls almost on a daily basis, but when a week passed without any further reports, I wondered how Claude had dealt with the problem. I happened to catch him outside the post office one afternoon.

'You've found a way of dealing with Billy?' I smiled.

'He's escaped, Constable, that's why. Disappeared overnight, run away.'

'You mean you've dumped him somewhere, Claude? Taken him on to the moors and left him? You know it's a criminal offence to abandon an animal in circumstances likely to cause it unnecessary suffering?'

'I said the goat had run off, Constable, and if I say that, then that's what happened. Anyroad, goats are naturally wild, there's a herd of wild goats in Northumberland and some more in Wales, so if he's living wild, he'll cope. So long as there's no car headlights to distract him.'

With no more cases of headlamp butting, the saga of the Greengrass billy goat faded in my mind and I must admit I thought I'd heard the last of Claude's problem. Later, when I popped into the Hopbind Inn at Elsinby one lunchtime on a duty visit, I found the place full of regulars. The bar was always full, even on a midweek lunchtime, and when he saw me, Gilbert Kingston, the postman, called, 'Ah, Nick, have you heard about the White Calf of Elsinby?'

'I know the legend, yes.' I wondered what had rekindled interest in this ancient tale.

'Have you been about at night lately? In Elsinby?' asked Gilbert.

'On and off, yes, routine patrols, that sort of thing.'

'You've not seen the white calf then?'

'No,' I shook my head. 'Why? Have there been reports about it?'

'A few, yes, some locals reckon they've seen a white calf in Elsinby Forest, among those red deer, there's been day and night sightings, mostly at night though. The trouble is the forest is so dense and very dark at night, even where it borders the road, and the calf's lost very quickly. If you try to get near it on foot, it just disappears into the undergrowth.'

'If it is the fabled White Calf of Elsinby, then it's a revival of the legend,' I said. 'Does that mean folks are getting worried in case it visits the churchyard?'

'They are, Nick. Harold Poulter's down there every night, watching his ancestors' graves in case the white calf decides to pay a visit. Mind you, if it calls at any other grave, he'll soon let the relatives know.'

'I'll keep an eye open on my rounds,' I promised.

Legends of this kind are inevitably intriguing and it was quite surprising to find grown men in the 1960s who still believed in such things, but I knew better than mock the good folk of Elsinby. If, for any reason, the White Calf of Elsinby did visit the churchyard, I knew the villagers would be very alarmed and worried and so I decided to maintain my own vigil. I had no intention of spending hours on guard but I would keep my ears and eyes open for sightings whenever I was on patrol. If I did spot the animal, though, I decided not to alarm anyone by mentioning it!

Late one Friday evening, though, in pitch darkness, I parked my Mini-van close to the wall of the parish churchyard in Elsinby for I wanted to undertake a night foot patrol in the village.

There'd been reports of someone prowling around in the darkness, entering gardens and greenhouses and wandering in the fields behind the cottages, and so I wanted to merge into the shadows while I kept observations. I found nothing, but I think the occasional sight of my uniform was reassuring to those who saw me, and then, as I was returning to my parked van, I saw Harold Poulter running from the church-yard, clearly terrified.

'Oh, thank God, Nick,' he panted when he saw me. 'It's in there ... the white calf, foraging around the graves like the legend says ... I daren't look any more ... I daren't.'

'Are you sure?' I asked. 'It's not a dog or something, is it? And I reckon if it was a deer, you'll have frightened it away!'

'I didn't stop to look, I don't want to know if it's visiting my ancestors' graves ... anyway you go and have a look; you're not local, you've no ancestors there so you've nothing to lose and it'll confirm what I saw. I'll wait here.'

He had left the gate open and so I entered in silence, my night vision being sharp and my boots soft enough not to make any sound on the stone footpath. The reflected light of the village was sufficient for me to see my way between the tombstones and then I saw it – a white shape moving among the tombstones in the far corner. I froze. I had no wish to startle the beast and I did want to find out what it was doing, wondering why this young calf had left the herd which lived three or four miles away in the forest.

But the combination of darkness, dense undergrowth in that part of the churchyard, and the arrangement of the tombstones, meant I could not obtain a very clear view. But I could confirm Harold's sighting.

And then the animal leapt. With an agile bound, it leapt on to the boundary wall, halted for a moment, then dropped down the far side out of my sight, but it was on the wall top long enough for me to catch sight of its horns in a beam of light from a street lamp, and to note its crisp white coat. But young deer did not carry horns, did they? And hadn't its figure been rather too heavy for a young deer? Its legs too short? And its neck also too short?

I was sure I had seen Claude Jeremiah Greengrass's billy goat and my suspicion was confirmed when I heard the distinctive crash of glass – after leaping over the wall, it had found my van! Then even as I was galloping out of the churchyard, I heard the second crash of glass with Harold shouting obscenities. When I returned to my van, it had two smashed headlights and Harold said, 'It was a bloody goat, Nick, and it had a go at your van...'

'So much for the fabled White Calf of Elsinby!' I said. 'This is Greengrass's doing, turning it loose! Where did it go?'

'It ran along that lane and into the field, you'll never catch it.'

'But I've a witness! Claude will get a bill for this.'

'Well, at least it settles things for me. I know I haven't seen the white calf of Elsinby on my ancestors' graves, and that's a relief!'

'You can go home and rest in peace, Harold. And I'll go and book off duty, it's getting on for midnight. See you tomorrow.'

'Night, Nick.'

Although the glass on my police van's

headlights was broken, the bulbs were still in working order and so I could guide the vehicle slowly home. Tomorrow, I would have to persuade Greengrass to retrieve his goat before it did any more damage. Wherever it had chosen for its den, it seemed it was roaming around Elsinby at night-time, making the villagers think prowlers were at large. I thought the best way to persuade it to surrender was to line up rows of old cars so that it could attack each of them in turn, then we could catch it! Or Greengrass could...

All these ideas were flooding my mind as I chugged slowly home on my damaged lights, but then, as I turned a corner at the edge of the forest, a herd of red deer leapt out ahead of me and darted across the road into the trees at the far side.

And among them I was sure there was a splendid lithe white calf...

Chapter 4

Eric Robshaw lived all alone in a superb detached house at the eastern end of Aidensfield. From the front of his home, which was slightly elevated within its own spacious grounds, he enjoyed wonderful and far-reaching views towards the moors. A long, gently sloping valley lay behind his home and this was conveniently hollow-shaped so that it provided extensive views from his garden towards the distant North Sea. Called Shakespeare House after the whim of some previous owner, it was a solidly built stone house with a blue slate roof, the whole of which might have been designed by a schoolchild. From the front, it looked that kind of house – an almost square and rather plain shape with an oblong door in the middle of the ground floor front wall and large double windows, expensively curtained, at each side. The curtains were always closed at night, and all the ground floor windows bore net curtains; even the smallest windows in a rear porch had nets over them. There were three matching windows on the first floor too, also heavily curtained, with net curtains in position during the daytime hours. To add to the childish design there was a set of chimney pots at each end of the roof, although smoke rarely issued from them.

To the east when looking at the front door there was a single-storey building, an annexe of some kind, while to the west a similar shaped structure served as a double garage. Certainly this very symmetrical and somewhat simply designed house was very imposing in spite of its plain architecture and it was the sort of home many would like to own if they could afford both to buy and maintain it.

From its external appearance, it was clear that Eric loved his home because he kept it, and the surrounding garden, in pristine condition. In many respects, though, Eric was something of a mystery. He was not married, and so far as anyone knew, never had been. To my knowledge, he did not go out to work; he had never had a job since coming to Aidensfield, nor had he followed a profession of any kind.

He never popped into the pub for a drink, or mixed socially with the other villagers, although he did attend the Anglican church. He lived completely alone, there being no sign of his mother, father or other members of a family. Indeed, no housekeeper or local cleaner visited his home and when he had his groceries delivered, they had to be taken to the rear of the house and placed on a shelf inside the back porch. Likewise, parcels and other large deliveries were always left in that porch. No one local ever gained access to Eric's fine home and whenever he wanted work doing on the house, he always secured the services of an appropriate expert from some distance away; his expert helpers were always strangers to Aidensfield.

An expert horticultural designer looked

after his garden, expert decorators attended to the interior and exterior of Shakespeare House, expert mechanics looked after his ancient Armstrong Siddeley car, an expert tailor made his very smart clothes while an expert shoemaker tended his expensive footwear. With such expensive tastes, it was not unexpected that Eric was the smartest and most expensive-looking person in Aidensfield. There was not an ounce of countryman about him. He looked like an import from Chelsea, or some other fashionable area of London.

Indeed, he was the most exquisitely dressed man I had ever encountered, and his whole demeanour was one of effortless elegance accompanied by exquisite taste with, apparently, no expense spared. He was approaching sixty, I estimated, with a head of well-groomed hair, (tended by an expert in Leeds), which still retained some of its dark colouring, albeit etched with silver but showing no sign of thinning at the crown or temples. He wore gold-rimmed spectacles and I think he possessed all his own very white teeth; his complexion was pink and healthy and he boasted a lithe, slim body complemented by his impressive height of just over six feet. He walked with an easy grace, not using a walking stick, and he never seemed to be in a hurry.

His cut-glass accent contained more than

a suggestion of an aristocratic background and even when dressed for relaxation in his garden, or merely to go for a stroll in the countryside, he dressed as if he was attending a royal garden party, or on his way to meet some very important person. Sometimes, he wore a smart panama hat and carried a folded umbrella, but he never seemed to buy his clothes from local shops or visit the homes of Aidensfield people. He obtained his groceries locally however, and these were delivered to the rear porch of his house. It seemed he had no desire for anyone to enter his home and I knew of no one, other than his imported experts, who had progressed beyond the smart white front door with its gleaming brass knocker. Truly, the suave Eric Robshaw was a man apart; furthermore, he seemed determined to maintain his distance from other human beings, particularly those living in Aidensfield.

When he attended church, so I had learned from those who supported the Church of England, he occupied the front pew on the right when facing the altar, and he was always first in the line for Holy Communion, but he never lingered afterwards for a chat with the vicar or a cup of coffee in the church hall. He simply nodded a gracious thank you to the vicar and walked home in his lofty elegance. His other outings seemed few and far between, although on one occasion I noticed his lovely old Armstrong Siddeley pull up outside a smart hotel in Ashfordly, to discharge a splendidly attired Eric. It seemed he was attending a function of some kind, although in what capacity I never knew. On another occasion I saw him enter a solicitor's office in Ashfordly, leaving his car outside the front door.

His determination to live apart and in isolation from the rest of the village gave rise to rumours about his origins, but that's all they were – rumours – because no one knew anything about his background. Inevitably, his demeanour created gossip and specu-lation, but no one knew any hard facts about him. Probably due to his smart, expensive and rather exclusive appearance, some thought he had a titled background, others thought he was a secret millionaire, a major businessman, or a former film star; some wondered if he was anything to do with television while others felt he might be a famous author or composer working under a pseudonym, while yet more believed he was related to the royal family and some speculated that he had won a fortune on the football pools or was even a retired gangster. He was not from old Aidensfield stock – Shakespeare House had appeared on the market some years before I arrived as the village constable and Eric had bought it.

I think he had been a resident in the village for more than twenty years, but until his arrival in Aidensfield, no one in the village had previously met or encountered him. It seemed he had never visited the village, either on business or as a tourist. No one knew where he had come from – even the estate agent who had sold the house to him had dealt through a third party, although the removal trucks which brought his belongings had a Kensington, London address. Those who had caught sight of his belongings being unloaded all those years ago spoke of also seeing volumes of antique furniture, lots of oil paintings, rare books, sets of expensive chinaware and a wonderful range of silver plate – but apart from that, he might have originated anywhere.

But Eric fuelled the mystery by steadfastly declining to talk about his background or his origins and life before coming to Aidensfield. In spite of the curiosity of the villagers and in spite of living in the village for a couple of decades or so, he had successfully managed to retain complete confidentiality about his own affairs. If anyone was bold or cheeky enough to ask him a leading question about himself, he had the ability to avoid a direct answer, and he did so with a smile and with the utmost grace. Charm was built in to Eric, but no one – not even me – knew anything about him – and that was no mean achievement in any village, let alone Aidensfield. Part of that success, I was sure, was due to the fact that no one had ever been inside his house. One's home so often provides clues to one's personality, occupation, background and interests, and it likewise displays artefacts which provide topics for discussion. But Eric's relationship with Aidensfield offered no such titbits.

As a village policeman, however, there was usually cause to visit most of the homes on my patch at least once. Often, these visits were for trivial reasons, such as attending to a piece of lost or found property, or there might be more serious reasons, such as asking for sightings of passing villains or even attending a crime reported within the household. Other reasons for calling at houses included the renewal of firearms certificates, witness statements to obtain for other police officers, dealing with neighbourly complaints, offering crime prevention advice or interviewing householders for a wide variety of reasons. Sometimes I just popped in for a chat, especially if the householder was alone and vulnerable. But not once had I had cause to visit Shakespeare House for a meeting with Eric Robshaw and not once had he come to me for help or advice.

His only contact with me occurred whenever he met me in the street, in which case he would bid me 'Good day, Constable' as he walked past. And that was all. He seemed unwilling to gossip about the daily trivia of village life and even if something serious occurred within his knowledge, like a traffic accident in the village, or a farm fire, he would show no inclination to stop for a natter about it. Clearly, Eric lived in a world of his own, one which he had no desire to change.

Then something strange happened. PC Alf Ventress was on duty in Ashfordly Police Station one morning when I popped in to collect my internal mail and police circulars. As I was emptying my pigeon-hole, the telephone rang. Alf responded with 'Ashfordly Police Station, PC Ventress speaking' whereupon the caller identified herself as the supervisor in Ashfordly Telephone Exchange.

Alf listened for a moment, then said, 'Well, actually, it's fortunate that the local constable has just walked into this office, I'll put him on,' and he held out the receiver for me to take.

'PC Rhea,' I introduced myself.

'It's the telephone exchange, Mr Rhea, I'm the supervisor, Mrs Browning. I wonder if you can help?'

'Try me,' I challenged.

'We're getting strange noises on one of our lines, Mr Rhea, they sound as if they're coming from an empty house. It's an Aidensfield number, the phone's off the hook. There's lots of echoes in the background and what sounds like banging on a wooden floor and a man groaning, but our operator can't get any sense from whoever it is.'

'Empty house?' I puzzled. 'I don't know of any empty houses in Aidensfield.'

'And we have no record of any houses which have asked to be disconnected due to being empty or through people leaving. Anyway, the number is Aidensfield 376 and the subscriber is a Mr Robshaw at Shakespeare House. It sounds as if he needs help of some kind, Mr Rhea, so I thought I'd better call the police. We did ring your house, but got no reply.'

'My wife has taken the children to see some friends,' I said. 'OK, leave it with me.'

After explaining this to Alf, I left immediately and rushed back to Aidensfield in my little police van, driving straight along to Shakespeare House.

I parked outside the front door, knocked without response, tried it but it was locked, so I hurried to the rear, noting that all the curtains, upstairs and downstairs, were closed and that no unexplained vehicles or people were in the grounds. By now, it was around eleven o'clock in the morning and I would have expected the curtains to have been open, except for the nets of course, and I began to fear something terrible had happened to Eric. The rear door was closed and locked too; I knocked and shouted Eric's name without response, and so I did a complete circuit of the exterior, seeking either another door or even a window which might permit me to enter. I found nothing. Even though the account of an empty-sounding house or even just an empty room, was puzzling, I began to feel there had not been a raid on Eric's house. I feared he might be in some other kind of trouble. I resorted to further knocking on the doors, rapping on the windows and shouting Eric's name at each window and door, but gained no response to any of these tactics and so, before embarking on the alternative of breaking in, I radioed Alf from my van.

'I'm at Shakespeare House, Alf,' I told him as a form of sit-rep. 'I've done a recce, the place does not appear to have been broken into, all doors and windows are closed and locked with the curtains drawn. There's no sign of intruders. I've knocked on all doors and windows and shouted for Mr Robshaw, without response. Can you check with the exchange to see if the phone is still off the hook with those noises coming through it? If it is, it looks as if the houseowner is in need of help, so I'll have to break in.'

'Right you are, Nick. Remain on air while I ring, it'll only take a moment.'

His call to Mrs Browning confirmed the worst – the line was still open and odd noises were still emanating from Eric's receiver which was clearly off the hook. Repeated action by the exchange staff had failed to elicit any sensible response and so I knew there was no alternative. I had to break in and I had to do so with the minimum of damage. I selected a small rear window, probably a kitchen window although I could not see inside due to the closed curtains, smashed the glass with a hammer from my van's tool kit, loosened the catch and prised open the frame with a screwdriver. Before climbing in, I shouted my name because I did not want Eric Robshaw, if he was ill, to think his house was being attacked.

'It's PC Rhea,' I called several times. 'I'm coming in, Mr Robshaw, to see if you are all right... It's PC Rhea...'

Although many of the villagers referred to him as Eric behind his back, he was always Mr Robshaw to his face and I do not know how his Christian name came to be so generally known. I guessed it might have been through the postman or post office seeing his mail. Not wishing him to come and hit me over the head and shoot me as an intruder, I shouted 'Mr Robshaw' repeatedly as I fought with the closed curtains and struggled headfirst through the window to find myself in what appeared to be a utility room. It was quite empty, save for a yard brush standing in one corner. However, I did eventually reach the floor, stood up and brushed the dust off my uniform, then called his name as I began to explore the ground floor of this spacious house. As I moved along the tiled floor which led from the utility room, I found myself in the kitchen and decided to open the curtains.

Apart from a cheap table, a single chair and a few items of crockery on the shelves, the kitchen was empty and the tiled floor uncovered, but I had no time to stand and stare. Shouting his name, I moved quickly into the entrance hall, also empty and wondered how to find the staircase. I went into the lounge – it was deserted too, with bare floors and walls, and closed curtains. I opened them because I needed light and found another door leading into a rear vestibule and there I found Eric Robshaw.

There was a flight of stairs and he was lying at the foot in what appeared to be a very untidy heap with the telephone, which seemed to have rested on a ledge at the foot of the stairs, just out of his reach. I think he had grabbed the wire and pulled it off the shelf where it normally stood. In a moment, I was at his side, feeling his pulse and shouting at him in the hope that my presence and voice might do something to revive him. There was blood on the stone floor and blood on his head; he was dressed in grey silk pyjamas, I noted, with one slipper on and the other midway down the stairs – also devoid of a stair carpet. But he was alive!

I lifted the handset and hoped someone was listening at the other end – I felt sure the exchange would be keeping a close vigil upon this saga.

'Hello? Anyone there?' I asked hopefully.

'Hello, yes, is that Mr Robshaw?' I recognized Mrs Browning's voice.

'No, it's PC Rhea, Mrs Browning. I'm with Mr Robshaw, he's alive but he needs an ambulance urgently. Can you call one? Shakespeare House, Aidensfield, I'll wait with him. He'll need urgent medical care the moment he arrives at hospital.'

'What's happened to him? Are they likely to ask?'

'I think he's fallen downstairs and injured himself severely,' I said, having considered the general appearance of the scene and the abandoned slipper halfway upstairs. 'There's blood from a head wound too, so tell them that. I'll open the front door for the ambulancemen and will make Eric as comfortable as I can until they arrive.'

'Right,' she said, and I replaced the phone in case she wished to call me back.

Although police officers are taught first aid, there are occasions when it is unwise to move or attempt to treat a severely injured person. Movement might aggravate an injury, particularly if the spine, neck or head are involved and so, although I wanted to do something positive for Mr Robshaw, I decided it was unwise to touch him or move him. I talked to him, telling him who I was and that help was on the way, and I think he responded with movements of his eyes and fingers. As always happens on such occasions, it seems that the ambulance took an eternity to arrive but in fact it was probably less than ten minutes. I had no idea how long Mr Robshaw had lain in that awful position but felt it had not been all night – the telephone operator had probably alerted the supervisor very soon after Eric had knocked the handset off its rest in his vain attempts to raise help.

Within minutes, therefore, the casualty was being whisked off to hospital, apparently unconscious and badly injured, and I was left alone in Shakespeare House.

I rang Alf Ventress from Mr Robshaw's phone to update him, and said I would remain in the house for a while in an attempt to secure the window I had smashed, and then to secure the entire house during Eric's forced absence. Also, I had to try to ascertain whether Eric had any relatives who should be told. Probably, he'd have a desk or writing bureau containing his personal papers.

Opening all the curtains, I began with the ground floor, but the house was empty. There was not a stick of furniture in any of the rooms, no three-piece suite, no dining suite, no chairs, no carpets, mats or rugs, no pictures or ornaments. Nothing. So I went up the carpetless stairs (the ambulance men had taken the slipper with them for use in hospital), and began to search the upper rooms. With the exception of one, all were absolutely empty.

One of them was clearly Eric's bedroom for it contained a single bed, an armchair, a wardrobe and chest of drawers; there was a brightly coloured rug on the floor too and on the walls were several oil paintings - valuable ones in my opinion and a radio set. In the adjoining room were several bookcases with dozens of novels and history books, but nothing else. I peeped into the bathroom; it was plain and simple with a handbasin, a toilet, a white enamel bath but no shower unit. The only place I might find names of next-of-kin was therefore the bedroom and his chest of drawers, but in spite of a careful search, I found only his spare clothes, all neatly washed and ironed, but no personal papers. As if to completely satisfy my curiosity, I made a thorough search of every room in the house and found nothing. Eric had no one.

His house was like him – he was all show and style but appeared to be otherwise empty. His house was the same – an empty shell, outwardly handsome and interesting, but utterly barren and deserted inside. So what about all those antiques and valuables the local folks had reportedly seen entering the house upon his arrival? Where had they gone?

But I could not spend time pondering the mystery of Eric Robshaw. Before leaving the house, though, I rang Mrs Browning at the exchange to thank her for being so helpful and to explain what had happened to Eric; then, from my van, I radioed Ashfordly Police Station to provide Alf Ventress with an up-to-date account. But Sergeant Blaketon answered my call.

'Was Mr Robshaw attacked, Rhea? Was he attacked and has he had property stolen, do you think?'

'No, Sergeant, there was no sign of a break-in. The house was locked when I arrived. I think he fell downstairs, one of his slippers was abandoned on the steps.'

'Even so, you'd better go and have words with him in hospital, Rhea, when he's fit to be interviewed, just to confirm he's not the victim of a crime.'

'I'll do that, Sergeant.'

'And make sure the house is secure before you leave.'

I found a set of keys hanging in a kitchen cupboard and located a piece of plywood in his garage which would secure the window I had smashed. I spent a few minutes boarding up the window, went around the house to open all the curtains, albeit leaving the nets in position for security reasons.

With the bunch of keys, I let myself out of the front door, locked it and took the keys with me. I would deliver them to Eric Robshaw when I went to the hospital and in the meantime, would keep a watchful eye on the premises.

After checking with the hospital by telephone that afternoon, I learned that Eric was severely injured and the ward sister suggested I did not bother him that day, nor indeed the following day; he had a broken skull, two broken ribs and severe bruising on most of his body, but she did say he was as comfortable as he could be. He'd been lucky, she said; if he had lain much longer without discovery he could have died. It was a miracle he'd managed to grab the telephone's cord and pull it from the shelf so that his plight could be heard – that, and the action by the operator, had saved him. She did ask if I knew of any next-of-kin and

I had to tell her that, to my knowledge, there was none.

It would be three days later when I went to interview Eric about his fall – I wanted to be sure he had not been attacked – and with his doctor's permission, went during normal visiting hours. Because he had no relatives, Mary suggested I take him something and so I bought some grapes and magazines, along with a bunch of flowers for the ward. And I dressed in civilian clothes so that my visit would not look too formal. As I walked down the long ward, I could see Eric propped up on his pillows with a bandage around his head and his face looking as if he'd survived ten rounds with a heavyweight boxing champion. But he was elegantly clad in his silk pyjamas, the ones in which I had found him, and in spite of his bandages, he looked the perfect gentleman.

'Mr Rhea.' The charm oozed from him even in his plight. 'How kind of you to come.'

'Hello, Mr Robshaw. It's nice to see you sitting up and looking so cheerful; you're certainly much better than when I last saw you.' I settled on a chair beside his bed and gave him his presents, then returned his house keys to him, explaining that I'd had to break in and that the window needed a proper repair.

'I'll see to that. But how kind of you, Mr

Rhea, to do all this for me. I must thank you most warmly for everything you've done...'

'It was Mrs Browning at the telephone exchange,' I told him. 'She raised the alarm, she's the one to thank.'

'She has been in touch with the hospital, Mr Rhea, isn't that thoughtful of her? She said she will be coming in to see me and her staff have bought me something too, they sent that card, signed by them all. Isn't that nice ... I had no idea people could be so nice and the nurses here are wonderful. I've never had so many people fussing over me ... never in my entire life.'

'Is there anyone you'd like to be told?' I had to ask him. 'Relations? Friends?'

He shook his head. 'No, no one. I'm all alone in this world, Mr Rhea. I shall survive, I am a survivor, you know.'

'I have to ask you what happened, Mr Robshaw, to complete my report.'

'I tripped when my slipper came off and I fell, Mr Rhea, nothing more sinister or com-plicated than that. Happily, I was able to pull the phone off the shelf by grabbing its wire, otherwise I might have been there yet.'

'My concern is to establish whether it was an accident or whether you were attacked, Mr Robshaw.'

'Attacked? Good heavens no. Who would want to attack me?'

'People do sometimes get attacked in their

own homes, by intruders looking for valuables.'

'I have nothing worth stealing, Mr Rhea, as I am sure you now realize ... you will not tell anyone, will you? About the house?' And now he looked worried, as if I might be responsible for revealing his secret to the world.

'Tell anyone what?' I asked.

'Well, about the state of it, being so empty with no furnishings, no beauty inside.'

'That is no one's business but yours,' I said. 'It is nothing to do with anyone else and I have no intention of gossiping about it; it has no bearing on what happened to you – now I know your belongings haven't been stolen!'

'I am ashamed of it really, Mr Rhea, my lack of furnishings.'

'You have no cause to be ashamed, Mr Robshaw.'

But it seemed he wanted to tell someone and it just happened that I was conveniently on hand at that time.

'I have no money, Mr Rhea, not a penny and no skills. I looked after my parents, you see, they were both handicapped. Physically, I mean, so I cared for them. Dad made money, he was clever with the stock market, and when they died, I got the house and all their wonderful antiques. Dad invested in antiques. It was my inheritance, they said,

132

but there was no money, no cash. Not when the various debts had been settled. And so, with no work skills, I have used those antiques to pay my way ... sometimes I pay tradesmen with antiques, a sort of bartering system and sometimes, I would sell a nice piece to raise money ... that is how I have lived, Mr Rhea, but I keep up appearances. That is so important, isn't it, to maintain standards; and keep up appearances. That is why I employed specialists from afar, Mr Rhea, you see I could tell them I was just moving in or just moving out and so my gradually depleting stock of furnishings would not look unusual. My parents always insisted on that, that standards had to be maintained whatever the cost.'

'But surely not if you impoverish yourself in the process!' I smiled.

'There is still the house,' he said. 'If necessary, I shall sell it and move into something smaller, and use the profits to pay my way. But soon I shall get a state pension ... how nice that will be. I have managed to maintain my contributions, you see: it will be my first regular income. My parents told me it was not fitting for someone in my position to work, you see ... so I never have worked at a job, other than looking after them. So there you are. A mystery solved. You thought someone had broken in and stolen all my possessions, didn't you?'

'It has been known to happen,' I had to admit, thinking my response might make him happy. 'We've had instances where entire houses have been cleared by thieves equipped with furniture vans! I'm pleased it did not happen to you and thanks for being so open with me.'

'So thanks to a loose slipper my charade has been exposed. Maybe I should not have been so silly, struggling to maintain appearances, but having had such a limited background, what can one do?'

'You've survived a nasty fall, Mr Robshaw, so now you have some time to think about your future.'

'My experience in hospital has already taught me that it would be nice to be able to invite people in for a chat and a glass of whisky or something, and to have real friends, without worrying about the furnishings ... or lack of them.'

'Now that you've reached that decision, I am sure you will find a way. Now, shall I tell the vicar about your accident?'

'Do you think he would be interested?'

'I am sure he would, and I am sure he would pop in to see you, and perhaps someone from the congregation might come along too...'

'Yes, that would be nice. Thank you, Mr Rhea.'

When he came out of hospital, Mr Robshaw went to stay in a convalescent home recommended by the vicar, and while he was there, he put Shakespeare House on the market. It sold very quickly to two families who wanted to turn it into a small guest house and with the proceeds Mr Robshaw was able to buy and furnish a small cottage in Thackerston. I popped in to see him on a regular basis, and Mrs Browning – a widow – became a very frequent visitor. Eric once told me he'd never been able to form friendships, due I think to his childhood, but Mrs Browning persuaded him to go out for meals, to concerts and for outings to the countryside.

But Eric Robshaw never lost his ability to be stylish. Whenever I saw him with his new lady friend, I noticed that he walked with a silver-topped black cane.

But if Shakespeare House contained its very own secret, then so did South View, a charming olde worlde cottage on the approaches to Thackerston. South View stood back from the road with a paddock in front of it and, as the name suggests, it commanded wonderful views to the south. It was a small cottage built of the local mellow limestone and it had a roof of red pantiles. A rustic arch had been constructed over the front door and this was rich with wild roses and honeysuckle during the summer, while the garden around the house was always a riot of colourful blooms. People passing the house would regularly stop and take a photograph because, even in the depths of winter, the cottage always looked so charming and appealing. It was the sort of pretty country cottage for which so many townspeople long.

For a time after my arrival as the village constable, South View was owned and occupied by an elderly gentleman who lived alone. His two sons and one daughter, themselves in their late fifties, lived away from Thackerston. His wife had died fairly recently, but he had continued to live in the house and to care for himself, fortified by regular visits from his children and their children. His name was William Stoney who was well into his eighties, and he was a retired quarry worker. After his wife's death, he cooked his own meals, washed his own clothes and cleaned his own house with remarkable success.

He maintained that beautiful garden which had resulted in so many photographs of his home. Then William died, the house was sold and new people bought it. The new owners were Leonard and Sally Heaton, proprietors of a fashion shop in nearby Brantsford and their first task was to modernize the house, something they wanted to do without spoiling its charm and beautiful appearance. Their plans included bringing the bathroom and upstairs toilet facilities up to date, refurbishing and extending the kitchen, fitting wardrobes into all three bedrooms, incorporating a downstairs toilet, having the timbers protected against woodworm and improving the damp course. They retained their previous house in Brantsford while this work was in progress, thus allowing the contractors to work without having to cope with people living there. The builders responsible for the structural improvements were a small local firm called Hodgkinson Builders, based in Crampton, whose proprietor – Jack Hodgkinson – worked alongside his three employees.

It was a scorching hot August day, at lunchtime, when I heard a frantic knocking on my front door. I was in the garden, enjoying an out-of-doors lunch with my growing family. I'd enjoyed a morning off duty prior to beginning a late shift, one which entailed working from 2 p.m. until 10 p.m. With the heavy and rather frantic knocking, however, it sounded as if I was going to start work earlier than expected and so I walked around the outside of the house, in my shorts and sandals, and with a bare chest, to find Jack Hodgkinson standing there with a very anxious expression on his face.

'Hello, Jack,' I said. 'You look all hot and bothered!'

'So would you if you'd found what I've found!' He didn't smile, and did not comment on my casual attire. Whatever was on his mind, it must be very serious, I realized.

'So what have you found?' I asked.

'A skeleton,' he said. 'A human skeleton, a child by the look of it.'

'A skeleton?' My heart sank at the news. 'Are you sure?'

'I'm as sure as I'm standing here, Nick.' He wiped his brow. 'That's why I'm reporting it.'

'Where is it?' was my next and most obvious question.

'South View at Thackerston,' he said. 'We're working there right now, extending the kitchen, and we found it under an outhouse, one we're demolishing.'

'I'll be there right away, Jack,' I said. 'Give me five minutes to put my uniform on. Do you want to wait here, or shall I see you there?'

'I'll wait in my van and follow you down, I don't fancy going back there by myself. I've sent the lads home, by the way, they've another job to be getting on with while we get this sorted out.'

Minutes later, I escorted him to South View where we parked in the space beside the cottage.

'Round the back,' he said with signs of nervousness, but leading the way nonetheless. He led me to the rear of the cottage where one of the small outbuildings was in the process of being demolished to make way for the extended kitchen.

A pile of dressed stones, tiles and roofing timbers occupied what had been part of the vegetable garden and the only remaining part of the former shed was the concrete floor, partially broken up by a pneumatic drill. 'There.' He pointed from a distance.

At first, due to the broken-up nature of the concrete and the rubble beneath it, I could not recognize anything that looked like bones, but when I crouched on my haunches for a closer examination, I could see the distinctive shape of a skull among the dry earth and rubble. It was the same colour as the earth in which it lay and almost entirely covered, but as I brushed a small amount of soil away with my fingers, I realized that, beyond doubt, this was a human skeleton, much smaller than an adult, but a genuine well-preserved skeleton nonetheless. For reasons yet to be established, it had been buried under that concrete floor. At this very early stage, I could not see whether it was a complete skeleton or whether it comprised only the skull and some vertebrae; some vertebrae were visible among the undisturbed earth.

'How long's it been here do you reckon?' I asked Jack. 'Any idea when this floor would have been laid?'

'I wouldn't have a clue,' he admitted. 'It's not recent, though, that concrete is pretty old, I'd say, not like modern stuff. I'd say that floor was added after the house was built; these old houses had earth floors you know, even until the last war in some cases, and outbuildings especially didn't have concrete floors until fairly recently.'

'I wonder why it was concreted over?' I was thinking aloud now.

'This is an old house, Nick. That out-building we're knocking down was as old as the house – two hundred years old I'd say – but that concrete floor's not as old as that. I'd say it was more than twenty or thirty years old but not two hundred years old, if that's any help.'

'It's a wide gap but our experts will be able to tell us something, I'm sure,' I told him. 'Well, I'd better call in the cavalry!'

'Cavalry?' he smiled anxiously.

'The troops,' I smiled. 'This is something for our experts to investigate, not a job for a mere village constable. Sergeant Blaketon, our Scenes of Crime experts, a pathologist and even forensic scientists could come, I guess, and among them will be someone who can tell us how old the skeleton is, whether it's male or female, elderly or

140

youthful, whether he or she died naturally or was killed, how long it's been buried and so on, and then we'll have to dig up the rest of that concrete, very carefully, to see what else lies under there.'

'You think there might be more?'

'Who knows?' I shrugged my shoulders. 'So let's get started.'

'Shall I stay?' he asked.

'I'll need a written statement from you, Jack, to record how you came to find this, I can catch you later if you've things to do, but I could take the statement right now while I'm waiting for my support teams to arrive. It'll take ten minutes, that's all, I'll take it down in my pocket book, and you'll have to sign it.'

'Let's get it over with,' he said.

'We can sit in the van,' I offered and he agreed.

Before recording Jack's account of the discovery, my first task was to inform Sergeant Blaketon. The moment he received my radio call, he began to panic in case we'd uncovered a murder victim and he told me not to touch anything until the experts arrived. He would call out Scenes of Crime, he said, and a pathologist, and I had to guard the scene until their arrival – and he would attend as soon as he could. In the meantime, I interviewed Jack Hodgkinson who told me how he had been operating the pneumatic drill to break up the concrete base and how he'd caught sight of the skull, happily halting his work before any real damage was done to the bones. He'd satisfied himself that it was not a joke, that no one had planted the object there for him to unearth, and that was all. He'd halted work immediately to inform the police and in the statement, I included his estimate on the age of the concrete floor. Then he signed the statement.

'What about telling the owners?' I asked him. 'Have you done that yet?'

'I'll have to tell them,' he said. 'They ought to know and it will mean work's going to be delayed until this is sorted out.'

'If the telephone is active, I can ring them from here,' I offered. 'I can't do it by radio, though!'

'The phone is live,' he told me. 'They did that so they can call me here or I can ring them.'

Jack offered to remain and help remove the rest of the concrete if that was necessary, but I said our own teams may prefer to do that.

He said he had another job only a ten-minute drive away, and so I suggested he left to attend to that. We could recall him if it was necessary – besides, it might be a long time before our officers wanted the remaining concrete removed. Somewhat relieved, he said he would leave now but left a contact number in case he was required. I then rang Mr Heaton at his shop.

'It's PC Rhea,' I announced myself. 'I'm ringing from your house at Thackerston.'

'South View? Not bad news, Constable, I hope!' but his voice revealed his concern.

'In a way, yes,' and I explained what had happened, adding that police teams were already *en route*.

'Oh, my God this is all I need ... it's taken me months to get those builders in and now they'll be off on other job ... but how serious is this, PC Rhea? Are we talking of murder, or is it some skeleton buried centuries ago?'

'We won't know the answer to that until we've had the bones examined in a laboratory,' I said.

'I won't come to make a nuisance of myself, PC Rhea, but you will keep me informed of progress, won't you?'

'I will,' I assured him, then settled down to await Sergeant Blaketon. He arrived in the official Ashfordly police car and looked rather flustered as he bustled to the rear of the house where I had waited. I led him to the remains of the concrete floor and showed him the discovery.

'I hope this is not a murder case, Rhea, I can do without a murder enquiry in my countdown as section commander.'

'I think it is a child's skeleton, Sergeant,

it's very small but I'm not sure how much of it there is under the concrete.'

'Our Scenes of Crime wizards are *en route*,' he said. 'And I was lucky to catch Dr Prescott; he's already on his way from Scarborough. We've about an hour to wait. So, have we any missing children on our records? Missing in the last, what, thirty or forty years or more.'

'I haven't done any research into that, Sergeant, not yet.'

'Give Ventress a call on your radio and get him to search the records as far back as he can go. Children missing from home, that sort of thing, or even a small person missing. This could be a small adult although I think it is a child. Mind, you can't really judge a person's height from only part of a skull, can you? At least, I can't. Experts might.'

The Force Scenes of Crime officers comprising Detective Sergeant Gideon and Detective Constable Linford, were first to arrive but, after a superficial examination of the discovery said they would await the pathologist. Things surrounding the remains, like pieces of stone, earth or other artefacts might be relevant in determining the age of the skeleton. Within a further half-hour Dr Jim Prescott, the forensic pathologist, arrived eager to begin his examination. After establishing the story of the discovery, he knelt beside the remains and began to examine them, first with the naked eye and then through a magnifying glass.

Eventually, he said, 'We need to remove as much soil as we can, and as much of the remaining concrete as possible.'

'I can recall the builder,' I offered. 'He has the necessary equipment.'

'I see no harm in using his skills, under our guidance,' said Prescott. 'Right, Constable, see if he can help us. We need to break up and remove this concrete blanket piece by piece, very carefully.'

Jack said he would arrive in ten minutes and so extraction of the remains commenced, a curious mixture of gentle archaeological technique and powerful drilling tools. But, as the work progressed, with the remaining concrete being broken into small pieces by Jack's powerful and noisy drill before being carefully set aside, those of us watching realized that this was a complete skeleton and that it was a child, a young child by the appearance of the bones. Younger than a teenager, we reckoned. But in time, all the concrete and rubble had been removed, and Gideon, aided by Linford, began to scrape away the layers of dry soil.

Slowly, but surely, the skeleton of a small child was revealed, lying in a bed of dry earth. There was no sign of any clothing or coffin and no adornments to the body. Prescott's gentle hands skimmed the surface of the skull, seeking signs of injury, the kind that might result from a blow to the head, but he found none. He looked at the neck bones too, for signs of manual strangulation, and then the vertebrae down the full length of the spine. Ribs, arms and legs were examined too, for this was a complete skeleton unaffected by the attention of wild animals because it had been securely buried under its concrete covering.

It took over two hours to reach this stage, but Prescott was extremely careful and very patient as he uncovered the remains inch by inch. Finally he stood up, stretched his back and said, 'It is the skeleton of a child, gentlemen, I am pretty certain about that. Age? Difficult to say. Four or five at death perhaps. Not a teenager and not a baby, that is certain, this is not a stillborn child. Sex? The bones are female, I know that from the pelvic area. Cause of death? There are no marks of injury on the bones, no signs of strangulation or skull damage, no broken ribs or smaller bones, and so I would say it was death by natural causes although I cannot rule out poison until I have examined the bones in laboratory conditions and had samples analysed. How old are the bones? At this stage, I do not know. I'd hazard a guess by saying they were not buried here during the last fifty years but they might be considerably older. I shall let you know once I have the results of my laboratory tests.'

'So we're not looking for a murderer?' smiled Blaketon with some relief.

'It is very difficult to be sure, Sergeant, but there may be an unauthorized burial, or unrecorded burial. Who was the child? Who has lived in this house – who buried the child and why? And was the concrete floor laid to conceal the grave, or did some later resident put down the concrete, little realizing what lay beneath? You have some puzzles to solve, gentlemen. Meanwhile, I shall ask that the remains be taken to my laboratory so that I can examine them in more detail.'

It took a while to arrange transportation of the remains to the pathology laboratory and, with Jack's help, we excavated further just to ensure no more skeletons were buried behind South View. There was a suggestion the area could have been a Saxon graveyard, or even a more modern Quaker burial ground but no further bones were discovered. We decided the discovery was the only skeleton buried here.

Sergeant Blaketon instructed me to inform the coroner about the discovery and then asked me to investigate the lives of

147

previous owners and occupiers of South View but I decided not to question anyone still living until I had the pathologist's confirmed opinion about the age of the bones. I had no wish to imply there had been a criminal act by some living person or the deceased relative of some living person until more evidence was available.

It would be some three weeks later when Dr Prescott rang me.

'I have carried out a very careful study of the South View skeleton,' he told me. 'Perhaps the most significant finding is that arsenic is present in the bones. Now, Constable, you may be aware arsenic can be present in soil in which case it might contaminate any skeletal remains covered by it, and in any case, all human bodies contain microscopic amounts of arsenic. The presence of arsenic does not necessarily imply a crime. But in this case, there is a substantial amount. I'd say that child – a female – died from arsenic poisoning, Constable, and that she was around four or five years old at the time. Whether the arsenic was ingested accidentally or fed to the girl deliberately is something we shall never know, but arsenic poisoning in England was very prevalent a century ago. Indeed, in 1851, the Arsenic Act was made law to restrict the purchase of arsenic. I'd say it was around that time when she died.'

'So we might have a murder victim, Doctor?'

'Quite possible, Constable, quite possible. But I doubt if you'll be able to record the crime as solved. Tests on the bones suggest they are at least a century old. As I said, I think this girl died around 1850, give or take a few years either side of that date. I shall send my written report very soon, and you might wish to inform the coroner of this call, pending his receipt of my report.'

I told Jack Hodgkinson of this and then the Heatons, with Mrs Heaton now wondering whether she could live in a house under which a body had been buried, and I updated my verbal report to Ashfordly Police Station, saying my written report would follow. Some weeks later, at the subsequent inquest on the bones, the coroner recorded an open verdict and the bones were eventually buried, at public expense, in Thackerston churchyard.

I did make enquiries into the previous ownership of South View and learned the house had once been called Rose Bower but the mystery of that dead girl remains unsolved. None of the local papers in the middle of the last century reported a missing girl, the case did not appear in any of our old records and I discovered absolutely nothing suspicious about any of those long-dead occupants. Nor did I find a record of a young girl living there at the material time.

There the matter ends – except that the villagers raised funds for a gravestone for the unfortunate child.

In the absence of a known name, we called her Rose Bower and the inscription said she had passed from this earth aged five, *c*1850. Someone produced a nice epitaph for her – it said 'Finally at Peace' and her tombstone can still be seen in a quiet corner of Thackerston churchyard – with South View watching over it. The Heatons decided to sell the house, however, and some people from Hastings bought it. No one told them about the skeleton. They don't know to this day.

Chapter 5

Some of the houses I visited in the course of my duties were veritable private museums of a small but very specialized nature. One lady collected blue thimbles, or thimbles with blue adornments upon them, and every suitable shelf in her house was occupied by her collection which seemed to be fashioned from a variety of materials. In spite of her all-consuming passion for such objects, I never discovered the reason for her particular interest. Another man collected watercolours by a local artist called Scott Hodgson, but when that man died, his collection was dispersed to relatives – but as a sole collection for this under-rated Yorkshire artist, the collection would have been unique had it remained intact. I have no doubt some art gallery would have welcomed that kind of donation and although most of the collections I was shown were fairly mundane, there were some which were unusual and probably unique in some particular, or even valuable from both an artistic, historic and even commercial aspect.

Even everyday objects can appear interesting when they form part of a cherished collection. I was shown collections of things like matchbox labels, cigarette cards, beermats, mugs bearing place names, out-of-date cameras, inkwells and ink bottles, fountain pens, dolls, teddy bears, perfume bottles, comics, series of magazines, books by particular authors, or every edition of a classic novel, glassware, china, wooden carvings, whisky artefacts and drinks memorabilia such as toucans and models of Johnny Walker. Without exception, each treasured article had a story behind it, something of blessed memory to the owner.

And if I called at any of these houses for

whatever reason, I was usually shown at least part of these proud collections and regaled with stories about the most treasured items. Certainly, most collections were a talking point and an icebreaker, some resulting from a lifetime's work.

Even police officers joined the fun by collecting helmet badges, cap badges or police uniform buttons from around the world. Some even managed to collect entire uniforms, enough to fill several large houses, while one old friend of mine collected traction engines and steam rollers. Saving old cars, motor bikes or even pedal cycles were popular hobbies too, while another friend of mine has what is surely the world's biggest collection of post marks. These are from post offices around the world, many of which have since been absorbed into larger units so that those small village post marks have become obsolete and thus no longer obtainable. Many are now rarities and my friend makes a good living writing and lecturing about his unique collection.

Whatever is manufactured or created is quite likely to become part of the specialist collection of some ardent admirer and, hopefully, such treasures eventually find themselves permanently housed in a formal museum.

Some collections do seem utterly useless

however. I had to visit the home of an old lady in Ploatby and could hardly get into the place because it was full of old newspapers. They were neatly folded and piled high on the floors, tables, sideboards and under the table and on the staircase and in the pantry. In more than one place the piles reached the roof of the room, and in some instances, she had to scramble over piles of newspaper in order to reach cupboards or even her staircase.

I have no idea when or why she started to collect newspapers, but she told me she had never ever thrown a newspaper out, and had never used one to light her fire. She lived alone and I wondered what would happen to the newspapers when she died. She was still living in that little paper-packed cottage when I left Aidensfield so I have no idea what became of her and her tons of newspapers.

Perhaps the most appalling collection I ever encountered was in a terraced council house where every feasible space, even the sides of the staircase, window ledges, mantelpiece, tops of wardrobes, kitchen shelves, every inch of floor space and anywhere else, was full of pint milk bottles of the old, tall, slender-necked type – and each was full of the male householder's urine. Even the downstairs toilet was full of them and the stench was unbelievable. I discovered this awful hoard when I had to interview the householder during my enquiries into the sudden death of a neighbour, but I asked him to sit in my van for my interrogation. There is no way I could have spent even the shortest time in that dreadful stinking house. I have no idea why he behaved in such a peculiar manner, but later I dropped a quiet word into the ear of a local council official. Clearly, the fellow had a problem of some kind – and some dairy or milkman was missing a few bottles!

But another prized collection provided me with something of a professional puzzle. On a hillside overlooking Elsinby stands a fine brick-built Victorian mansion which commands extensive views across the village to the front and the moors to the rear.

In its own spacious gardens and grounds, it was built around 1845 by a highly successful businessman and included a range of stables, loose boxes, a conservatory complete with vine, greenhouses, potting sheds and sundry other very useful outbuildings. As I became gradually more knowledgeable about the people living on my patch, I learned that the house – called Elsinby Manor – was currently occupied by a wealthy gentleman and his wife, each of whom had wide business interests in this country and overseas. They were Geoffrey and Isabella Cunningham, a sophisticated and popular couple in their mid-fifties who had purchased Elsinby Manor several years prior to my arrival as their village constable.

Among Geoffrey's business enterprises was a flourishing wine importing company specializing in reds and white from the Loire Valley but he had many other interests, including a furniture production company in Sunderland, a perfumery in Portugal and a motor-car franchise in northeast England. His wife was also a businesswoman with a sports outfitters in York, a restaurant in Harrogate and an up-market shoe shop in Leeds specializing in personal fitting for ladies.

They were a busy, successful but very pleasant couple with no children who lived alone in that huge manor house, albeit with help in the form of a cleaner, a secretary, a couple of gardeners, an occasional handyman and also an occasional cook, all recruited from the village. With Geoffrey's overseas interests, he spent a lot of time away from home, something that did not appear to worry Isabella because she could usefully employ herself with her own business interests and a busy social life.

She liked to entertain at home and her dinner parties were widely known and enjoyed by like-minded people from the locality. Sometimes Geoffrey attended her parties but quite often when he was away on business, Isabella used those occasions to bring in her own friends, rather than tolerate their joint friends or business acquaintances. Although, to some extent they lived separate lives, they were very happily married and overtly a very close couple.

Not quite six feet tall, Geoffrey was prematurely white-haired, stockily built and rather stooping in appearance which made him look older than he really was. He behaved rather like a man older than his years too; he loved his dark-red Jaguar car, his two yellow labrador dogs, his wine, his cigars and the occasional visit to the local pub for a chatter with the local menfolk. He claimed such visits kept his feet firmly on the Yorkshire ground. By contrast, Isabella was dark-haired with more than a hint of Mediterranean blood within her. She wore her plentiful glossy hair very long, often with a bright ribbon tying it back in a ponytail, and she loved brightly coloured clothes, often wearing skirts of bright red, yellow, blue, orange and green, or a mixture of all colours, along with frothy white blouses. She behaved in ways which suggested she was ten years younger than her genuine age. Tall and buxom, she loved Spanish dancing, for example, holidays in the sunshine and loud modern music while Geoffrey preferred to relax with Beethoven, his slippers and a glass of brandy beside the fire. In some respects, they were as different as chalk and cheese, but they were a happy and contented pair who complemented one another in their private and business lives.

Or, perhaps to be truthful, their outward appearances suggested a happy and contented marriage because, as I was later to discover, there was some kind of discord within the happy household. I think it was a rather minor discord but it took me a while to appreciate its precise form or source, but things began to happen while Geoffrey was overseas on a wine-buying mission. Unfortunately, as many of us know, if a problem manifests itself early in the day, then that problem increases, expands and intensifies as the day progresses, usually compounding itself and adversely affecting other matters as the day proceeds until, as night falls, we realize the day has been one long series of linked disasters. And all because we could not find one of our shoes when we overslept, which meant we missed the train to work and then the boss arrived at the office earlier than expected that morning and he urgently wanted figures from the file which we'd left at home in our panic to catch the train...

And so it was with Geoffrey and Isabella on that noteworthy occasion. Perhaps, in order to provide the full flavour of this incident, I ought to first refer to Geoffrey's passion. He was an avid collector of paintings in watercolours and oils; he collected pastels too and even colour photographs but only one subject interested him: it was nude women – provided they were redheads. Whenever he saw a picture of a naked redhead, he felt compelled to purchase it and then display it in Elsinby Manor. This meant that most of the walls bore pictures of redheaded nudes, some in the form of huge oils, others in miniature style and some as colour photographs, and there is no doubt Geoffrey's fine collection was unusual – and very interesting to his male visitors.

Unfortunately, as I was to learn, Isabella did not wholly approve of his passion. In fact, there were times she positively fumed at some of his more erotic purchases, something she often mentioned to her friends in the district (which is how I came to hear about it), but Geoffrey steadfastly refused to abandon his aim to keep adding to his collection and displaying them in the house. He ignored Isabella's regular protests about their presence – he did listen to and obey her in practically all other matters, even down to the decor and style of furniture. I believe this was part of his ploy to keep his pictures! When it came to redheaded nudes, therefore, Geoffrey was adamant. He would buy pictures of them whenever he wanted and he would display them in the house wherever he wanted. Most of us knew that Isabella disliked his hobby because she was never afraid to say so, but whether this was because she was a raven-haired beauty of continental appearance, or whether Geoffrey had once shown undue interest in a redhead, fully dressed or otherwise, is something I do not know. I believe, however, that this was the only true discord between this happy and fortunate couple, but on one occasion it provoked a rather complicated series of occurrences.

A day or so prior to one of Geoffrey's overseas trips, he made a walking tour of his property with one of his gardeners – Jim Barnes – and discovered that many of the outbuildings were full of old junk which had accumulated. Over the years, these cast-offs had been dumped there because it had been the most convenient solution at the time.

The rubbish comprised all sorts – discarded furniture such as drawers, wardrobes, settees and chairs, old gardening implements, a dead wheelbarrow, some children's toys left by a previous owner, broken and useless planks of wood, cracked vases and plant pots, bits of old cars and motor bikes, ancient fireplaces, a discarded bath and toilet basin, and more besides. Determined to clear the rubbish, Geoffrey had instructed the gardener to find some-one – like Claude Jeremiah Greengrass – to shift every piece of it. He wanted the sheds cleared of every piece of discarded junk and he would happily pay for its removal; if the clearance man was able to earn himself a little extra by selling some of the items, well, that was to his benefit. Geoffrey simply wanted rid of the accumulated clutter.

Geoffrey then showed Jim which sheds had to be cleared; there were three at the end of the garden near the greenhouses. Jim said he understood perfectly and would see to it without delay. The place would be clear of junk before Geoffrey's return from the Loire Valley. It was a chore long overdue.

Knowing Geoffrey's business plans well in advance, however, Isabella had planned an important dinner party during his absence. It would include some of her influential friends from the locality, but also the two directors of a prestigious department store on Tyneside through whom she hoped to sell her custom-made and rather expensive ladies' shoes. Geoffrey's absence was to be from one Friday morning until the follow-ing Thursday evening, and so Isabella – with Geoffrey being fully informed of her plans – arranged her event for the Tuesday evening between those Fridays.

Being a good businesswoman, however, Isabella had undertaken some research into the two lady directors from Tyneside, only to discover they were twin sisters, both married, who did not drink alcohol, did not smoke, attended chapel every Sunday, thought Hollywood films were immoral, abhorred women appearing in public in bathing costumes and refused to stock items of lingerie because men were regular customers in their shop. They did not think men should be free to look at women's underwear. Isabella was not surprised to learn the sisters belonged to some kind of puritanical religious sect with its roots in the Scottish wee-frees. Mrs Hester Fisher and Mrs Rebecca McDonald, however, were very successful in the business world and Isabella discovered they had no objection to other people enjoying a glass of wine or a cigarette on formal occasions – but they did not themselves indulge.

In spite of their quirks, Isabella felt she could safely entertain the sisters, who would be staying at an hotel in Ashfordly for a semi-holiday, and she therefore went ahead with her plans, but with discreet warnings to her closer friends about the sensitivities of Mrs Fisher and Mrs McDonald.

As her plans were nearing completion, however, she suddenly remembered Geoffrey's nude redheads which adorned every wall in the house; the dining-room had a particularly seductive beauty on the west wall while every picture-hanging space on walls around the table was filled with a nude redhead in some pose or other. The drawing-room boasted three massive gilt-framed charmers; the downstairs toilet was full of miniatures and the cloakroom had that very detailed colour photograph taken in what appeared to be a jungle or perhaps a greenhouse.

With something approaching horror-stricken panic, Isabella realized there were nude redheads at every place the puritanical sisters would be visiting. Bearing in mind the background knowledge she had acquired about them, and unable to consult Geoffrey due to his absence, Isabella decided the nudes must be removed. None of Geoffrey's pictures must jeopardize a possible business deal of such lucrative and socially acceptable possibilities. Isabella knew she could hire replacement pictures from some of the local galleries at short notice, and in any case she had some of her own in the attic. Her collection comprised lots of Mediterranean scenes and English rural landscapes, and so, in a last-minute rush of conscience, Isabella set about the removal of Geoffrey's nudes. Aided by her two cleaners and her handyman, the pictures were swiftly taken down during Monday, but because Isabella did not wish them to clutter her stylishly furnished reception rooms, she told the cleaners to store them, temporarily, in one of the outbuildings.

'Put them in a nice dry place,' she told them. 'And we can replace them before Geoffrey returns.'

And so it was that Geoffrey's renowned collection of redheaded nudes – dozens if not hundreds of them – found themselves placed somewhat unceremoniously in a dark but dry outbuilding behind Elsinby Manor. They reclined among an array of discarded furniture including an old wardrobe, two washstands, some broken dining chairs and an old sideboard.

It so happened that Claude Jeremiah Greengrass had been commissioned by Jim Barnes to clear the outbuildings of their rubbish.

Claude had assured Jim that he and his helper, David, would arrive mid-morning on the Monday to load their vehicle but Claude's trusty rusty old truck, had suffered some kind of relapse which took Bernie Scripps a considerable time to repair. The outcome was that Claude could not remove the junk on the Monday, but he was able to do so the following Wednesday.

Although Geoffrey always told Isabella about his business commitments he had not said anything to her about clearing the garden sheds and so this minor hiccup – the

Greengrass delay – was not known to Isabella either. She had no idea that Geoffrey had decided to clear the sheds and was more than happy that the nudes should remain in one of them, out of sight, until they could be returned in advance of Geoffrey's return to the Manor. Even though she disliked them, she did allow Geoffrey to display them – after all, he was tolerant in all other respects, not even complaining when she played loud music or played with her castanets.

On that Wednesday, therefore, Claude Jeremiah Greengrass and David Stockwell, his willing learner-driver assistant, arrived to carry out their commission, driving around to the rear of the premises where they were met by Jim Barnes. Jim said everything had to go and he had recruited assistance from some of his pals and so, under directions from Claude as to the sequence of packing the rubbish, the band of men began to empty the sheds. Claude, however, had made a preliminary reconnaissance of the sheds and had spotted the stack of nudes. Realizing these were rather special, he decided they should be first into his truck – he'd drive away to dispose of them before returning for the remaining items.

I am afraid I am unable to record the delights expressed when the men handled

164

the hoard of nudes, but I was later to learn that the Greengrass lorry had been seen speeding into York with dozens of pictures on board. Claude, it seemed, knew an art dealer who would cheerfully buy anything of quality presented to him without asking too many embarrassing questions about the source, and so Claude managed to sell Geoffrey's wonderful collection for £550 – cash. Claude then returned to concentrate on the old pieces of furniture. It was a good day's work for Claude Jeremiah Greengrass.

Because Isabella's hired pictures had to be returned to the lender on Wednesday morning, her helpers cleared the walls and packed them ready for return, returning her own pictures to the attic at the same time. At 10 a.m., a hired van appeared at Elsinby Manor and removed the hired pictures; Isabella had the rest of the day to recover Geoffrey's nudes and all day Thursday to hang them in their original places, but at 10.30 a.m. on Wednesday she received a phone call from her mother. That call completely ruined her plans. In her anguish, Isabella forgot about Geoffrey's nudes when her mother demanded her immediate presence because she (mother) was desperately ill. Pausing only to pack her nightdress and toiletries, Isabella therefore rushed off to Wolverhampton to tend to her mother who was suffering from a stomach disorder but who was not as ill as she had pretended. Nonetheless, Isabella thought it wise to stay for a couple of days, and had the foresight to leave a note for Geoffrey to explain her absence. In it, she said she would ring to let him know mother's progress. She left it on his desk in the study.

Geoffrey, therefore, came home to an empty house on Thursday evening, let himself in and found lots of bare walls and no sign of his precious nudes. His first reaction was that his home had been burgled by someone who knew the value of the paintings, but as he gathered his shocked wits, he realized there was no sign of forcible entry and no other damage or tell-tale signs of an intruder. That suggested the culprit was Isabella! As he brewed himself a coffee while trying to look objectively at the situation, he tried to remember whether, prior to leaving for France, he'd said anything or done anything which might have inflamed her open dislike of his pictures. Had she disposed of them in a fit of pique? Was this some way of securing revenge for something he'd done or omitted to do? As he wandered around the house trying to come to some logical conclusion, he found Isabella's note on the desk and decided to ring her.

'It's Geoffrey,' he had said, with strained politeness. 'I'm back, darling.'

'You got my note?' she asked. 'I'm sorry I had to leave in such a rush, but mother was ill...' and she provided him with an account of her activities while asking about the success of his trip. Not once, he noted, did she refer to the pictures. When she had finished, she promised she would return home on Saturday and it was then he decided to ask about his missing pictures.

'Oh, my God!' she cried. 'Oh, Geoffrey, I am sorry. I removed them...'

'Removed them?' he bellowed. 'Why, for God's sake?'

She explained about Mrs Fisher and Mrs McDonald and he listened, his anger subsiding as Isabella's reasoning sounded perfectly feasible under the circumstances.

'So where are they?' he asked in due course. 'I've searched the house looking for burglars, but didn't find any of my pictures.'

'I had them put in that garden shed, Geoffrey, the one with the green door. On Tuesday.'

'Locked, was it?' he asked.

'Oh, no, none of those sheds have locks as you know, but we've never lost anything.'

'That's because they were used to store junk,' he said. 'No one's likely to steal junk! Those paintings are worth a fortune! Anyway, I'll go and find them now, then get help rehanging them. But next time you have people in for dinner, make sure they don't object to the finest of art, and if you have to remove and store them in the future, make sure you keep them in the house, in a secure place.'

'Yes, of course, Geoffrey, I'm sorry,' and their conversation ended.

He hurried out and searched all the garden sheds, only to find every one of them empty. As instructed, Jim had arranged their clearance, and even though Geoffrey examined the shed with the green door, it was empty too. Growing increasingly worried, he searched every other out-building on his premises, every parked vehicle, every room in the main house including the attic and even the vegetation beneath his hedges and around the extremities of the property. But there was no sign of his precious nudes. Now very unhappy, he rang Isabella again.

'Isabella,' he said, 'you did put my paintings in that shed, didn't you? The one with the green door? You're sure about that?'

'Yes, of course I did, Geoffrey. Why would I say so if I hadn't done so?'

'They're not there now,' he said. 'In fact, they're nowhere to be seen. I've searched all the outbuildings, the garden, the vehicles, the house, the attic ... they're nowhere to be seen, Isabella. They've gone. Is this some kind of joke you are playing? I know you dislike those nudes but they are my pride and joy and...'

'I should be your pride and joy, Geoffrey, not some painting of a naked woman with red hair! But I put them in that shed, like I said. If they are not there, I have no idea where they are! You'd better speak to Jim about it. He might have moved them somewhere else.'

'He's not around, he's finished for the day.'

'Then go and see him all the same!' and she slammed down the telephone.

Jim Barnes, who lived in Elsinby, was at home when Geoffrey knocked on his door shortly before nine that Thursday evening and after they discussed the timetable of events, it was evident that the pictures had been inadvertently cleared by Claude Jeremiah Greengrass along with the rest of the junk. Geoffrey was mortified that anyone might consider his pictures worthless junk but his anger turned into anxiety as he realized two clear days had elapsed – where on earth would the pictures be now? Burnt to cinders? Thrown on to a council tip? Sold to a dealer? There was time enough for them to have reached the Continent or even to be packed ready for transportation to the United States.

He hurried around to the Greengrass ranch but Claude was not at home and there was no sign of his truck.

Geoffrey thought he might be in the pub and so he headed in that direction, only to meet me on the forecourt as I was about to pay one of my official visits.

'Just the man!' he breathed when he saw me. 'Just the man, Constable. Now, I am not sure whether I am about to report a crime to you, or whether I am the victim of sheer bad luck, or whether there is a conspiracy of some kind surrounding contentious articles of my property...'

'I'm all ears!' I invited him to explain.

We walked along the lane beside the pub, away from interested ears, and he told me the whole story in considerable detail, hence my ability to provide this account. When he had finished, I said, 'Well, Greengrass is in the pub, his truck's on the car-park so we can have a word with him, but if he removed the paintings in all innocence, as part of the other stuff he was asked to shift, then he's not committed a crime. Your only recourse is to take civil action to recover the pictures – unless he willingly returns them to you.'

'I hope he's not dumped them some-where!' He was hoarse with emotion now. 'Or sold them to some unscrupulous dealer. I mean, Constable, if Greengrass recognized the value of those paintings, he'd want to sell them for what he could get, wouldn't he?'

'He would indeed,' I had to admit. 'You did imply that whoever removed your rubbish could sell anything they took?'

'I did, I don't deny that, but never in my wildest dreams did I think my wife would place my art collection among the rubbish.'

'So let's talk to Claude,' I said. 'It's not really a police matter, I ought to say, but when dealing with the Greengrasses of this world, a police uniform is always helpful.'

Claude was drinking with his cronies when I found him and first protested at my intrusion upon his leisure time, but when I referred to the alleged theft of some valuable paintings from Elsinby Manor he agreed to accompany Geoffrey and I upon a little walk away from flapping ears.

'I never stole them!' He spoke with force and passion when I put the situation to him. 'I was asked to clear those sheds and told I could sell anything I wanted if I could get a bob or two for it, otherwise it all went to the council tip. You ask Jim Barnes, he got me to do the job.'

'We know that, Claude,' I tried to pacify him. 'All Mr Cunningham wants to know is – where are his pictures? They shouldn't have been put in those sheds, you see, it was an accident.'

'Well how was I to know that?' Claude bristled. 'I just did what I was told.'

'Yes, Claude, we're not saying you did

anything wrong,' Geoffrey now spoke to him. 'All I want is my pictures back, that's all. So where are they?'

'Well,' Claude blushed. 'I sold 'em, to a chap in York. A dealer. Art and antiques dealer. He reckoned he had a couple of customers who were looking for a range of pictures like that...'

'How much did you get for them?' was Geoffrey's next question.

'That's a matter between me and him,' said Claude. 'Us entrepreneurs don't discuss our profit margins or details of big deals, you should know that, Mr Cunningham.'

'One has to respect confidentiality in business matters, Claude,' smiled Cunningham. 'But if you got less than five thousand pounds, you were robbed!'

'Five thousand?' blasted Claude. 'That cheating sod gave me five hundred and I thought I'd done well...'

'They're insured for eight thousand pounds, Claude, and I want to get them back. That's all. You're not in trouble. All I need to know is that dealer's name so I can go and talk to him.'

'And what do I get out of all this? A load of expense and trouble and you asking for your money back!'

'That dealer owes me the right kind of money; they're my pictures not his. I need to see him – and I need to do so very urgently before he parts with them. And now I know what he paid you, I can do business with him, I'm sure.'

'Aye, well, it's a chap called Rattenby; he's got an antique shop just off Coney Street in York.'

'I know him,' said Cunningham. 'Thanks, Claude. I'll go immediately, I know his home address.'

I was not involved in any more of that incident but Geoffrey Cunningham did secure the return of his collection intact, although he had to pay £500 to reclaim it from Rattenby.

Claude, however, was not forced to return his money – that was a measure of Geoffrey's relief at tracing his beloved works of art. The odd thing was, though, that Rattenby told Geoffrey that two ladies, twin sisters who had a department store in Newcastle, had shown great interest in the entire collection. It seemed they were redesigning their famous store and wanted a more modern image – even though they didn't touch alcohol or stock lingerie, it seemed they loved classic art and had no objection to the nude form, whether male or female, provided it was tastefully portrayed in an artistic manner. They really would have loved that collection of nude redheads but Rattenby had to tell them the sale had been withdrawn for personal reasons – and I don't think Geoffrey mentioned any of that to Isabella.

Another problem arose through a wealthy incomer to Crampton, a village which lay a couple of miles from Aidensfield. This new arrival to our patch of rural peace high-lighted a problem which continues in many villages even today – that of naming houses. Because many of the villages around the North York Moors tend not to have main streets, the houses are not numbered con-secutively. Some houses don't have names and they have become known by the name of an occupant or some distinguishing feature, such as Miss Fenton's House, the White House, Three Chimneys or The Blacksmith's Cottage, and there are many obvious ones such as The Police House, The Vicarage, The Surgery, School House, Old School House, Old Vicarage, Station House, The Post Office House, The Poplars, The Oaks, Beech House, Church View or Honeysuckle Cottage.

Many are tucked away along quiet lanes, lots of them don't bother to display a name-plate and thus deliverymen and even the emergency services have difficulty finding these places. This is especially difficult on a dark, winter night when the village roads are deserted and there is no one from whom to ask directions. To add to the problem, some villages contain more than one house or cottage with the same name – The Cottage can appear several times in one village. Rose Cottage is another favourite which is often used for several places within a very small area and to those I could add Beckside, Riverside, Moorside, Ash Cottage and dozens more. In time, the local people are able to easily distinguish one from the other, invariably relying upon the identity of the occupants, but even so, there can still be difficulties.

This was highlighted when I discovered three farms all called Abbey Farm, and all within the same locality on my beat. Added to this problem was that two were owned by people called Gilham and the third by a man called Gilholm. If there was one redeeming feature, it was that Arthur Gilham's Abbey Farm lay within the parish of Aidensfield while Adam Gilholm's Abbey Farm was just across the river in Crampton parish. Then Alan Gilham built a new farm and called it Abbey Farm.

The reason for the name arose because, in medieval times, the land upon which all the farms stood had once belonged to Crampton Abbey. When the abbey was destroyed and totally eradicated in that first wave of attacks upon the Catholic Church, the building which had been the grange (the place where the monastery's grain crops were stored) survived Henry VIII's destruction. It was the only part of the former abbey to have survived; the rest had been razed to the ground.

After standing derelict for two centuries, the grange was reoccupied and developed into a farm, making use of some of the former lands of the abbey. Unlike the Victorian craze for calling such places The Grange, this farm had become known as Abbey Farm, Crampton.

Directly across the river, however, was the former site of the abbey church and, somewhere in the early eighteenth century, the owner of the land sold it to a developer who had been surprised to find tons of beautiful stone buried under the mounds around the river side. These were the stones of the old abbey church and so he built a splendid farm with outbuildings on the site – quite logically, this became known as Abbey Farm too, but because it was across the river from the other Abbey Farm, and in a different parish, no one was unduly concerned. After all, one Abbey Farm was in Crampton and the other in Aidensfield, even if they were separated only by the width of a small river. The similarity of owner's name did not appear until shortly before my arrival in Aidensfield when Abbey Farm, Aidensfield was owned by Arthur

Gilham, with its neighbouring Abbey Farm, Crampton being owned by Adam Gilholm.

The problem was exacerbated after World War II when the local estate decided to sell off some of its land. Parcels of land offered for sale included some which bordered Abbey Farm, Aidensfield but because Arthur Gilham could not afford to buy, it was offered on the open market – and bought by a man called Alan Gilham. He was not related to Arthur.

Then this incoming Gilham undertook some research and excavations which revealed the foundations of the former monastery including the dormer buildings, refectory and kitchen, all domestic quarters of the monks who had inhabited the former abbey. He wanted to built a modern farmhouse but with such a reservoir of good quality dressed stone, he decided to build his new home of old stone, using as much as he could find buried on site. And so a new farm appeared on that part of the former abbey – and Mr Alan Gilham decided to called it Abbey Farm.

Arthur protested loudly at this proposal, but Alan persisted, using the argument that his was the rightful name because Arthur's farm stood on land formerly occupied by the church part of the abbey – so Arthur should really call his premises Church Farm. In spite of Arthur's long protests, supported by his pal Adam Gilholm from Abbey Farm, Crampton, the completed new house and its modern outbuildings were named Abbey Farm, Aidensfield. It seemed there was no law to prevent the use of identical names even if there was confusion within the post office, the council offices, the water companies and others with official interests in the properties. All were able to offer suitable advice to Alan Gilham, as I understood they did in no uncertain terms, but he was not legally bound to take any notice.

One minor problem occurred on a regular basis when one or other of these farmers telephoned anyone. Gilham and Gilholm sound almost identical, particularly when spoken quickly in the dialect of the North Riding of Yorkshire. In both cases, the name sounds rather like 'gillum' although whenever they did make a phone call, they stressed their Christian names. In Adam's case, he made sure the recipient of his call knew that he was ringing from Crampton, not Aidensfield.

And so, when I arrived in Aidensfield, I had three Abbey Farms on my beat, all standing within little more than a couple of square miles, two of them occupied by Gilhams with an Aidensfield address. While acquainting myself with the history of these places, it took me a while to sort out in my mind which person owned which but, like the other local people, the problem faded as familiarity grew. Even so, there were times when I had to ponder whose firearms certificates were due for renewal or whose stock registers were due for quarterly inspection and, in the long term, I think the two A. Gilhams suffered most, if only because each regularly received mail belonging to the other -which was opened more often than not – and because business callers like commercial travellers, vets and others sometimes arrived at the wrong place.

There is little doubt the local people felt that Alan Gilham, in his new home, was at fault for his insistence on naming his construction Abbey Farm, but he was determined never to change its name. History was on his side, he claimed. A likeable if stubborn character, he got on surprisingly well with his neighbours and there was no reason to believe there was enmity between the two Gilhams in Aidensfield, or their near-namesake across the river in Crampton.

Then a major problem arose. One dark night, fire broke out in a haystack and one of them dialled 999, gasping out the address which sounded like 'Gillum, Abbey Farm' before the rest of the address was lost in the trauma of that moment.

The fire brigade was locally based and comprised a band of gallant volunteers rather than full-time fire officers and so, when they received the call-out, they were told by someone at Fire Headquarters that the emergency call had come from 'Gillum, Abbey Farm' with the rest of the address being lost. The recipient of that call, a part-timer at Brantsford, assured headquarters he knew Gilham at Abbey Farm, Crampton, and so they would head for that farm. As the first fireman to arrive at the station was an agricultural machinery mechanic who had also dealt with Adam Gilholm at Crampton, it was perfectly logical for him to support that decision, and so the Brantsford Fire Brigade appliance set out for Adam's Abbey Farm at Crampton.

As they approached Abbey Farm, Crampton with blue lights flashing and sirens sounding at ten o'clock that night, it became increasingly obvious they had gone to the wrong place, because there was no fire at this farm and a large blaze could be seen in the distance, across the river. That meant a considerable detour but their arrival had alerted Adam Gilholm and he rushed out to see what the commotion was about. He was quickly able to tell them that the fire was at Abbey Farm, Aidensfield but from this distance, in the dark, he couldn't be quite sure which Abbey Farm! He offered to telephone one or other of them to find out, but the firemen said there was no time and besides, the farmer would not be sitting by his phone – he'd be out there with his hosepipes and hayforks. Adam said that Arthur Gilham's Abbey Farm was first on their route from here and so the brigade turned out and bolted into the darkness with all lights and sirens in full action.

The fire wasn't at Arthur's farm either, and it took a further four or five minutes for the brigade to find their way to Alan's new buildings in their remote setting, by which time the haystack was well alight and throwing sparks among the neighbouring buildings with a freshening wind threatening to drive the flames towards the house itself. I was called out too – I could see the blaze from my hilltop police house and knew which of the Abbey Farms was at risk. Police officers attended all fire service call-outs where there might be suspicion of arson or malicious damage, but when the brigade eventually brought this blaze under control, their experts felt it was a case of spontaneous combustion, a common cause of fire among haystacks.

However, it had been an extremely worrying time for Alan Gilham, particularly as, in the darkness of that night and from his slightly elevated viewpoint, he could see the blue lights of the fire appliance twice heading for the wrong farm. At one stage, he did think he was going to lose his new house but when the fire service later rang him to say the confusion had occurred due to the similarity of neighbouring names and addresses, it prompted him to rename his farm. He called it Abbey View Farm and, as a gesture of solidarity, Arthur renamed his Abbey Church Farm, although Adam retained the original name. After all, he was in a different parish anyway.

Now, though, they've all left those farms on that ancient abbey site. All the new owners are now called Smith.

Chapter 6

It is often claimed that one of the roles of the police is to rescue members of the great British public from the results of their own stupidity. Certainly, some people – supposedly adults – do behave in a rather childish fashion, particularly when they are on holiday, and this often results in them requiring the aid of the emergency services. They do things like getting swept out to sea on rubber dinghies, lost in fog or snow in the mountains, trapped by the tide on beaches and setting fire to forests and moors; such dilemmas often occur through sheer carelessness, base stupidity or ill-preparation but it is the public who usually fund their rescue. It has often been suggested that fools should be made to pay for their own mistakes, but how can a daft working man afford to pay thousands of pounds for a combined air-sea rescue when his inflatable has been washed out to sea because he fell asleep in it, or his actions in lighting a campfire to cook his sausages and baked beans resulted in the loss by burning of thousands of acres of heather and peat moorland?

In similar vein, the fire brigade would say that a high proportion of chip-pan fires occur at tea-time when women leave them on full heat while gossiping, cars fall on to men working beneath them because they are not properly jacked up and do-it-yourself merchants sometimes find their houses collapsing around their ears because they haven't been sufficiently careful in their 'improvement' work. It is beyond doubt that the police, fire brigade and ambulance service spend a lot of their time – and a lot of public money – going to the assistance of total clowns and coping with the lamentable behaviour of idiots.

Having said all that, it is also a fact of police life that some silly incidents occur, not through carelessness or stupidity, but through an unfortunate and unpredictable combination of circumstances. And, like those who are fools, it is often the police or some other emergency service, who have to remedy the matter.

For example, consider the case of Cuthbert Crombie who became known in Aidensfield as Crombie the Zombie. Cuthbert was what might be described an idealist; he was very left-wing and voted Labour; he wanted to ban the bomb, nationalize all systems of production, have no private ownership of property and live in a happy clappy world where everyone was equal, except those who were more equal than the others because they had more brains. They would be the leaders of his new world, and he would be among them showing others how to lead the ideal life. Full of socialist zeal of the more loony kind, he left the urban haze of industrial Rotherham to live in the fresh moorland air of rural Aidensfield where he could convert the unbelievers, or just sit and think, or perhaps just sit.

In his late twenties, bearded, long-haired, be-sandalled and fond of wearing jeans, Cuthbert was married to Clarissa and they had two sweet children, a boy and a girl, aged five and three respectively, who were called Clement and Cleo. They lived in a small but gloriously untidy rented cottage behind the main street of Aidensfield; the cottage had a paddock and a large garden, both of which were overgrown and the couple kept hens, geese, several pet rabbits and three cats. They also tried to grow food such as potatoes, carrots, lettuce and cabbages, but the weeds invariably won the battle for space and food.

It seemed Cuthbert thought garden produce would look after itself once it had been planted, as weeds do.

Cuthbert worked as a lecturer in Rural Studies in a local polytechnic college, travelling to the deepest West Riding of Yorkshire in his battered old car two or three times a week, during term time, for his few stints behind the lectern. At home, he liked to pop into the local pub for a pint of ale and a chat with the local yokels and, from these talks, the villagers understood that it was his dream to become self-sufficient. The locals knew it was impossible with such a small patch of land, but as an academic and lecturer in Rural Studies, Cuthbert was not expected to know that.

When he was not expounding the theory of rustic living to his little band of enthusiastic students, it seems he spent the rest of his time at his cottage producing learned articles about various rural topics. These included his plans for a socialist future full of maypole dances, happy people who worked wholeheartedly for the state and ultimately a future where it was not necessary to do any work at all, and where a classless society allowed everyone to earn the same money, eat the same food, buy the same clothes, live in the same houses and never refer to other people as sir, Your Grace, Your Worships or Your Majesty.

In addition, though, he did spend time wondering how to become a thoroughly rural person – in truth, his vision was impossible. He envisaged a socialist countryside, something that could and would never happen. Most of us got the impression that, rather than lecture about rural matters, he wanted to actually live within the theories he perpetually expounded to his eager students.

To give him due credit, he was a charming fellow who wouldn't harm a soul and he did take an active part in village affairs, becoming a member of the committee of the village hall, a member of the parish council, secretary of the local CND committee and chairman of the Aidensfield Labour Party of whom there were three members. One was his wife and the third member was a former guard with British Rail who had been sacked or 'victimized' for sleeping while on duty. With a really Socialist Britain, so it seemed, no one would ever be sacked from their state-controlled job whatever they did or did not do.

If Cuthbert was to achieve his dreamlike mission, he knew he must become a countryman. From his visits to the pub, we knew that was his way of infiltrating the simple rural people, but it seemed they were happy to enlighten him because he began to learn a little rural realism from the local farm workers and landowners. He felt he had won a minor battle when, over a few pints, they persuaded him to attend the local agricultural shows which would be held during the summer while his college was on holiday. There he could look at animals and vehicles, new methods of controlling pests or fertilizing crops, and learn something about the financing of rural life, not forgetting the drawbacks such as diseases of animals, the need for slaughter-houses and knackers' yards, the necessity of fox-hunting, rat-poisoning and other vermin control.

From time to time, I enjoyed an off-duty drink in the pub, or perhaps a visit during the course of my work, and even on those occasions, I could see that Cuthbert was losing his battle.

He thought he was winning the conversion stakes, but in fact the regulars were steadily converting Cuthbert into a capitalist/countryside way of thinking. They were clever enough to let him think he had thought of some of the startling new ideas he began to propound, such as 'It's not really a capitalist idea to own a pig' or 'No man is an island' and 'Money is a sort of fuel, it helps the economy to function'.

Somehow, through all his pontificating, they had persuaded him that it would be a good idea to create a herd of dairy cattle, there to provide the finest of sustenance to the masses, and they persuaded him it was easily achieved through sales of milk, sales of animals for meat, selective breeding and, of course, the wonderful subsidies offered by the government.

Thinking about it, Cuthbert realized he would need a field to accommodate his cows, but, as he had no desire to be known as a landowner, he could rent the necessary grazing land, but he would require buildings and equipment, then there would be veterinary fees and umpteen regulations to obey, all of which could be financed from sales of milk without necessarily making a capitalist profit.

And so it was that a somewhat enlightened Cuthbert went off to Brantsford Agricultural Show one hot summer Thursday, there to try and learn at least a little of the true benefits of owning cattle, perhaps a dairy herd, or even fatstock for eventual sale. Such was his new enthusiasm for all things rural and all things farming, and such was his desire to actually be able to call something his very own, that he entered a typically rustic competition, the first prize of which was a fully grown Charolais bull.

The competition was easy – one had simply to guess the weight of the huge creamy-white bull itself, and it was standing there in a pen, looking almost cuddly, as competitors examined it.

I was on duty at the show, initially in the car-park and later patrolling the show-ground during the course of the event as a deterrent to drunks, pickpockets and other socially unacceptable offenders. During the event, I did have a passing chat with Cuthbert, but was later amazed and shocked when I discovered he had won the Charolais. His name was mentioned over the loudspeaker system. I knew that some socialists did not like people owning valuable objects and I wondered how he would deal with that idealistic problem, but I discovered that winning things, without actually working for them, seemed to be acceptable within that ideology. And so it was that Cuthbert padded off to the secretary's tent to claim his prize bull. While he went to claim his animal, I moved to the exit gate so that I could supervise the departing traffic and while I was there, he came up to me.

'Nick,' he said, his face a picture of misery,

'I've won that bull ... I mean, what on earth can I do with it? I've been to claim it and they say I have to move it from the showground. It's my responsibility because it's my animal and it can't stay on the showfield; they're starting to clear it already and then there's the question of food and transport and things...'

'There's George Boston over there.' I pointed to a parked Landrover belonging to an Aidensfield farmer whom I knew well. 'Have a word with him.'

'He's only got a Landrover!' whispered Cuthbert.

'Yes, but he's likely to know someone who might transport it away for you for a small fee of course, but where are you going to put the bull? It can't go into that little paddock of yours.'

'I was wondering about that field behind the village hall.' His brow was furrowed in deep thought. 'Temporarily, of course, until I decide what do with my bull.'

I knew the field concerned. It stretched from the back of the village hall and sloped down towards the beck at the rear. About an acre in extent with good grass, it was secure on all sides with stout hedges and fencing and the gate from that field led into the lane beside the village hall. That meant there was good access. In fact the field was owned by the village hall. Years ago, when the land had been purchased for the building of the hall, that field had formed part of the whole plot and now it was retained should there be a need to expand, perhaps as a car-park or even a children's play-ground. Apart from the fact that the double-doored emergency exit opened on to that field, it was surplus to current requirements and I thought Cuthbert's idea was sound.

If necessary, he could pay rental to the village hall committee, and being a member of that committee, he might persuade the chairman to give him a decision immediately. Tonight, the village hall might have a bull as a neighbour and I wondered whether, if the bull remained there for an extended period, Cuthbert would have to erect a 'Beware of the bull' notice.

I saw Cuthbert in earnest conversation with George Boston and then the pair of them disappeared among the stalls and marquees as I decided I should do a spot of traffic control duty. The crowds and the traffic were leaving and unless the rush of vehicles was regulated, we'd have a bottle-neck of cars trying to reach the exit together. It was about an hour later when I saw Cuthbert, who now looked quite pleased with himself and, as he left the showground in his battered car, he called to me. 'George found someone with space in a trailer, Nick, they're taking the bull away for me. I've seen Rudolph too, he's at his auctioneer's stand over there and he says I can put the bull in the village hall field until I've got myself sorted out.'

Rudolph Burley, Aidensfield's resident auctioneer, was also chairman of the village hall committee and it seemed he had applied common sense, and the chairman's prerogative, to Cuthbert's urgent and unusual request. And so, at least for a while, the village would have a resident bull, and I must admit, from what I had seen of the beast, it appeared to be a charming, docile creature, if a little on the large side. It looked like a huge cuddly toy, although one kick from its feet or a butt from its massive head was likely to do serious injury.

Although I performed my traffic duty until the car-parks were virtually empty, I left the showfield well ahead of Cuthbert's bull, but had to call at Ashfordly Police Station before returning home in order to deal with a few routine matters. Later, when relating the day's highlights to Mary over my evening meal, she told me that, while coming home after visiting a friend, she'd seen a cattle trailer disgorging a huge creamy bull into the village hall field.

In my mind, that confirmed that Cuthbert's bull had been placed in the village hall field and I must admit, I thought no more about that saga. The following night, however (Friday), was important for the village because Aidensfield String Orchestra was performing a concert of classical music in the hall to raise funds for its (the hall's) modernization scheme. It was hoped there would be a full house, but, although the tickets sold very well, the hall was less than half full on that evening – the hot, warm weather was blamed. People did not want to be cooped up in a hot village hall when they could be out in the countryside or enjoying a barbecue in their own garden. For some, the act of buying a ticket was more of a donation to the cause than a promise to attend the function.

Nonetheless, the concert began at 7.30 p.m. with a stirring rendition of Vivaldi's 'Summer' from his Four Seasons and although it might be said the double bass lingered rather too long upon some notes, that the lead violin's 'A' String was a bit flat, that some of the notes did not quite appear to be in the correct sequence and the woman playing the cello was showing rather too much of her red knickers, it was a lively start to the proceedings. This was followed by a varied and interesting selection of popular and almost recognizable pieces with Rudolph Burley brightening the evening with a solo rendition of some Irish dance music. The first half was scheduled to conclude Tchaikovsky's '1812 Overture', complete with loud drums and mock explosions.

Later, I was told that the sounds within the hall, when heard from the outside, were rather horrific.

We had no idea just how awful it must have sounded until the double emergency exit doors at the end of the hall, just to the right of the stage, suddenly burst open. They were smashed like matchwood from the outside, then amid screams and shouts and the sound of dwindling violins, coughing cellos and a wheezing double bass, in charged Cuthbert's angry Charolais bull which hurtled inside for a few yards, then halted and stood glaring at the orchestra whose members had by now, and without exception, ceased their stringy noises. The lack of music seemed to calm the bull – clearly, it had been very annoyed at the constant din just behind the doors and the banging and clattering of the '1812' had been sufficient to persuade the bull to do something about it. And it had worked. The minute he battered down the door, the music stopped and peace was restored. I have no doubt that clever bull thought he had solved his own problem. Our problem was what to do next.

'Nobody move!' shouted Rudolph Burley who knew about these things. 'Just stay where you are ... they don't like sudden movements ... keep very still...'

And we did.

Every one of us froze in our seats, the orchestra froze, the doorkeeper froze and Rudolph Burley, now in his capacity of a man experienced in auctioning bulls rather than the conductor of a string orchestra, stopped waving his hands and stood immobile, watching the huge head of the bull as it studied the interior of the hall, snorting from time to time but not yet venturing further into the building.

'Nobody move!' came Rudoph's voice yet again, because the handsome Charolais began to walk the length of the hall, crossing in front of the stage and then padding along the centre aisle towards the main door. This was standing open due to the heat and when the doorman made a move to close it to prevent the bull's gentle exit, Rudolph shouted, 'No, Jack, stay put ... leave him ... we can round him up outside, it'll be safer than trying to do it in here ... let him go...'

And so the giant bull moved steadily along the aisle, with the ring in his nose glinting in the reflected lights of the stage and he glared at the rock-steady audience in their chairs before disappearing into the street beyond.

'Right,' said Rudolph. 'Stay in here, all of you. I'll follow the bull. Nick, you ring Cuthbert, or better still find somebody with a dog or two who can head him off, or drive him into a field or barn or something. We don't want him stampeding into a gallop or butting his way into the pub or anything.'

My own house was only a few minutes away so I hurried to my telephone and rang George Boston. Of my local farmers, he was the one living closest to the village and I knew he had well-trained dogs which were accustomed to driving cattle. He would come immediately and I explained that the Charolais was padding down the main street with Rudolph in careful pursuit. Cuthbert was at home too, and after some indication of initial panic, said he would come to see what could be done. I told him to look out for a large whitish-cream bull taking a walk down the main street, adding that Rudolph was stalking it from behind and that George Boston would try to steer it to a safe haven with his dogs.

I'm not sure that Cuthbert heard any of my latter remarks but he seemed in such a state of worry that he slammed down the phone and rushed out. I was aware of the likelihood that police marksmen might have to be called in if the bull showed signs of being dangerous, but that would have to be as a last resort. Meanwhile, I told Mary what had happened, got out my police van and used it to return to the scene of the drama. I needed a place from where I could

196

establish contact with any other helpers, and the radio in my police van was ideal. I drove carefully into the village, anxious not to scare the bull, wherever it was, but in time I could see it padding sedately towards the pub, and decided to leave the van. I then trotted along the street to catch up to Rudolph who seemed very happy at the way things were progressing.

'What we need is for him to be driven into some kind of enclosure, like the pub car-park or the school playground, then we can fasten him in,' said Rudolph. 'But so long as nobody frightens him, he'll be no trouble. I hope those concert-goers stay put in the hall and the band doesn't strike up again.'

'I've got George Boston coming with his dogs,' I told Rudolph. 'Maybe we can persuade the bull to head into some kind of barn or field.

'There are some stables behind the pub,' I remembered. 'They're not used these days.'

'Good idea,' he said. 'Hello, who's this?'

And there, heading towards us from the opposite direction was the bearded figure of Cuthbert Crombie.

He was walking down the centre of the road directly towards the bull which was also heading down the centre of the road. Several cars had stopped behind it, recognizing the mini-drama now being enacted in Aidensfield village centre, but Cuthbert seemed to think he was heading towards a stray kitten, not a huge and unpredictable tonnage of mobile bull flesh.

'Cuthbert,' called Rudolph. 'Keep away, we're trying to divert him into an enclosure or the stables behind the pub; George is coming with his dogs...'

But Cuthbert either did not hear us or refused to listen because he continued towards his bull, and then he called, 'He's my bull, Rudolph, and I must learn to deal with him.'

'Yes but he's on the run; he's been frightened into doing this. He's unpredictable; he's not sure where he is or what's happening to him; he's not the lovable chap you won in that raffle...'

'Yes he is!' And Cuthbert continued down the centre of the road towards a direct head-to-head confrontation with his bull.

'This is suicide...' muttered Rudolph.

But it wasn't. As the bull halted to observe the approach of his master, Cuthbert reached out and took a gentle hold of the ring in his nose and said, 'Come along, Clarence, its time for bed.'

And the bull followed him like a little dog.

'Well, I'll be damned!' said Rudolph. 'Either Cuthbert is as daft as they say he is, or he is very, very brave, or he's got a way with animals, but look at that, the bull's following him like a dog on a lead!'

'Where are you taking him?' Rudolph called.

'Home,' responded Cuthbert. 'He can stay in our paddock tonight, then tomorrow I shall have to find somewhere more permanent. But he's a lovely chap, isn't he? So docile and calm...' And the happy pair disappeared into the darkness as George Boston and his dogs arrived. The drama was over. We could all go home.

Next morning, I saw Cuthbert walking up the street towards the surgery with his hand bandaged.

'You did very well last night, Cuthbert,' I said. 'You were calm and in full control, you prevented what might have become a tricky situation.'

'I think I have an affinity with animals,' he said. 'You know, Nick, I think I might enjoy life in the countryside; I might give up my city job and go in for breeding livestock, with my bull. A herd of Charolais ... what a lovely sight it would be!'

'Did your bull do that then?' I pointed to his injured hand.

'No, the rabbit bit me. Clarence is far too gentle to hurt me. Well, I must be off, I have to see about getting those village hall doors fixed and I understand Henry Watkinson at Moor End Farm has some grazing to rent, and a spare stable where Clarence can live. I am seriously thinking of buying a female

Charolais next, you know...'

Regular complaints received by the police, particularly those operating in rural areas, invariably included grumbles about low-flying aircraft. Most of us appreciate that in order to be trained to protect our realm, Royal Air Force pilots must practise their skills in all kinds of conditions, amongst which is flying low over agricultural land and remote moorland regions. Accepting this, most country folk do not complain, but incomers do; city dwellers who have opted for the quiet life in the countryside do not take kindly to being roused by jet aircraft whooshing overhead at little more than chimney-pot height, or disturbing their Sunday afternoon nap in the garden in repeated pseudo-bombing raids on the White Horse of Kilburn or Whitby Abbey.

In too many cases, a sense of priority does not prevail, although we received complaints from a range of rural dwellers, ex-townies and country folk alike, about the noise causing favourite cats to run away, startled hens to lay eggs without shells, worried cattle to stampede from their fields, terrified horses to leap over fences and disappear into the great unknown, or to throw their riders, while greenhouse windows shattered and ear-drums buzzed with the force of the jet-propelled noise.

There was little the police could do about low-flying RAF jet aircraft and we simply passed the complaints to the nearest RAF base or sometimes to the Air Ministry. So far as civilian aircraft were concerned, a similar code of conduct applied, except that we contacted the Ministry of Aviation in the event of a complaint, but it was very rare to find a jet airliner flying low over Aidensfield. If that happened, the pilot was either lost or in dire trouble.

What we did get was the occasional light aircraft pottering above the countryside, often with a local man acting as pilot who was flying low over his family home. But even a slow moving propeller-driven aircraft can be alarming when it buzzes across the countryside to skim the hedges, scatter the livestock and put the wind up old ladies.

It is a criminal offence to fly an aircraft so low that it causes unnecessary danger to people or property and there are well-defined rules about the flying heights permitted for aircraft, including helicopters, crop-spraying planes, gliders, airships, balloons, kites and other undefined flying machines. Civil aircraft registered within the UK all carry a registration mark comprising the letter G and a further four capital letters and this makes it possible to trace any offending plane, provided the witness notes that series of letters. The snag is that few can prove the aircraft has flown below the specified height and even if the complainant says he or she can easily read the registration mark, the authorities rarely accept that as undisputed proof of the plane's height above the ground. Most of us are pretty useless at estimating the height of a passing plane. There are times, however, when I wonder that if a plane's wingtips chop the tops off my poplar trees, such a thing is proof that the aircraft was flying lower than it should have been.

Then one afternoon, I was stopped in Aidensfield main street by a man called Toby Matthews. About fifty, he was stoutly built and balding, with a round face and chubby cheeks. He habitually wore navy-blue suits, red ties, white shirts and black shoes and looked rather like a clerk in a solicitor's office.

In fact, Toby was a very successful architect who worked as a partner within a practice in Ashfordly which was responsible for designing some ghastly modern buildings. Happily, most of these were far away from the moors, deep in distant city areas such as York, Leeds, Middlesbrough, Sunderland and Bradford – they built things like awful concrete tower blocks or multi-storey car-parks which looked as if they would collapse the moment a strong wind blew, or huge shops several storeys high with immense glass windows which baked customers and staff in the summer and always looked dirty because they were so difficult to clean.

In spite of this, Toby lived in a very traditional and splendidly secluded farmhouse in a hollow on the moors about a mile out of Aidensfield. Once a working farm, it was called Rowan Tree Farm but most of the land had been sold separately for grazing and Toby had bought the house, along with some twenty acres of the meadowland. His wife, Angela, bred Cleveland Bay horses and so she worked from home, sometimes going away to agricultural shows or horsey events to display her animals. She'd converted the outbuildings into a fine set of stables and undoubtedly ran a thriving business. Between them, therefore, the Matthews were a very successful couple, with each of them running a beautiful Mark II Jaguar saloon. Toby's was sky blue and Angela's was bright red.

Although Toby could hardly be described as glamorous, his wife, in her mid-forties, was a beautiful blonde with a stunning figure, lovely legs and a smile that would cause most men to go weak at the knees. I've no doubt her highly attractive appearance contributed to the success of her business. Inevitably, with such an attractive woman spending much of the day alone in her moorland retreat, there was gossip about male visitors. People who respected Angela regarded them merely as customers, people with the same horsey interests as herself, but once or twice I caught snippets of conversation which suggested the visitors were not always interested in the horses. A delivery man had called once and although there'd been a red Jaguar on the forecourt and a smart green MG sports car tucked away between two buildings, he'd not been able to get any response to his calling and hammering on the doors. He had noticed that some bedroom curtains were closed, and asked me if I knew whether or not the Matthews were away. I had to say that, so far as I was aware, they were not on holiday, although Toby would be working away from home. Then a chance conversation with Gilbert Kingston, the postman from Eltering who delivered to Rowan Tree Farm, alerted me to the fact that the red Jaguar had been at the house while a white Rover had been seen parked between the buildings, curiously enough in the same place as the smart green MG. Gilbert had noticed it because he'd searched the outbuildings for Angela as he had a registered letter and required her signature. He did add that knowing the farm very well due to his deliveries, a vehicle parked between the buildings in question could quietly leave the complex upon the approach of the unsuspecting husband, and never be seen by that husband. It was the ideal place to conceal a vehicle because by the time the unsuspecting husband arrived on his forecourt, the departing vehicle would be screened by the extensive range of farm buildings and it could leave the farm without the husband ever knowing it had been there.

Gilbert had made those calculations claiming to know the character of Angela Matthews and the rumours which surrounded her, and, of course, his own detailed knowledge of the layout of the premises. Although these incidents had occurred very recently, with no similar reports of past misdeeds, it was this sort of thing which sparked off speculation, if not rumours, and I am sure Gilbert was, in his own way, quite a gossip. I'm not sure his gossip had any factual basis. Nonetheless, in my personal view, the growing rumours about the love life of Angela Matthews were reinforced on two quite separate occasions when I was called to Rowan Tree Farm to settle what we term a domestic dispute. On both occasions Angela had called me by telephone, and in something of a panic, because Toby had gone berserk, according to her, and was attacking her. On both occasions, however, by the time I arrived she had changed her mind about involving the police and did not want any further action on my part. That sort of outcome was quite normal for such domestic disputes.

'Toby is fine.' She met me at the door both times and did not want to admit me. 'Sorry to have troubled you, Constable. He's been under a lot of pressure lately and he's had too much to drink. I can deal with him.'

However, on the occasion Toby met me in Aidensfield, he did not wish to discuss architecture or horses, nor did he wish to comment about his wife's conduct (he did not mention my previous involvement with his married life), but he did want to complain about a low-flying aircraft.

'Tell me about it,' I invited.

'It flew over Rock Howe two or three times,' he grumbled. 'It was flying so low I'm surprised its wheels didn't clip the telegraph wires in Nettledale just below. Then it went along the floor of the dale, still very low, skimming over the farms...'

I took details of the date, time, direction of flight and precise location, and a brief description of the aircraft, a single wing, single propeller aircraft, probably a two-seater, silver-grey colour with red tail markings. Then I asked, 'Toby, did you get its registration mark? Four letters preceded by G and a hyphen.'

'No.' He shook his flabby cheeks. 'No, sorry.'

'I've not had any other complaints,' I assured him. 'But I'll enter it in our records and we'll send a report off to the Ministry of Aviation.'

'I don't really want to make a fuss,' he said, 'but I thought it was dangerous, I've never seen a plane fly so low. Skimming the moors, it was; it's a wonder it missed some of the trees in the valleys. I even thought it was buzzing me and my client.'

'Your client?'

For a fleeting moment I wondered if Toby had been enjoying a romantic sojourn on the moors with a lady who was not his wife, and I felt I had better establish that small matter.

'I had a client with me,' he said. 'He wants me to build a new house for him on a site in Nettledale. We were looking at the site from hills above, trying to anticipate the sort of complaints we might get and the reaction from the planning authority and, of course, I need to examine the surrounding land-scape so that I can make sure the design blends well with it.'

' And your client? Did he get a better look at the aircraft?'

'No,' but Toby gave me the name of his client – a businessman from Scarborough – if I wanted to pursue the matter. I assured him I would report the incident and inform him of any developments. As I patrolled the village that same afternoon, I received two further comments about the low-flying plane. From the descriptions I obtained, there was no doubt it was the same light aircraft and both people – one a smallholder with premises along the Elsinby road and the other a farmer from the moors who had come into Aidensfield for some petrol – told me about the low flying aircraft. Neither wished to lodge a formal complaint, but both expressed an opinion that it was flying much lower than seemed normal and that its crew of two seemed to be paying undue attention to the village, especially the houses and farms spread around the outskirts. Neither witness recalled the registration mark, however, although the descriptions they provided convinced me it had been the same aircraft.

Those were the only complaints I received about that incident of low-flying and so, having entered details in our records and completed the necessary formalities, I thought no more of the matter. If any further action had to be taken, it would be done by the Ministry of Aviation rather than the North Riding Constabulary.

Then one Saturday morning, I received a phonecall from Sergeant Blaketon.

'Ah, Rhea,' he grunted into the telephone, 'that report of low flying near Aidensfield.'

'Yes, Sergeant.'

'We've had a response from the Minister of Aviation. Well, from his office to be precise. It seems the aircraft was taking aerial photographs of the district and it has been given an exemption to fly low for that purpose.'

'So it wasn't breaking any rules?'

'Not on this occasion. Exemptions from the general rules about low flying can be granted when aircraft are used for land surveys too. So it was all in order. We can forget the matter.'

'Thanks for telling me, Sergeant. I'll inform Mr Matthews.'

But before I could ring Rowan Tree Farm to see whether Toby Matthews was at home, there was a loud hammering on my office door and when I opened it, I found a stranger on the doorstep. It was a man in a dark suit, with rather long hair; he'd be about thirty-five and looked terrified. His car was parked on the road outside my office.

'Thank God!' he said. 'Look, you've got to get up to Rowan Tree Farm, Constable, or that chap'll kill his wife ... he's got her locked in one of the stables. I managed to get out...'

'Slow down a moment,' I said. 'Who are you for starters? And just what is happening at Rowan Tree?'

He gave me a business card with the price of pictures written on the back, as he continued, 'Look, so far as I am concerned, it was just a routine visit; all I did was call at the house, like I'm calling at other houses in the district, asking if householders want to buy aerial photographs of their homes.'

'Aerial photographs?' I queried.

'Yes, I work for a business that takes aerial photos. When I showed that chap and that blonde bit of skirt of his the picture of his house, he blew his top ... he shouted something about being caught in the act and the next thing I knew he was hustling her off to one of the stables and he'd locked her in. He told me to send him a bill and to get off his premises right now ... so I did. Got off his premises, I mean. And I haven't been paid for the photograph.'

'Where is the photograph?' I asked.

'He's got it, it's in colour, and framed as well. A very professional job if you ask me. But I thought I'd better tell somebody in case he does something to that woman.'

'I'll go straight away,' I said. 'Thanks. I have your card if I need to contact you,' and I slipped his business card into my wallet.

'So what's his name?' asked the man whose name was Russell. 'So our head office can send him a bill.'

'Matthews,' I said. 'Toby Matthews, Rowan Tree Farm, Aidensfield. If you give me a spare card, I'll see he gets it; he's a decent fellow, would you believe, I'm sure he'll pay you.'

And so I hurried in my police van to Rowan Tree Farm and when I arrived, I could hear Angela shouting from one of the stables and rattling the door as I saw Toby sitting on the back doorstep with his head bowed and a large framed photograph in his hands.

'Toby,' I said, approaching him with care.

'Oh, God,' he muttered. 'What have I done ... look, Nick, sorry. I don't want to get you involved. It's between me and her, a personal matter. Nothing to do with the police.'

'I was sent here. I have to make sure there's going to be no breach of the peace,' I said. 'No harm done to you and Angela, that sort of thing.'

'I won't,' he sighed, getting to his feet but hanging on to the large photograph. It was the size of an average framed picture, some two feet by fifteen inches or so, with a good quality wooden frame. 'I promise.'

'I think you should release Angela; she could complain about illegal imprisonment.' I thought I had better try to shock him into adopting a more reasonable attitude. 'Where's the key? Shall I let her out?'

'If you say so.' He appeared to begrudge this action but dug his hand into his trouser pocket and handed me a key to the padlock which secured the bolt. 'Look, I'm sorry, this is not how I behave as a rule but, well, I don't know what to do, it's such a shock. I don't know how to handle it; I don't know what to do....'

'How about putting the coffee on?' I interrupted him. 'For you, Angela and me.'

'Coffee?' He looked rather baffled.

'Milk, no sugar for me,' I said and he trudged indoors, still clutching the framed photograph.

I went to the stable door and before I opened it, I said, 'Angela, it's PC Rhea. I'm going to let you out. Toby's gone to make us a coffee.'

'Coffee?' she almost screamed from behind the solid wooden door. 'What's got into that man? I'll give him coffee when I get my hands on him ... what's he think I'm doing? Honestly, PC Rhea, he's been behaving like a moron lately.'

'If I let you out, will you promise to remain calm?' I put to her.

'It won't be easy,' she shouted. 'How would you like to be treated like this, locked up in a stable?'

'Promise,' I said loudly. 'Promise to remain calm. Toby's making coffee and I want you and him and me to sit down to find out what all this is about. I have no idea what's going on...'

'Neither have I!' she screamed. 'Lately,

he's been accusing me of seeing other men, sleeping with my clients, deceiving him while he's at work, and then he had half a bottle of whisky and threw his glass at me – that's when I rang you. Twice he did that... I mean, I've done nothing. I know he's working hard and I know things aren't easy at work, but there's no need to lose his head like this.'

'You've not been seeing other men?' I had to ask the question.

'Of course I haven't!' she snapped. 'I would never do that ... is that what he thinks?'

'I don't know, we'll have to ask him,' I said. 'But I want you to remain calm, that's important. But if you've not been deceiving him, what else might he be getting upset about?'

'How should I know?' She was speaking in a more rational manner and so I decided to unlock the door. She emerged looking pale and with her hair awry but considerably more calm than when I arrived.

'It won't be easy, remaining calm,' I said.

'You act as mediator,' she said. 'I mean it, you be referee, but I would like to know what's bugging him. He's never ever been like this until these last few weeks.'

'Let's talk,' I said, leading the way indoors.

Toby had brewed three mugs of coffee and they were sitting on the kitchen table as we entered. He had the photograph on his

213

knee, with its back towards us and so I sat down next to him, motioning to Angela to sit opposite.

'So, Toby,' I said. 'What's all this about?'

'This!' he snapped, banging the picture on to the table. 'This photograph.'

'What about it?' I put to him, with Angela deciding not to say anything at this point.

'This car, see? Between those buildings ... hidden so nobody could see it ... I know whose that is, it's Alec Black's, I'd know it anywherc. A white Rover with a black top ... see? It's as plain as a pikestaff...'

'Yes,' said Angela. 'That is Alec's car.'

'And I've heard about others being here, on and off, folks talking in the village and in Ashfordly; somebody said they'd seen Jeff Wilson leaving. Now what's he doing here? He's not one of your clients, he's not one of mine and he has no cause to come here when I'm out.'

'You think I've been having affairs? Is that it?' She spoke very quietly.

'Well, it's obvious, isn't it? All this odd behaviour, secrecy, phone calls when you thought I was at the other end of the house, letters you don't want me to see ... you think I haven't noticed all these things? You stopping conversations on the phone when I've come into the room, then cars coming to the house while I'm out, and now this one hiding in the buildings so he could get away without me seeing him ... if the policeman wasn't here, I'd wring your neck, Angela, after all these years ... all these years,' and he started to weep.

'Oh, Toby.' She rose from her chair and went to his side, putting her arm around his shoulder and nestling her cheek against his hair. 'Poor, poor Toby.'

He began to sob and I thought it was time to leave, but Angela pulled a chair to his side and sat next to him, kissing him on the cheek and hugging him with obvious love and affection.

'Toby, listen. And PC Rhea. I didn't want to break this news to you, Toby, but in view of what you're going through, perhaps I'd better be open with you. PC Rhea, in six weeks' time, Toby is fifty. I've been trying to arrange a surprise for him, a secret party, with a marquee, caterers, music ... that's what all the calls and secrecy have been about. I thought I could arrange things here, without you knowing. You'd have seen me in town and people would have talked ... we didn't want you to know...'

He looked up at her with his eyes full of tears, then rubbed them away and said, 'Have I made a fool of myself?'

'No more than usual,' she laughed. 'That's why I love you so much.'

'So I needn't have drunk myself into a state, or thrown things, or gone all moody and angry and morose...'

'No, of course not.'

'I should have trusted you,' he said.

'Yes, you should,' she told him firmly. 'Then I could have arranged a lovely surprise for you. Now, you know all about it. Anyway, there's nothing I can do now so let me see this photograph? Was it taken by that little aeroplane that was buzzing around here a while ago?'

'Yes,' I said, and then I remembered the salesman's visiting card. I placed it on the table between them. 'If you keep the photo, they'll want money from you. The price is on the back.'

'I might buy you this for your birthday,' she said, then added, 'Oh, and PC Rhea, would you and Mrs Rhea like to join us? I'll send an invitation.'

'We'd love to,' I smiled, wondering how many other secrets had been revealed by those cameramen in the sky.

Chapter 7

There is little doubt that the duties of a village constable in the 1960s were extensive and embraced a broad range of responsibilities, but there was a part of our work which was ill-defined and which might not have been considered police duty. It entailed visiting people who were alone and vulnerable, often for nothing more sinister than a chat or a cup of tea, but sometimes involving extra chores such as lighting the fire, cutting the lawn, doing bits of necessary shopping, or taking the cat to the vet's surgery. When doing this kind of thing, it might be said we were exceeding our role as law enforcement officers, or that welfare of the community was not our job or responsibility, or that we should not interfere with the private lives of others, but in remote rural parts there was often no other person with the time or opportunity to carry out this vital kind of on-the-spot social work. It was not, as some left-wing critics tried to pretend, a means for the police to go snooping or spying upon the private lives of others; it was, and still is, nothing more than a desire to help those less fortunate than ourselves. And, I might say, such offers of help or practical demonstrations of active support and interest by the local constable were always appreciated.

During my patrols around the spectacular countryside on my Aidensfield beat, I had my 'regulars', people upon whom I called every time I was passing, provided, of course, I was not engaged upon some more urgent matter. In many cases, those people lived very ordinary and mundane lives, but from time to time, I realized that some of these people had wonderful stories to tell, or secrets to reveal.

There was a war veteran who had lost both legs while fighting for this country; he loved to regale me with tales of his wartime experiences and because he never left the house, I was one of his few contacts with the outside world. We chatted and drank tea beside his fire and he wished for nothing more than the opportunity to talk and laugh with other human beings.

Another was an old lady who lived alone and who always had trouble getting her fire lit; there was an 87-year-old man who weighed eighteen stone and who kept falling out of the bed to which he had been confined. I made regular visits to lift him back, a difficult task for me but an impossible one for his seven-stone wife, and there was a lonely man who could never get his grandfather clock to function properly even when he wound it regularly. I visited a retired farmer who wanted help with his income tax forms, an elderly lady who always asked me to put oil and water into her car engine, a shopkeeper who could never get one of his rear windows closed because he was too small to reach it properly, and a young woman who was terrified of the peculiar character who had fallen in love with her and who sent bunches of forget-me-nots at least once a week.

Most of these visits were to very ordinary people who had led very ordinary lives and for whom the world of the policeman was exciting and romantic; for that reason I would tell them tales about my own varied work, albeit without revealing professional secrets, and most of my regulars enjoyed this modest escape from their very plain existence.

Among my regulars, there were many who came to rely, if only in part, upon frequent visits by the passing constable and one was a lovely old lady, a widow of many years, who was confined to her cottage and whose younger son had died several years prior to my arrival in Aidensfield. Her name was Josephine Ingram and she would be in her early eighties, I reckoned; her husband had been called Ted and he had worked for Crampton Estate until his retirement, but he had died rather suddenly within two years of retiring. I never knew Ted, and Josephine had been a widow for about fifteen years, she told me. The cottage belonged to the estate, with Josephine being allowed to live there for a very low rent as long as she needed.

During the summer months, she would sit in a battered but comfortable armchair in the open doorway of her home, hoping to attract the attention of passersby, if only for a momentary chat or to join her for a cup of tea and a cake. That is how I got to know her. I was patrolling the quieter parts of Aidensfield shortly after my arrival as the constable when she hailed me and asked if I would post a letter for her. I did so, and thereafter stopped for a chat every time I was passing. Over the months, I got to know her quite well and, as autumn approached, she had to retreat indoors due to the chilliness of the changing weather, but she left her door standing wide open as an invitation to possible callers.

Over the winter months, however, the door had to be closed to conserve the heat of her fireside, and this meant she hated the winter – as she told me, 'Once that door's shut, folks don't bother to come and see me. It does get lonely, Mr Rhea, believe me. You will keep popping in, won't you? In winter?'

'I will,' I promised, and promptly made a conscious effort to pop in whenever I could. There was always a kettle on the hob and she made exceedingly nice jam tarts, scones and fruit cakes! As time went by, she began to tell me more and more about herself and her family and I was surprised to learn she had had two sons, one of whom was currently working in Canada and the other who had been a Catholic priest.

'We're not Catholics,' she told me one day. 'None of us, but Simon got it into his head, even as a young lad, that he wanted to be a Catholic priest. I have no idea what made him want to do that because neither me nor Ted were Catholics and not even church-goers or religiously minded. Anyway, he was set on the idea and that's what he did. We never tried to stop him; he knew what he wanted and that was important. A lovely man, he was, so gentle and kind. He became a Catholic and then a priest after studying for a lot of years, but it was funny calling him Father Simon. He joined the monks at Maddleskirk Abbey, you see...'

'So where is he now?' I asked.

'Oh, he died. It was so sad. He was only thirty-two, Mr Rhea. It was leukaemia. But he died happy, that's what's counts, isn't it?'

'I'm sorry.' I did not know quite how to react to her sudden revelation.

Then she said, 'Would you like to see his photographs?'

'Yes, of course.' I had a few minutes to spare and I thought it would please her if I shared her memories.

'I'll get them, they're in a box in the cupboard under the stairs,' and she pottered away to bring them to me. 'Sit yourself at the table so you can spread them out,' she told me.

She returned with a large cardboard box

and plonked it on the table in front of me. Inside, there were several albums of black-and-white photographs, all the photos being carefully fixed and bearing titles. Even before she handed me the first album, I could see these were not pictures *of* her priest son as I had thought; they were photographs *by* him, hundreds of them, and from what I saw in those first seconds, they all looked like scenic views – trees, lakes, moors, mountains, rivers, ruined abbeys, castles, country cottages, village scenes, blacksmiths at work, farmers milking, women baking and washing, men and women at harvest time and more.

'If he hadn't been a priest, he said he would have been a photographer, Mr Rhea. He loved the countryside, you see, and the people who worked in it; he'd get on his bike and take his camera with him, taking pictures wherever he went.'

As Josephine was chatting, I was flicking through the first album and although I do not claim any particular knowledge or expertise in the art of photography, I did think this collection was out of the ordinary. All the photographs – each in black and white, half-plate size – had an air of quality about them; where people were at work, he had captured the expressions on their faces, the movement in their arms or backs, the satisfaction of doing a worthwhile task or, sometimes, the sheer drudgery of it all. There was a wonderfully atmospheric shot of a man weeding a turnip field and he looked utterly bored and fed-up.

One of Simon's abilities, when he chose to photograph a country scene, was to make water appear to be wet, the leaves of the trees seemed to be alive and fluttering, the meadows had an inviting appearance as the grass looked genuine, the moors looked rugged enough to deter all but the most determined and the snow scenes looked cold but beautiful. Beyond doubt, he was a very talented photographer.

'Did he ever show these to anyone?' I asked. 'Or try to get them published?'

'Oh, no,' she shook her head. 'He wasn't interested in money, it was a hobby, he said, his work as a priest came first and the photos reminded him of the places he'd visited and some of the wonderful people he'd met.'

'They're not local scenes, then?' I asked.

'Not all of them,' she told me. 'Some are but quite a lot are not. If you take the pictures out, you'll see where he took them, he made notes on the backs of the pictures.'

She indicated one I was examining. It was marked 'Water's Edge' under the black-and-white print and depicted a scene which might have been in the English Lake District, or Scotland, or Wales, but when she removed it from its place, the back was endorsed 'Loch Tay, Scotland, 25th June, 1951.'

'He cycled all over the place, exploring the countryside,' she was telling me. 'Even when he was a priest. They do get holidays, you know, priests and monks I mean, and he would tour Scotland, sleeping at monasteries up there but always with his camera. He never went anywhere without it.'

'I think this is a wonderful collection.' I meant every word. 'It's the kind that would make a valuable published record. These pictures are of a period which is passing us by, Josephine, a unique record of country life. I'm sure some publisher would love to reprint them, and to pay you a fee, of course.'

'Oh, no, Mr Rhea, Simon would never have wanted me to do that. They're for the family. When we die, they will go to our other son, Thomas, he's in Canada and he has two children, you see, so the albums will remain in the family. And in keeping with Simon's wishes, nobody will try to make money from them or to show them to the public.'

I did not have the time to carefully examine all the photographs but flicked through a second album as I told Josephine I had to leave as I had a commitment to interview someone in half an hour's time.

But as I was preparing to end my viewing session, one photograph caught my eye. It was a watery scene with what appeared to be a large animal partially submerged; its back was out of the water but its belly and legs were concealed. Its neck was arched with the head beneath the surface and the entire picture was full of ripples or wavelets around the creature.

'That's the Loch Ness Monster,' said Josephine in a most matter-of-fact voice. 'Simon nearly got a picture of it when it came out of the water, but by the time he'd got his camera out and focused, it was going back under the waves.'

'The Loch Ness Monster?' I couldn't believe this but when I looked at the caption, it did say 'Loch Ness Monster' and the rear of the picture bore the legend 'Loch Ness – 10th August, 1951'.

'It was his summer holiday and he was staying at that monastery near Loch Ness, Fort Augustus it's called. He was walking along the shore with another visitor when the Loch Ness Monster came out of the loch. They both saw it, Mr Rhea, and because Simon's camera was in his haversack, it took a few moments to get it out. By the time he got it ready, the monster had gone back into the water and was submerging.'

'Did he tell anybody about this?'

'No, he didn't want to make a fuss. He said nobody would believe him, even if he was a priest and even if he had a witness with him, but he did get that picture. He said it was a bit like a hippopotamus with a long, slender neck, but he didn't want a fuss made. He knew what he saw, Mr Rhea, even if no one else does.'

'But if this picture is genuine...' I began.

'Oh, it's genuine, Mr Rhea, I mean, a priest wouldn't lie about such a thing, would he? There's no point in lying, is there? Not when you're not going to tell anybody.'

'It must have been some other animal,' I said. 'A seal of some kind.'

'Some of the other monks have seen the Loch Ness Monster, Mr Rhea, and they never talk about it. Anyway, our Simon got a picture of it and it was that picture, just the one. He had no time to take another, it had gone under the waves by then.'

'And the witness? Who was it?'

'It was a man staying at the monastery, Mr Rhea, a man from America, not a priest. Just a traveller of some kind, a visitor staying there for a day or two during a tour of Scotland and England. Simon called him Ray. That's all I know. I do know that Simon tried to contact him later, but no one knew who he was or where he'd come from. He didn't leave any address at the abbey.'

This was beginning to look just like any

other Loch Ness Monster story where the evidence is not quite complete, where witnesses cannot be traced and where no positive photograph can be found. From what I could see of the creature in Simon's photo, it appeared to be a large and somewhat cumbersome beast with no hairs on its body, and thick skin rather like a hippo or an elephant, but because this was a black-and-white print, it was impossible to determine the colour, neither was there any other object in the picture from which to gauge the size of the animal. Something like a water fowl or tree trunk in shot would have helped enormously. The portion of its neck, which was visible, was quite distinct, but it was arched because the head was under the water which meant I could not see what the head looked like, nor did it give any indication of the length or thickness of the neck. I could not see a tail either, because the rump was beneath the surface. So was this a genuine photograph of the famous Loch Ness Monster? Was it a cow or bullock bathing in the Loch, or a seal of some kind such as the huge grey seal or some other kind of deep sea animal? And how big was this creature? And what did it really look like? A large head, a small head, a head with horns, or a tail which was short and fat or long and thin? There were many questions to answer.

But I could not upset Josephine by insisting she had the photograph analysed by photography experts, nor could I risk there being any publicity about the picture if it got into the wrong hands. I smiled and closed the album.

'I wish Simon was here to tell me about it,' I said.

'Yes, it would be nice,' she said quietly. I did not look at the photograph on any other occasion and while Josephine was alive, I never told anyone about that picture. Sadly she died not long afterwards and I do not know where the picture is now. I can only assume that it was passed to Simon's brother, but he might not have been interested in the collection and it might have been dispersed or thrown out. But to my knowledge that photograph has never been published and it has never been reproduced in any book or feature about the Loch Ness Monster. I have always waited for its appearance in the public arena and am still waiting.

Perhaps, one day, it will surface for us all to admire and discuss. Just like the monster itself, I suppose.

Another man upon whom I called on a fairly regular basis was a very fit and active retired military gentleman, a former lieutenant colonel whom I think had served in the Green Howards. Everyone in Aidens-field referred to him as the Colonel and he was not the sort who insisted that people addressed him by his full military rank. He seemed to be quite happy being known as the Colonel and would even use that term whenever he rang me – 'Hello, Constable, it's the Colonel here,' he would announce himself.

His wife, Lucille, was still very much alive too and very able to look after the house, herself and her husband, as well as the garden. Her small but exquisite garden was a picture, a truly beautiful display of flowers and shrubs which changed throughout the year. I found it amazing that such an elderly, tiny woman could maintain such a won-derful display of plants.

The couple were in their early eighties and the Colonel's real name was Lieutenant Colonel Joshua Kilburn-Bardsworth and he was from an aristocratic background, some-thing which was evident in both his speech and bearing. His wife called him Josh and he had fought at the Somme during the First World War, being awarded the Military Cross as a junior officer and later the Dis-tinguished Service Order, added to which he had been mentioned in despatches on several occasions.

After a successful army career, he had retired on pension from the service some thirty years before I came to know him and had then enjoyed a second but rather shorter career with a subsidiary of a major British petroleum company. The subsidiary company, known as OSO Ltd, was then searching for oil and natural gas throughout Britain, both on shore and off shore, and a good deal of its exploratory work was in and around the North York Moors.

For all his bravery and military experience, the Colonel was a quiet gentleman who preferred to remain in the background of village life, not volunteering to chair or join committees, organize events or turn up at parish council meetings to complain about things. Lucille was of like mind, although she had once been president of Aidensfield Women's Institute.

The Colonel was quite content for others to 'run the show', as he put it, believing he had done more than his bit for England during both his military career and in the time he had spent searching for oil in the UK. It was that second career which led me to become one of his regular visitors. Every month he received his pension cheque from OSO Ltd, but, somewhat oddly, it had to be countersigned by what was termed 'a responsible person' who was not a relation of the pensioner or an employee of the pensioner's bank. The purpose of this signature was to prove the pensioner was still alive at the time he cashed his cheque and that no one else was committing a fraudulent act by cashing the cheque or paying it into some other account. Lieutenant Colonel Kilburn-Bardsworth told me that people like the vicar, the doctor, a Member of Parliament, a Justice of the Peace, a police officer or someone of similar standing was able to satisfy the company's desire that this chore should be done by 'a responsible person'. As I was out and about in the village perhaps on more occasions than other acceptable signatories, I found myself being asked regularly to confirm the Colonel was still alive and kicking. And, of course, I did not object to this – it was one way of meeting the variety of people who lived in the village.

If I chanced to be passing the Colonel's detached home at the end of the month, I would pop in, and if I didn't pop in as expected, he would telephone me to ask whether I could oblige. Sometimes I was away on some urgent task, or even on leave, or attending a course for an extended period, and in those cases he would find some other 'responsible person'.

Whenever I did call, however, my visit involved a modest ritual which involved at least one glass of sherry while being entertained by the Colonel in his study along with a cup of coffee and a chocolate biscuit. Inevitably, this was all accompanied by the old man's vivid account of his time in the Somme or some other aspect of his long career, and so that modest cheque-signing chore tended to occupy us both for an hour or more on every occasion. Lucille would disappear during this ritual, either to do something in the house or to tend her beloved and beautiful garden.

We did embrace something of police work during these chats because the Colonel knew what was happening in Aidensfield and district and at times he was able to acquaint me with details of suspected law-breakers, such as unknown young men visiting the home of the elderly for doubtful purposes, the activities or latest scheme of Claude Jeremiah Greengrass, or gossip pertaining to various facets of Aidensfield life. In short, the cheque-signing was useful to both of us.

From time to time, the Colonel referred to his earlier life, usually indirectly or in fleeting moments when he wished to emphasize a particular point and it was at those odd times that I realized he had come from a privileged background. He might refer to his public school, for example, or the gamekeeper on the estate upon which he had lived, or perhaps a titled person who turned out to be an uncle or aunt, or customs like dressing for dinner and passing the port to the left, or even holidays with

Lord and Lady Somebody-or-Other.

But even if he did briefly refer to that aspect of his youth, he did not show any signs of boasting about his family tree or ancestry, and seemed more content with and proud of his military career than any of his noble relations. Even his house was nothing like a country mansion – it was a nice detached house in its own medium-sized garden, with modest accommodation while being tucked away behind the main street. Just the sort of place you'd expect to find a retired military officer keeping a low profile, I thought.

It was during one of those visits that he asked what commitments I could expect to deal with during the coming weeks and I mentioned Ashfordly Fair. This was held twice a year, once in the spring and once in the autumn, invariably in May and October as specified in a charter dating to the fifteenth century, and it attracted a considerable crowd. The modern fair was probably nothing like the original; today's fair comprised a host of fairground attractions like dodgem cars, shooting galleries, bingo and a lot of games involving skill and machines, although some of the villagers did attend in the hope of selling their handiwork – artists, wood carvers, basket-makers, embroidery experts, jam-makers and others, even some musicians came along to

233

add to the festive atmosphere. The original fairs would have been very commercial, with sales of livestock, farm produce, fruit and vegetables, cakes and bread, tools and equipment and all manner of handicrafts, but it would also have attracted music, feasting and dancing.

'You're there to keep the peace, I suppose?' he smiled.

'There's rarely any real trouble,' I told him. 'But sometimes young lads get a bit high spirited, some have too much to drink and you can guarantee there'll be a dispute of some kind over a girl! We try to keep things calm.'

'Nothing changes!' he smiled. 'My family were granted a charter to hold a fair in Bardsworth, that was years ago of course.'

'Bardsworth?' I didn't know the town or village.

'In Shropshire,' he said. 'It's a smallish village now but it used to be a substantial market town and the Bardsworth family sought permission to hold a fair. My ancestors, that was. Some kind of organized outlet was needed for the country people so they could bring in their wares and sell them, and of course, it meant they could let their hair down twice a year. There was feasting and dancing, with a good deal of drinking and courting too, I have no doubt. But it was good for local trade, Constable, and it attracted custom from a very wide area, even from France and Spain. Bardsworth Fair was renowned in its time, but it faded away about a century ago.

'And the charter was granted to your family?' I asked.

'Yes, that's how it was done in those days. The lord of the manor had to approach the king to ask that he grant a charter for the town to be allowed to hold a fair. We provided the dates we thought best – usually saints' days – and hopefully the king would grant us a charter. Once it was granted, of course, no one could halt it or rescind it, and I do know instances where modern local authorities have tried to abolish ancient fairs. It's not on, Constable. The charter gives permission for eternity.'

'So your family were Lords of the Manor of Bardsworth?' I asked.

'We were. The Earl of Bardsworth. That was my father's title; I don't carry it because I'm not the eldest, and I don't bother with all that stuff about the honourable and so on. I'm the Colonel, that'll do me!'

'That is a world quite foreign to me,' I smiled. 'But when was all this?'

'The grant of the charter, you mean? 1476. Getting on for five hundred years ago. Stow-on-the-Wold received its fair charter at the same time, from Edward IV. Ours, Bardsworth I mean, was granted the same year by Edward, of course. I have the charter here, perhaps you'd like to see it?'

'A copy of it, you mean?'

'No, the original, signed by Edward IV in his own fair hand. Come along, Constable, I'll show you where I keep it!'

He led me from his study and across the spacious hall with its parquet floor and Persian rugs, and I thought we were heading for the library or some other grand room, but he opened the downstairs toilet door and said, 'In there, hanging on the wall. It makes good reading for anyone who has the time and knowledge to decipher it.'

He switched the light on and I saw an oblong length of parchment, very yellowed and dark, with closely written words in what I thought was Latin, and I could just distinguish the signature and seal at the foot. It was in a glass-fronted frame and appeared to be in excellent condition.

'It's hard to believe this is nearly five hundred years old and that that is the actual signature of Edward IV,' I had to say. 'I would have thought this would have been in a museum.'

'I might donate it to one before I depart this earthly life, there are few responsible Bardsworths left, but we keep it in the loo because the darkness suits it and the temperature is just right. And it provides good reading during those long moments...' he chuckled. 'The frame is fairly modern, though, and air-tight, but the charter's been in the family since it was granted. It was granted to the family, you see, not the town, and I'm delighted to have it here, in my house. I don't think it has any commercial value, Constable, it's not the sort of thing a thief would want to get his hands on, but from an historical point of view, I think it is valuable.'

'I'll bet there are not many people with a royal document hanging in their toilet!' I laughed.

'There's more than you think, Constable!' was his reply.

But even now, all those years later, it is difficult to believe that an ordinary house in Aidensfield contained such an historic treasure. When the Colonel died, his wife did donate the charter to a museum, but it did make me wonder what else was hidden behind the curtains of Aidensfield.

It was not only houses, or perhaps attics, which contained surprises. In the country-side especially, the outbuildings and barns of remote farms and distant cottages would often produce gems of furniture, valuable paintings, old grandfather clocks, antique kitchen equipment, discarded family letters, unwanted objects like farm and dairy machinery, old typewriters and sewing machines and a host of other fascinating treasures. I knew one man who bought a house and in the attic found a huge collection of postage stamps which the outgoing owners had left behind because they did not want them. Another found a beautifully carved wooden statue of St Cuthbert which had lain undiscovered in a shed during the occupancy of several other houseowners. It was the work of a well-known artist who had earlier lived nearby. Another found some valuable seventeenth-century silver spoons concealed in his thatch and from time to time, householders found things like wells in their garden, old motor bikes in the garden shed and hoards of money hidden beneath the floorboards. The cast-off rubbish of one generation had become the antiques of another.

As the village constable I was usually aware of these discoveries because the question of ownership might arise. Generally, the finders of such things, even on the premises they now owned, did not wish to be accused of theft or dishonesty of any kind by retaining the found objects and so they took steps to remedy any defect in the question of ownership. In some cases, the outgoing householders had forgotten all about the stuff they'd abandoned and the goods were returned to them; in other cases, they had not wanted the clutter they had left and had no wish to have it restored to them.

On occasions, this left the new occupiers with the problem and expense of disposal, but from time to time the new householders found themselves owners of a valuable or interesting object. In the case of the silver spoons in the thatched roof of a cottage, this was reported to me so that I could inform the coroner because it might be treasure trove – in fact, the spoons were declared treasure trove because they had been hidden there. The owner of the house in question received their valuation from the state and the spoons found their way into the British Museum. That was a very satisfactory outcome.

In one case, though, a fascinating object became the focus of my enquiries. For reasons which were never evident, a very successful grain farmer from Suffolk decided he wanted to become a sheep farmer on the North York Moors and while looking for suitable premises, discovered the deserted and windswept High Whin Farm in the hills above Elsinby. This was a stone-built long house with a blue tiled roof and plenty of outbuildings, some of more recent construction than the house. Although it had been unoccupied for years, it was in surprisingly sound condition. It was within his price range, too and offered the range of household accommodation along with the extensive moorland and numerous buildings he thought he required, and so he bought it – lock, stock and barrel, as the saying goes. The isolated house, owned by the family of the last farmer to live there, had been empty for some ten years and it needed a lot of improvements but the buyer was a wealthy man and soon the domestic quarters were undergoing a long-overdue modernization. The outbuildings could be dealt with once the new owner had moved in.

From the near wreck of a moorland farm, therefore, High Whin was changed into a highly attractive home and so the sheep farmers and market traders of the moors found a newcomer among them, a man who might have to be taught the rudiments of moorland sheep husbandry. His name was Julian Beresford and his wife was called Christine. Both were in the mid-forties and both were keen to establish themselves in their new and challenging life. They had no children, but Christine did have several golden retrievers because that was her hobby – she bred them and showed them and, I was later to learn, she was extremely successful in this specialized field.

Shortly after they moved in, I paid a call just to introduce myself, and was invited to have a coffee with them. I found Julian to be a powerful man, both in appearance and personality; well over six feet tall, he had dark hair and thick eyebrows, broad shoulders and a figure which suggested he kept himself very fit, while Christine, a blonde, was a good looking, slightly overweight woman with immense charm and a cheerful smile. Clearly, they had ambition and determination and I knew they would be successful – each had that confidence which leads to success. They told me about their plans, what they'd done to the house, what they were going to do with the outbuildings and how they planned to immerse themselves in the life and community of the moors.

It would be a couple of months later when I received a phonecall from Julian Beresford, asking if I would pop in to see him next time I was passing. He said it was not urgent, there was no need to make a special journey to High Whin.

He did not explain the reason for his call except to say he'd welcome my advice on a little problem, and so, a couple of days later, I was in the Elsinby area and drove along the bumpy, narrow lane to High Whin. Julian had noticed my approach as he'd been working out of doors and when I eased into the parking area in front of the house, he was awaiting me. It was about eleven o'clock and, as before, he invited me in for a coffee. Christine was inside the house, busying herself with decorating the dining-room, but she welcomed the opportunity for a short break.

After the small talk, he said, 'Well, Mr Rhea, you'll be wondering what all this is about, but I wanted to ask you this – what's the position if you find yourself in possession of property which might be worth a lot of money, but which isn't yours and which you did not know about? Could I be charged with a criminal offence if I keep it?'

'Like finding hidden treasure, you mean?' I was wondering if he'd found something during the alterations to his buildings.

'Sort of,' he smiled. 'I don't mean treasure trove, I know how that system works because I once found some Roman coins on my other farm. This is different. We bought this farm as it stood at the time – empty for ten years and in dire need of modernization, but with lots of old furniture littered about the house and loads more junk and old machinery in the outbuildings. We bought it lock, stock and barrel, as they say. The lot, including the junk.'

'Then I'd say whatever you find here is yours, surely? You haven't discovered a Rembrandt in the attic, have you?'

'Something along very similar lines,' he smiled. 'When you've finished your coffee, I'll show you.'

With Christine accompanying us, he led

me to one of the outbuildings and as we approached it, he said, 'This old shed was full of rusty machinery, a broken mangle, old horse collars, broken lengths of fencing, bits of tree trunks which had been stored for timber but never cut – you name it, Mr Rhea, and it had been stuffed into this shed. That's how it was when we bought High Whin. Because we did not need to use this shed, we left it alone until we had time to clear it out – and we started not long before we rang you.'

'And you found something?'

'Right at the back, under all the other clutter,' he said. 'I'll show you.'

He opened the door and led me into the dark interior; there were no windows and the only light came through the open door, but as my eyes became accustomed to the gloom, I saw the outline of what looked like a curious trap – the pony and trap type of vehicle. Painted blue, it was complete with two large red wheels and elegant blue shafts, and included a black-roofed cab directly over the axle. There was seating space for two passengers on leather upholstered seats and two brass coach lanterns, one at each side of the cab, near the glass windows.

'A trap?' I smiled. 'You'll be able to take people for rides at our fairs and garden parties! All you need is a pony.'

'It's in surprisingly good condition,' he

243

said. 'A clean up and a bit of carpentry should make it roadworthy, maybe with a spot of paint where it's been knocked.'

'So what's the problem?' I put to him. 'If you bought the farm lock, stock and barrel, that surely implies that whatever is on the premises becomes your property.'

'That's what my solicitor said, I had a word with him before I rang you.'

'Then I can't see there's any problem,' I had to say. 'Certainly there's no need to worry about criminal proceedings; you've not stolen this trap if that's what's bothering you. If it's been here, abandoned for all those years, it's a case of finders-keepers. Both civil law and criminal law would support that.'

'It is bothering me just a little,' he admitted. 'That's why I wanted this chat. You see, Mr Rhea, this is no ordinary trap. It's a cab, a Hansom Cab to be precise, designed by Joseph Aloysius Hansom.'

'He was born in York,' I said. 'An architect by profession.'

'That's the fellow, Mr Rhea. Christine's done a spot of speedy research into his life and work.'

Christine now said her piece. 'We found a letter, you see, Mr Rhea, tucked into a pocket in the cab's leatherwork. It's still there, we put it back where it was found because we think it should never be parted from this cab.'

'And?' I invited her to continue.

'Well,' she said. 'I did a bit of checking at the reference library in York and in view of what's in that letter, I think this is a prototype of Hansom's first cab. If it is, then it is very rare and highly collectable, unique in fact, and therefore far more valuable than any other of his cabs which might still exist.'

'So what's in the letter?' I asked.

She went across to the recumbent cab, opened a door and pulled a tatty piece of folded yellowing paper from a pocket in the interior wall. She passed it to me. I opened it to find it was plain paper bearing the date 12 August 1834, and dark-ink handwriting addressed to 'Dear George'. It said: *This is the vehicle I envisage, large wheels beneath the centre of the cab's body to give stability with the driver at the front up aloft, louvre ventilators, a small covered cab for two persons and drawn by a single horse – and a good looking vehicle too! Sincerely, J.A. Hansom.*

'This is wonderful stuff,' I enthused. 'But if this is Hansom's very own prototype, how does it come to be hidden on this farm?' I handed the letter back to Christine.

'From 1820 until 1855 the farm was owned by a close friend of Hansom's, George Swainton,' Christine had clearly delved into the mystery in the short time available. 'I think he came here to build his prototype away from prying eyes, so no one would copy it. Hansom was a devout Catholic, too, and he spent a lot of time at Maddleskirk Abbey – which is how I know about his link with this farm. Their librarian was very helpful. Hansom and his friend would walk across the hills to the abbey, to attend mass. I'm sure this is the George mentioned in this letter.'

'It all makes sense,' I said. 'So who have you told about this, apart from your solicitor and me?'

'No one,' Julian said. 'We thought that once the history of this cab became known, there'd be all kinds of people coming here to claim it, and so I wanted to be as sure as possible about my rights, just in case!'

'Look at it this way,' I suggested. 'If that cab was built on this farm in 1834 or thereabouts, it's been here for more than a hundred and thirty years. How many changes of ownership has the farm witnessed in that time, I wonder?'

'Eight,' said Christine without hesitation. 'I've checked.'

'And that cab has been owned by them all, without any kind of claim being made – and now it's your turn. But you've discovered something about it that no one else knew – or perhaps no one else cared about. I cannot see that anyone else can have any claim to this, certainly not retrospectively in view of its unique character and bearing in mind the terms of purchase of the farm. And, of course, you have done all within your power to trace the owner – and the true owner would seem to be no less a person than Joseph Aloysius Hansom himself. It seems he left it there in 1834 and he's not going to make a fuss about it.'

I advised Julian and Christine to make a written record of their discovery and the research they had undertaken, and then to lodge it either with their bank manager in a safe deposit box or with the deeds of the house, just in case there was any future counterclaim. In time, though, there was no claim and they donated the splendid cab to the Northern Museum of Horse Drawn Vehicles by which time its pedigree had been verified by experts. It was Hansom's very first attempt to build his famous cab, although his original design was later amended by a man called John Chapman who patented his own design in 1836. But those little cabs have always been known as Hansom Cabs. And Julian and Christine did become highly successful moorland sheep farmers.

Chapter 8

'If there's one thing I shall not miss in my retirement,' Sergeant Blaketon said one day when he was in an affable mood, 'it is that army of self-righteous people who persistently complain about things. Look at this lot!'

It was the Ashfordly Police Station file entitled 'Persistent Complainers' and every year it was filled with letters and abstracts of telephone calls or a log of such callers at the police station. They complained about anything under the sun which annoyed them, but the most regular grumblers were about litter in the street or in people's gardens, noise, especially that which emanated from dance halls, pubs and neighbours' music centres, traffic, especially that which parked outside their house or aroused them during the night, neighbours who were a nuisance, policemen not doing their duty, teachers not disciplining children out of school, indiscriminate parking of prams and pushchairs outside shops, window boxes that dripped water on their heads, visiting cats digging up gardens for latrines, shop awnings that were too low, footpaths with gaps in the paving stones, the language used by some radio and television presenters and the proliferation of road signs.

Quite often, there was little or nothing the police could do about the complaint, often because it was a civil matter between two warring factions and not a matter in which the police service should involve itself. This was self-defeating, however, because the persistent complainer simply returned to repeat the complaint, this time adding another to the effect that the police were doing nothing about it. And this file related specifically to those who do *persistently* complain.

The occasional complaint was sometimes justified in which case the police would attend to the matter in whatever manner was appropriate, but persistent complainers were never satisfied. They just kept on complaining and used tactics like writing to the newspapers, their MP, the prime minister, the queen, the pope, the chief rabbi, the home office, the foreign office or anyone else in authority who might look kindly upon their grumbles. Sometimes, their letter would be sent back to the local police station for a constable to investigate the matter, provided it was justified of course, and so the whole merry time-wasting exercise started all over again.

The main problem with these people is that they never give up. They are persistent complainers who repeatedly grumble about anything that annoys them, but genuinely feel they are doing something beneficial for society whereas in reality they are nothing but a nuisance themselves. Some of them bear a grudge of some kind or suffer from a defect in their personality; I felt sure others suffered nothing more than crushing loneliness so that complaining was a means of attracting attention and perhaps getting a visitor, even if it was a police officer. But so many of them were very bitter towards their fellows. For some reason, they saw themselves as arbiters of public morals and behaviour while themselves being anything but perfect – as Christ himself said, when he was shown the woman who was an adulteress. In his time, the penalty for adultery was being stoned to death, but when Christ looked upon the woman, he said to the militant crowd, 'Let him who is without sin cast the first stone.' No one took up the challenge. Persistent complainers should be issued with that story on a little piece of paper! But it wouldn't stop them. They'd complain about the size of the print, the colour of the paper, Christ's abdication of responsibility, or something. In listening to these non-stop complaints, the police had to be patient and polite, otherwise a complaint would be lodged against the officer involved, and most of the time we did our best to examine the matter and, if necessary, took the appropriate action. From time to time, though, we wished the ground would open up and swallow some of these pests, or that some of them would be hoist by their own petard.

Happily, I did see Sergeant Blaketon deal effectively with one of Ashfordly's more persistent complainers. He was the appropriately named Harold Nutter who lived in a semi-detached house at 47 Brantsford Road in Ashfordly. He was a small, slightly built man with half-moon spectacles, a pinched face, a thin mouth and a massive bald pate above a patch of dark hair. He tried to disguise his baldness by spreading long strands of thin hair across the expanse of skin, but that only served to emphasize his hairless state. Harold was a retired civil servant who had come to Yorkshire because he'd read about the peace and tranquillity offered by its rural areas and it seemed he had persuaded his mouse-like wife, Lydia, to accompany him.

In his retirement, though, Harold had become quite famous, or perhaps notorious, because he was a regular letter writer to the newspapers, but his letters were always connected in some way with the roads or the traffic they carried. In the newspapers, he complained about a lack of attention to the roads in winter, blocked drains, ineffective snow clearance, too long a gap between a fall of snow and the arrival of the ploughs or not enough gravel or grit on the ice.

In the summer, he complained about traffic congestion, indiscriminate parking by tourists, noisy motor bikes, councils repairing road surfaces in hot weather, cyclists weaving about, children pulling faces through car windows, caravans, slow-moving farm vehicles, harvesters, cattle trucks going to agricultural shows, horse boxes and pig containers. If he was not writing about this kind of thing, he found something else to amuse him, such as grumbles about children kicking footballs into his garden, putting chewing gum on park benches, leaving litter in the bus shelter or using bad language.

However, a wonderful new development occurred which provided him with even more opportunities to complain to the newspapers and the police. The authorities decided to impose a 30 m.p.h. speed limit on Brantsford Road, and it was effective on the stretch which ran right past his house. Harold believed he was responsible for that limit being imposed because, over the past five years or so, he had campaigned for a speed limit in countless letters to the papers, to his MP, to the county council and rural district council and of course, to the police. His dream had come true; his efforts had been worthwhile, and Harold now had a speed limit right outside his front door. The snag was that no one took the slightest bit of notice. Traffic moved along Brantsford Road just as it had done prior to the imposition of the restriction.

I was on duty in Ashfordly Police Station one morning when Harold arrived at the counter.

'Constable,' he said in his slightly high-pitched voice, 'you really must do something about traffic along Brantsford Road. I thought the new restrictions would have reduced their speed, but not so! They hurtle past my house just as they used to, lorries, buses, cars, motor bikes, all ignoring the signs.'

'We need to catch the speeders before we can prosecute them,' I said. 'We have to prove they are exceeding the limit; we can't prosecute them if we merely think they are going too fast. We need evidence good enough for the courts to impose a conviction. I do know that our traffic patrols regularly monitor speed limits throughout the county, and pay especial attention to newly imposed speed limit areas. We have the situation in mind and I am sure our Road Traffic Division will be staging a speed trap there before too long.'

'You need a uniformed presence all the time on that road, Constable, to deter them, to remind them of their responsibilities. I shall write to the chief constable to suggest a constable be permanently placed on duty there, to deter speeders.'

'We do have other things to deal with, Mr Nutter, like crime and attacks upon old people, children and so on. We cannot spare an officer full time for that kind of duty.'

'That is no excuse, Constable. I pay my rates so that I can get a good service from the police. What are the police for, if they are not going to enforce the law? I shall write to my Member of Parliament, and to the Home Office, and I shall inform them that Ashfordly Police are not taking their duties seriously enough!' And with that, he walked out.

I told Sergeant Blaketon of our exchange of words and he advised me to make an entry in our occurrence book, detailing my comments and outlining Mr Nutter's grounds for complaint. 'And,' he added, 'give Road Traffic a ring to find out when their next speed trap will be located on Brantsford Road.'

I rang Road Traffic and spoke to Sergeant Browning.

'We've a provisional listing for three weeks on Sunday, Nick,' he said. 'Two hours on

Brantsford Road between 10.30 a.m. and 12.30 p.m., peak times for Sunday speeders!'

'Thanks,' I said, and explained the reason for my call.

'We'll catch a few,' he said, 'but it won't deter the others. But a show of police uniform followed by a few court cases will do some good.'

Later, I was told that that particular speed trap had caught only three drivers, and they'd only been travelling at 40 m.p.h. or less in the 30 m.p.h. area; they would not be taken to court for driving so little above the limit but would be given an official caution. It seemed, from that exercise, that there was no great speeding problem along Brantsford Road. Unfortunately, Harold had been away for the whole of that weekend and he had therefore not seen the police officers checking the drivers.

I was again on duty in Ashfordly Police Station, this time with Sergeant Blaketon at my side, when Harold arrived at the counter.

'Ah!' he said when he saw Blaketon. 'The man in charge! Now perhaps something will get done!'

'Yes, Mr Nutter?' I could sense just a hint of resignation in Blaketon's voice, but he produced a sort of smile for his customer.

'Speeders on Brantsford Road, Sergeant. I

demand action, and I shall not tolerate any lack of commitment by you and your officers.'

'We ran a speed check recently, Mr Nutter, and found only three vehicles had exceeded the limit, all travelling at less than forty miles an hour. Three offenders in a two-hour stint of duty in which more than five hundred vehicles passed our check-point.' Sergeant Blaketon looked at Nutter. 'That is hardly a cause for concern.'

'I live along the road, Sergeant, and I know what the drivers do. I watch them! Now, am I right in thinking you need to follow a speeding vehicle for a considerable distance in order to assure yourselves it is not a momentary lapse?'

'We do that as a matter of practice, Mr Nutter, yes.'

'Then I have the evidence you need, Sergeant,' and Nutter pulled a piece of writing paper from his pocket. 'A sports car travelled for a mile and a half along Brantsford Road this morning, averaging fifty-two miles an hour for the entire journey. I have its registration number here. It entered the speed limit area at sixty-five miles an hour and reduced its speed throughout the journey, but always exceeding thirty, varying between forty-five and fifty miles per hour. As a witness, I demand that you prosecute the driver.'

Sergeant Blaketon took the piece of paper upon which details had been recorded and it showed the date, time and place of the alleged offence, the registration number of the red MG sports car and a description of the driver, at least from the neck up!

'This is very good, Mr Nutter,' smiled Sergeant Blaketon. 'Just what we need in fact.'

'I am not a fool, Sergeant. I know that is all you need for a successful prosecution and I am prepared to go to court to give evidence against the accused.'

'You did say you would not tolerate a lack of commitment by me and my officers?'

'Indeed I did say that, Sergeant, and if you do not prosecute this man, and make him an example to the motoring public, I shall write to the Home Secretary and the Minister of Transport to demand an enquiry into your conduct.'

'Well spoken,' beamed Blaketon. 'But how can you prove this car was driving at the speeds you allege?'

'Because I followed him right along the road in my own car, Sergeant. I checked his journey every inch of the way, with a stop watch too.'

'Ah!' smiled Blaketon and I saw the glint of satisfaction in his eyes. 'May I see your driving licence, Mr Nutter? And your certificate of insurance?'

'My licence and insurance? Why?'

'Because I cannot shirk my duty, Mr Nutter, and if you admit to averaging fifty-two miles an hour in your car through a thirty miles an hour limit, as you just have done, then I shall have to report you for exceeding the speed limit in a built-up area.'

'Me, but—'

'You have just admitted it, Mr Nutter. I could not have a more voluntary confession than that! Now, your licence please.'

Blaketon's mood changed swiftly. Nutter realized what was happening but it was too late. Blaketon was going to teach him a lesson. Nutter delved into his pocket and pulled out his wallet, extracted his driving licence and passed it to Blaketon who opened it and studied it.

'You haven't signed it, Mr Nutter.' He pointed to the blank space where Nutter's signature should have been.

'Oh, well, I can do it now,' he said, reaching for his ballpoint.

'No, that is no good. It should have been signed upon receipt of the licence, Mr Nutter, and I see the commencement date of yours was 21 March last year. It is an offence not to sign your driving licence, Mr Nutter, so I shall retain it as evidence. I know you would not want me to shirk my duty. Now, your certificate of insurance?'

'It is at home, Sergeant, I can bring it in.'

'You must bring it in for me to inspect, Mr Nutter; you have five clear days in which to produce it at the police station of your choice.'

'Oh dear, well, yes, I'll bring it to Ashfordly. Look, Sergeant, I think you have made your point ... I was only trying to do my public duty...'

'I cannot ignore offences against the law, Mr Nutter, as you well know, and I do know that you would not want me to fail to do my duty however painful that might be. I would not wish you to write letters of complaint about my dereliction of duty. Now, shall we examine your car?'

'Examine it?'

'Yes, as a police officer, I have the power to examine your car for defects in its brakes, lights, steering, exhaust, windscreen wipers, direction indicators, tyres and other matters. I am only doing my duty, Mr Nutter.'

Nutter followed the striding sergeant outside to where Nutter's Ford Consul was parked on the street, and I followed. Blaketon then asked him to start the engine as he listened to the sound of the exhaust pipe, then requested him to switch on the lights, the indicators and wipers.

'Your offside headlamp is not working, Mr Nutter, and the blade on the nearside windscreen wiper is defective.' Blaketon was making notes as he continued his detailed examination of the vehicle. 'I see your car is taxed and that your excise licence is up to date, but I wonder whether our Road Traffic Vehicle Examiners should look at your car? They execute a much more detailed and professional technical examination than I can give at the roadside, Mr Nutter, things like testing for dangerous parts and accessories, the brakes and so on.'

Nutter said nothing, but Blaketon smiled and said, 'I think I have enough for the time being, Mr Nutter. I shall report you for the offences of exceeding the speed limit in a built-up area, failing to sign your driving licence and for having a defective headlamp. You are not obliged to say anything, but what you do say will be taken down in writing and may be given in evidence.'

Nutter said nothing. Blaketon said, 'I will keep this piece of paper with your notes upon it, it will be good evidence, Mr Nutter.'

Nutter left the police station without saying a word, so I asked, 'Sergeant, will you prosecute him for these things?'

'He might complain if I neglect my duty, Rhea!' grunted Blaketon with a knowing grin. 'But people like him need to learn that we are not all perfect. I shall recommend a written caution from the superintendent, although I doubt if a prosecution for exceeding the speed limit would have succeeded either against him or the chap in the sports car. I trust he has learned some kind of lesson, though, and I hope his insurance is in order.'

It was. Nutter brought it to the police station within the specified five days and Ventress checked it. But that was the last time Harold Nutter came into Ashfordly Police Station to make any kind of complaint.

Another persistent complainer was Robina Barton, a spinster of the parish of Aidensfield who lived alone in Beehive Cottage. A retired matron from Ashfordly Hospital, she was a tall, severe and very large woman who terrified the children and indeed the rest of the population. Her dark greying hair was worn short and from a distance it looked like a deep sea diver's helmet clamped around her head. She wore curious little spectacles with round lenses and thin wire rims and those people who had been very close to her swore she sported signs of a shaved moustache. She never wore make-up and habitually dressed in a long dark-grey skirt, a white blouse and a black cardigan, clothing which was almost a repetition of her matronly uniform. Formidable might be an apt description of Robina and in addition to her demeanour, she had a very loud and very sharp voice which demanded instant obedience.

If, for example, a child got in her way in the shop, she would snap, 'Out of my way, child!', and the startled child would leap out of her way without question. Similarly, if she attended a parish council meeting and someone raised a rather stupid point, she would bellow, 'Don't be silly, man! We don't want to know that. Give us something sensible to discuss', or if she crossed the street while a horn-blowing motorist was approaching, she would shake her fist and shout, 'People were made before cars, you know! You'll have to wait'.

In other words, Robina was one of the village characters and none of us was surprised that she lived alone without having married. I could not imagine the sort of man who would have had Robina as a wife, nor could I imagine her finding any man with whom she would be content.

I think she missed the drama of working in a busy hospital and, in her retirement, she developed a keen hatred of rubbish and litter. That is why she attended all meetings of the parish council where she complained about it persistently. She wrote to the papers too and compiled pieces for the parish magazine in which she grumbled about litter outside the post office, the shop, the pub and the bus shelter; she grumbled about litter in the street, the churchyard, the grounds of the village hall and other places of public resort especially the village green. As if that wasn't enough, she even resorted to grumbling about litter and rubbish in people's private gardens, particularly those which fronted the main street of the village and which could be seen by the passing crowds. Worse still, she made her objections to untidy gardens widely known throughout Aidensfield, which was, in my view, not a very wise thing to do.

In addition to the parish council, she harangued the rural district council, the county council, the vicar, the secretary of the village hall, the bus company and anyone else whose premises attracted litter in any shape or form. I don't think she actually wrote to the owners of the untidy gardens, but she did make veiled comments about them either verbally to people she knew, or in comments printed in the parish magazine. It seemed that her entire life was dominated by litter in the street and rubbish-strewn private gardens. The snag with her private campaign was that if she did not know to whom she should direct any particular complaint, she would come to see me, demanding my immediate attention and stressing that I must prosecute the offender or offenders without delay.

'When I was in charge of the wards in that hospital,' she would often say to me, 'I did not tolerate litter or rubbish of any kind, Constable. Everything has its place and the place for rubbish is the waste bin, and all my staff knew that. Mine was the cleanest hospital in this kingdom, I am sure of that because I made it the cleanest. It was spotless, night and day, no matter how busy we were, and I see no reason why this village cannot be the tidiest in the realm. The people need advice and training, Constable; they need to be told, quite forcibly, not to dump litter and that is your job!'

'We did win the best kept village competition,' I reminded her on one occasion. 'The villagers were marvellous, they worked really hard to keep the place neat and litter-free and thanks to their efforts we had the tidiest village in the whole of the North York Moors National Park area.'

'Well, it's evident they have not remembered those lessons!' she retorted, before stomping away to tidy up someone's discarded cigarette packet or chocolate wrapper.

One afternoon some time afterwards, she hailed me outside the Aidensfield Stores. Her face was thunderous as she snapped, 'Constable, have you seen the state of that garden at Number Ten, round the corner?'

'It's untidy,' I had to admit, 'but it's always like that. Those people are the scruffiest in the village, everyone knows that. You should see the inside of the house!'

'Untidy? That is not the word I would use, Constable. It is a disgrace. There's an old abandoned mattress, rotting armchairs, a pushchair with no wheels, a motor cycle without an engine, half a wardrobe and a chest of cheap drawers, a discarded toilet basin, old clothes ... really, Constable, it is disgusting. Why don't those people take their junk to the council tip? Or get the council to move it? You ought to do something about it. I shall complain to the parish council.'

'It is on private land, Miss Barton,' I told her. 'I have no jurisdiction over people littering their own private grounds with their own rubbish. It is illegal for anyone to throw litter into someone else's premises from a public place, like the street, or, of course, drop it in the street, but for me to be able to prosecute those people who do drop litter in public places, I need to catch them in the act or to have a witness who could provide the necessary evidence. And,' I added, 'I have to be sure they have abandoned the litter in question. If I tell the dumper to pick it up and place it in a bin, and he or she does so, there is no offence.'

'That is very silly, Constable!'

'Effective enforcement of the Litter Act of 1958 is not easy,' I added.

'That is your problem, Constable, your

job is to enforce the law, not to find pitfalls with it. If you are not going to do anything about it, then I shall! And have you seen the state of Number Fourteen? And Seventeen?' And off she stalked to go about her self-imposed task of tidying-up Aidensfield.

'Be careful if you're thinking of grumbling about those gardens! You've no right to complain about the state of people's private premises,' I reminded her as she strode away.

'We'll see about that,' was her battlecry.

In truth, she did have a point. Some of the gardens on the council estate were dreadful, a genuine eye-sore; not only were they completely neglected from a horticultural point of view, they were also the dumping ground for anything which could not be accommodated in the dustbin. They contained pieces of cars, vans and motor bikes, and even scrap entire cars and motor bikes, cast-off furniture and clothing, un-wanted items like broken fridges, television sets and lawnmowers, household bits and pieces – anything in fact which could not be placed in the bin was often just dumped in the garden and left to rot. If Robina could persuade those people to move their offal, she would be doing a service to society, and although the council had tried, they had usually failed. In spite of her fervour, however, I felt she should not involve herself with junk left in private gardens.

From what I was told, though, it seemed she could not restrain herself from letting her views be known to those whose gardens had become her most recent target for reform and, if the people concerned did not heed her grumbles, she would intensify her actions. She'd taken to regularly walking past the offending places and during such outings she would deliberately halt to peer over the fences and to wrinkle her face in disgust at the appalling sights which confronted her. I am not sure what she hoped to achieve by this personal display of disapproval, but it did lead to a noteworthy development.

The man who lived at 10 Council Houses, Aidensfield was called Elvis Wayne Satterthwaite and he was an unemployed labourer. In his early thirties, Elvis had no talents and no skills and could never retain even the most mediocre of jobs because he was useless at whatever he tried. Although it was doubtful whether he could read or write, he was very good at claiming the dole and used that considerable skill to keep his council house, his six children and his large, untidy and very dirty wife whose name was Tracy. He did tend to accumulate junk because if he bought a car, it would be a heap of old rusting rubbish for which he would pay very little with the inevitable

267

result that it broke down within days. Because he could not afford to repair it, he left it wherever it had breathed its last, which was usually his garden, and bought another – which also died within days of purchase.

And so it was that Robina chanced to be passing Elvis's home one evening when he was endeavouring to fit a new starter motor to his most recent acquisition, a battered and rusting Ford Anglia.

A neighbour, painting a bedroom with the window open, happened to note their meeting.

'I say,' Robina called to him over the fence. 'Don't you think it is time you cleared some of this junk from your garden, Mr Satterthwaite?'

'Sod off,' he replied, or words to that effect.

Robina, being an ex-matron of con-siderable experience, was not at all daunted by this unhelpful response. Some of her past patients had been similarly uncooperative.

'I shall not sod off until I get a civil reply from you,' she said, and promptly came to a standstill outside his garden gate. 'I am merely suggesting you consider those who live around you and rid yourself of this litter. It is most unsightly and it lowers the tone of this area and also the standard of the whole village–'

'I said sod off,' and Elvis continued to curse the broken starter motor as he tried to make the piece fit.

'And I said I shall not leave here until I get a civil response.' Robina, a towering form at the garden gate, folded her arms in a show of determination.

'All right, stay there, you silly old bat,' was Elvis's reaction as he continued his repair job. He continued to work on his car without any further reference to Robina, and she stood at his gate, arms folded, awaiting some kind of reaction. But she got none. She was there for quite a long time.

It seems she realized her presence was serving no useful purpose because she stalked away as darkness was falling. Round One to Elvis.

Her parting shot was, 'I shall demand the council does something about the state of your garden, and those others at Number Fourteen and Seventeen. They are a disgrace! I shall demand a response! I shall write to the chairman of the council and demand that he sends someone to examine your garden, and those others I have mentioned, Mr Satterthwaite.'

He had not replied, except to curse vilely when the spanner slipped and trapped his finger.

When Robina awoke next morning, however, she was horrified to find her own garden hidden beneath a mountain of household junk and old vehicles. There was an array of scrap cars and motor bikes, old electrical goods, armchairs and settees with the stuffing coming out, parts of demolished wardrobes – in fact, everything she had noted in all the council house gardens. At least, that is what she claimed when she came to visit me at eight o'clock that morning.

'It's that man Satterthwaite!' she said. 'He's dumped all his rubbish in my garden, Constable, and that from the other house. I demand police action. You must prosecute him!'

'How did he get the stuff into your garden?' I asked. 'Presuming it was him, of course.'

'By lorry, I would think, and delivered from my back lane, Constable, where else?'

'It's private, isn't it? Your back lane?'

'Yes, of course it is. It gives access to the back of my house, nowhere else. It is not a public right of way, not a footpath, if that is what you are asking.'

'Then there is no criminal offence under the Litter Act,' I had to tell her. 'It is a civil matter between you and Mr Satterthwaite, if indeed it was him.'

'Of course it was him! Who else could it have been? I had words with him about his garden and this is his response. It is typical of the man, I would say. You mean you are going to let him get away with this?'

'Strictly speaking, it's not my duty but I'll speak to him,' I promised her, wondering how one earth he had managed to dump such a huge lot of large and noisy items without arousing her during the night. She must sleep very soundly and it must have taken an hour or more to offload all this junk.

Before calling on Elvis, I looked at the other two junk-filled gardens, and both Fourteen and Seventeen were blissfully empty. Next, I paid a call on Elvis and also found his garden completely empty. He answered the door.

'Hello, Mr Rhea,' he beamed. 'Just the man. I was thinking of calling you because somebody has stolen all my belongings from the garden. Spare cars, bits of old radiators, fridge spare parts, bits of wood which are part of some old furniture, you name it and it's gone. And from my neighbours up the road. There's been a thief about, Mr Rhea.'

'Isn't that amazing?' I smiled. 'And by some coincidence, Robina Barton has got a garden full of things similar to the ones you've lost, they arrived overnight. Old cars, bits of furniture, derelict fridges and ovens...'

'You mean somebody's nicked it all from me and my pals and dropped it in her garden?' he smiled. 'Why would anybody do a thing like that?'

'Would you like to come and look at the stuff in her garden, just to check whether it is yours?' I asked, tongue in cheek. 'I can ask your neighbours too.'

'No problem, I'll come now. I know what my neighbours had, we often swopped bits and pieces, you know how it is. If I wanted an alternator for my Ford and only had one from a Hillman, him at Number Fourteen might do a swap,' and he walked with me as I returned to Robina's house. She saw us approaching and hurried to meet us.

'Well done, Constable,' she smiled. 'You've found the culprit.'

'Elvis,' I said. 'This stuff in Robina's garden? Have a good look at it. Is it yours? Or is part of it yours? Or does some of it belong to your neighbours?'

'No, none of that's mine, Mr Rhea. Nor my neighbours'. Not a scrap. I've never seen any of that old stuff before. Sorry. Those folks who took our stuff must have dumped this to make room for ours, that's what I think. I'd say there was a couple of lorry-loads here, Mr Rhea.'

'How can you believe him, Mr Rhea?' she cried. 'This is his; I saw it last night in his garden...'

'If it is mine, it must have been stolen,' said Elvis. 'You didn't steal it, did you, Miss

Barton? You don't look like a thief to me, does she, Mr Rhea? I wouldn't want to accuse a lady of stealing if she's innocent.'

'You're not accusing me of stealing from you, are you?' Robina shrieked.

'No, because that's not mine, Mr Rhea. I mean, I can understand her thinking it might be, after all one scrap car's just like another, isn't it? When its registration number's been removed? And can you say that old fridge is definitely the one from my garden? So sorry, Mr Rhea, I just can't help. I shan't bother reporting my goods stolen, Mr Rhea, it was just a load of scrap after all, and I know my mates won't want a fuss making about theirs, although you can ask them if you like.'

'Well, Robina,' I had to say, 'it looks as if you have acquired a lot of scrap and if Mr Satterthwaite and his friends say it is not theirs, there is not a lot more I can do about it. I'm sure Claude Jeremiah Greengrass will move it for you, it is rather unsightly. He might even give you a few pounds for any usable scrap metal he finds among it.'

'This is appalling!' and she stomped indoors. In spite of her non-stop grumbling, I did feel slightly sorry for her, but she had brought much of this upon herself by her constant interference and I could only watch as Elvis Satterthwaite walked away smiling.

'It's a funny old world we live in, isn't it, Mr Rhea?' he grinned. 'But it's quite nice, having a garden free from clutter. I might even get around to some gardening one of these days.'

'Don't push your luck next time!' I warned him.

'I don't think there'll be a next time,' he said, whistling as he walked away.

Among my regular complainers were Bertram and Prunella Osbourne who lived in Waterfall View, Aidensfield. Bertram was a representative for a firm of medical equipment suppliers and his wife worked part-time in a ladies' fashion shop in Ashfordly. Bertram's profession, selling all manner of surgical and hospital equipment, including splints, artificial legs and wheel-chairs, allowed him to work from home where he had a small office in a spare bedroom, and Pru's job also allowed her to spend some time at home. She worked three mornings a week, one of which was a Saturday. For this reason, they were often in and around their house and were always pleasant to people who walked past their smart garden. They were in their early fifties, and took part in village affairs, helping with things like garden fêtes, running the village hall, putting flowers on the altar in the church and so on.

Nice and decent as they were, the Osbournes were persistent complainers. Their chief grudge was sloppy workmanship, whether it was in the clothes they bought, the meals they ordered in restaurants, or the standard of workmanship from tradesmen like plumbers, bricklayers and builders in general. Anyone who had sold anything to the Osbournes or done work for them could expect to receive a complaint of some kind and I am sure they received many refunds, exchanges, free meals and cash remedies as a result of their non-stop activities. One counter-effect was that few of the village craftsmen and tradesmen wanted to carry out any work for the Osbournes, knowing that however professional they might be, the Osbournes would find cause for complaint, often with the purpose of claiming a discount.

Similarly, few of the villagers invited the Osbournes in for a meal, or joined them at concerts or other outings because the Osbournes would be sure to complain about something. They wrote to the newspapers about sloppiness on radio and television, and about spelling mistakes in the papers; they complained to film producers and television drama makers about mistakes in period costumes, continuity and a host of other minor details, and they wrote to authors and publishers about errors in books and magazines. Those of us who knew them wondered whether they actually enjoyed anything they did and the general conclusion was that the only thing they truly enjoyed was making complaints. It seemed to be their hobby.

Fortunately for me, few of their grumbles involved the police, although Pru did complain that PC Alf Ventress's bottom tunic button was undone while he was performing traffic duty in Ashfordly, while on another occasion Bertram wrote to Sergeant Blaketon to say that the Ashfordly police car needed a thorough wash. I received a few complaints too – they said I did not pay sufficient attention to the pub at closing time, that I did not prevent cars parking outside Aidensfield's two churches on Sundays and that on one occasion my police house noticeboard contained two out-of-date posters.

One day, however, I decided to pay them an official visit because all rural constables had received advance intelligence that confidence tricksters were touring rural areas in the North Riding and offering to do repair work on roofs, chimneys and gutters. These were not skilled operators but were cheap confidence tricksters who persuaded householders to pay high prices for poor and unnecessary work.

Their work was rarely, if ever, required –

the men pretended to have noticed broken slates, loose chimney pots or blocked gutters, offering to remedy the defects, but when the job was done, they demanded extortionate fees, with violence on occasions. They never gave anyone their names or addresses, never issued receipts or guarantees, and always demanded cash payments.

Invariably the 'work' or 'repair' was poor in the extreme and sometimes their victims were gullible old folks who paid a fortune for work that any competent handyman could do for a couple of pounds. Because this confidence trick had first been practised in the Leeds area, these characters were known as Leeds con. men. From time to time, we received advance notice that they were likely to be operating in certain areas and we would then warn as many people as we could and at the same time keep observations for likely suspects.

One problem was that the borderline between a confidence trick, bad workmanship and an unsatisfactory business transaction was very narrow and these characters could often operate just within the law, avoiding criminal charges by a careful use of language while knowing their victims could not or would not take action through the civil courts. The police, of course, did not involve themselves in civil wrongs. In any case, the crooks never left their names or addresses – which was why we always asked victims to secure the registration marks of vehicles they used.

Having received a warning that they were likely to visit my patch, I decided to alert the villagers because country properties did seem to attract these villains, possibly because of their remote setting plus the fact they could operate unseen.

It was with that in mind that I called at Waterfall View. Both Bertram and Pru were at home and invited me in. They offered me a coffee and as I sat in their kitchen to warn them of these undesirables, Bertram said, 'Oh, we would never employ people like that, Mr Rhea. We are very particular about our choice of workmen, we take the utmost care before allowing anyone to carry out maintenance on our house.'

'If you do receive a visit from anyone who might fit their description, could you make a note of their appearance and any other details, like names and car numbers? We want to put a stop to their antics.'

'Yes, of course, we will do all we can. But no confidence trickster will get a penny out of me, Mr Rhea! I'm much too careful for that sort of thing to happen – and so is Pru.'

We chatted for a time about village matters, with Bertram telling me he had complained to the highways department of the county council about the standard of workmanship on the roads because the most recent resurfacing had resulted in a lot of loose gravel which had not been collected, and he had also written to the rural district council to notify them of a spelling mistake in their latest rate demands. I left him to his little pleasures.

Over the following days, I called at many other houses and business premises in Aidensfield and in the other villages on my patch, making sure that the centres of community activity such as the shops, post offices, pubs and churches all knew about the likelihood of a visit by the Leeds con. men.

My colleagues did likewise throughout the rest of Ashfordly section and Sergeant Blaketon felt we had all done a good job. If the con. men did venture on to our patch, he was confident we would be told about them and he did express just a hint of the pleasure it would give him if we could arrest these villains. It would be a nice conclusion to his period as our sergeant, and of course, a nice way to end his career in the police service.

Over the next few days, we received no suggestion that the Leeds con. men had ventured into our territory and I began to wonder whether they had somehow discovered our advance interest and had gone elsewhere. Then, as I was walking past the post office shortly before it closed, I noticed Bertram Osbourne heading towards me with a clutch of letters in his fist.

'Good afternoon, Constable. Very quiet in the village, eh?'

'Very, Mr Osbourne. Just how it should be!'

'Those Leeds characters you warned me about never materialized, did they?' he smiled, almost relishing the fact that I had been proved wrong.

'Not yet,' I agreed. 'We've alerted the whole of the population around Ashfordly, so if they do come anywhere near here, we'll know about it!'

'You police officers may be tempted to believe that all visitors are wrongdoers,' he said. 'I am sure there are people who would alert householders to defects in their properties, and offer to rectify them, without necessarily being rogues and thieves.'

'I am sure you are right, Mr Osbourne, but that doesn't alter the fact that there are some very cunning and unscrupulous characters about, men who will readily take advantage of decent people.'

'Well, I had a young man call this morning, just as I was going out, and he was the exact opposite of what you have led me to believe.'

'Really?' I wondered what he was going to

tell me. 'And he was one of these nice people, was he?'

'Just as I was coming out of the drive in my car, he was passing and he stopped me to point out that one of the tiles on the ridge of my garage had slipped. He said he had noticed it when he was passing. It would let in the rain and no one wants that. Anyway, Mr Rhea, he offered to replace it for me.'

'Did he?' Now I was becoming interested. This had all the hallmarks of the Leeds con. men. It was how they introduced themselves to gullible householders. 'So what did you do?'

'Well, I was heading off to meet a very valuable customer and so I thanked him and said I would get a local builder to do the job for me. Then the man said he would be pleased to do it, it was the work of a mere five minutes, provided I could lend him an extension ladder. He said it would cost me nothing – the garage roof is easily accessible. I have a ladder in the shed, Mr Rhea, and so I said I was rushing off, but showed him where the ladder was. I said it was wrong that he should do the work for nothing, so I gave him a fiver, Mr Rhea.'

'And you went off to meet your customer, leaving him on the premises?'

'I did, and when I returned, the tile was back in place. That young man has saved me a lot of trouble from water seeping in and he did the job for a fraction of the price I would have had to pay a local man.'

'You've no complaints then?' I smiled.

'None at all.'

'And your ladder is back in its place in the shed?'

'It is, Mr Rhea, neatly hanging from the wall where I keep it.'

'Was Mrs Osbourne at home while he was working?'

'No, she was at work in the shop, and this afternoon she went shopping with a friend in York. I expect her back, by six or thereabouts.'

'And you have checked your house? No break-in? Nothing stolen from the garden or outbuildings?'

'There you go again, thinking there's evil in everyone! No, Mr Rhea, I did bear your warning in mind and I checked everything when I got home. Nothing has been stolen, my tile has been replaced entirely to my satisfaction and that is the end of the matter. I felt you should know that not every visitor is a confidence trickster.'

'I'm delighted to hear it,' I said. 'But who was this young man?'

'I have no idea, he had a West Riding accent. He was driving a small white van and he was quite smart with a white coat on, like a fish merchant might wear. In his late twenties, I'd say, with dark hair and a nice smile. A very nice young man, Mr Rhea.'

'But not a local person?'

'No, I can't say I have seen him before. But as I said, I have no complaints about his work. Now, I must get these letters into the post box and then get home to prepare a meal for Pru. We share household chores, you see. My turn to cook tonight!' And off he went.

I must admit I was rather worried about the mysterious and helpful caller because that visit had all the hallmarks of a confidence trick, but Bertram had assured me that nothing had been stolen and the job had been done to his satisfaction – and that alone was something of a miracle. As Bertram went off to post his letters, I turned for home, but even as I entered my office to book off duty, the telephone was ringing.

'Blaketon here, Rhea. Is everything correct on Aidensfield beat?'

'Yes, Sergeant, all correct.'

'No visits by Leeds con. men?'

'I've had none reported, Sergeant,' I had to say, but I added, 'although one man did have a visit this morning, from a stranger in a white van.'

'Did he?' and I could sense the interest in Blaketon's voice. 'So what happened? Who was that man and why did he see fit to tell you about it?'

I told Blaketon the story which had been related by Bertram Osbourne and when I had finished, Blaketon said, 'Well, Rhea, I think you had better go and have another word with Mr Osbourne. Ask him to check his roof again – and not just the garage.'

'He said the tile was fixed perfectly, Sergeant.'

'It's not the tile I'm thinking about, it's the lead flashing on his house roof.'

'He didn't mention that, Sergeant,' I had to say. 'He just said the house had not been broken into and the man had fixed his garage roof for a fiver.'

'Listen to this, Rhea,' said Blaketon. 'Your man has had a visit by a new gang of Leeds con. men.'

'There was only one man, Sergeant,' I told him.

'Only one man went to the house, Rhea, the others would be waiting out of sight. Now, this is what they've been doing, a new technique. A charming young man in a white van calls at a house just as the householder is leaving – they watch their target houses to establish this – and he then points out some defect on the building. That is usually fairly easy – blocked guttering, cracked or loose roof tiles, a chimney with the cement missing ... almost any house in the country has some kind of minor defect, and that young man offers to fix it. He says he's spotted it while passing and will repair it free. He persuades the householder to let him borrow a ladder and so the householder agrees – if the householder insists on being present and watching, then the defect is repaired and usually a token payment is made. Clearly, no attempt is made to steal anything in that case. But if a householder is rushing off to work or somewhere, they leave the charming man to carry out the work – after all the rest of the house is locked. The confidence trick is achieved when the man says he will fix the defect for no payment. That establishes his trust-worthiness. And once the householder is safely away, a lorry arrives at the house, with two or three men on board.'

'And they clean up?

'Steal from the garden, from outbuildings and lead from the roof. The lorry then disappears with its load.'

'And the man in the white van?' I asked.

'He remains a while, to further establish his bona fides by popping into the post office or shop to say he's done the job at Honeysuckle Cottage or wherever, so per-haps the shopkeeper/postmaster or whoever would tell the owners when they return? Everyone thinks he's a wonderful young man. No one is suspicious of him and in the meantime, the lorry with its load of stolen property is heading back to base, totally unsuspected. The way they operate gives the gang time to get well clear of the scene before the alarm is raised.'

'This is a departure from the usual way they operate, they don't steal things as a rule, just demand exorbitant fees for shoddy work, so are you saying the Osbournes' house has been raided, Sergeant?'

'It's a very distinct possibility, Rhea, so get yourself down to see Mr Osbourne immediately, and ask him if he's lost any lead flashing from his roof.'

'Can I ask how all this has come to light, Sergeant?'

'Through good police work, Rhea, by Ashfordly section I might add! And through a piece of good luck involving Mrs Ventress. She had unexpectedly called on a friend in Slemmington but the friend was out and a man with a white van was working on the roof. Because Alf had mentioned the Leeds con. men, she noted the number and as she was leaving, she saw a lorry parked along the road, so she took its number as well, then told Alf. When Alf checked, the householders told the story of the white van and the charming young driver who had offered to clear their gutters without payment, but when they checked the garden, a statue of Eros was missing.'

'An expensive one, no doubt?' I added.

'Worth in excess of five hundred pounds,

Rhea. Anyway, thanks to Alf and Mrs Ventress we circulated neighbouring sections and Force Control Room informed all mobiles – and our traffic patrols caught the white van and the lorry on the A19 just south of Thirsk, heading for Leeds. Both vehicles are registered at a Leeds address. We've got four men in custody and we've recovered Eros, along with a motor lawnmower, two garden rollers, a selection of gardening tools, a hedge trimmer, a pair of garden shears, a wheelbarrow – and a supply of lead. We're trying to find owners for those items – and it occurred to me your man might not have noticed he had lost the lead from his roof tops. I think he would have missed the gardening items, so we've further enquiries to make about the ownership of those.'

'Great stuff!' I said. 'Right, I'll go straight away.'

I told Mary I would not be away for long, and headed straight for Waterfall View where I found Bertram slaving over a hot stove in the kitchen. I could see he was not too pleased to be interrupted in his culinary duties, but he halted his work, removed his apron and came outside to talk to me.

'Mr Osbourne,' I said, 'following the visit of that young man you told me about, can I ask you to check your roof?'

'I did check it, Constable, I told you so.

The tiling work was done most satisfactorily.

'I mean the roof of the house, not just the garage. What about the lead?' I asked. 'The lead flashings?'

'Lead?' His face fell and I knew he had never given it a thought. He hurried into the garden to gain a vantage point and together we walked completely around the house as we stared up at the range of roof levels. It was a big house and the garage stood apart from the main building, but he'd never even considered anyone might strip his roof of its lead flashings. It wasn't the sort of crime you'd notice by chance. But as we stared aloft, I could see the tell-tale clean patches from where the lead had been removed – where some of the roof abutted walls and where other sections joined roof levels of differing heights. They had done a good job. Every square inch of lead had gone.

'Oh my God...' he said. 'Constable, what are you going to do about this? I shall write to the chief constable, I should have been warned...'

'You were warned,' I reminded him gently. 'And we have caught the thief in possession of your lead. That charming young man with the white van was an accomplice, Mr Osbourne – now, if you had listened to my advice and noted his registration number...'

'I don't know what Pru will say about

this,' was all he said. 'I just do not know...'

'I'd like to take particulars from you, please, for my crime report.'

'You'd better come in then, Constable.'

He led me into the kitchen and I settled at the table with my file of blank forms, then Prunella Osbourne returned while I was taking the necessary written statement from her husband. I must admit I was surprised at the anger in her voice when she realized what Bertram had allowed to happen. But as I located the right forms, I couldn't resist saying, 'I need a formal complaint from you, Mr Osbourne. That will authorize us to take action against the suspects.'

'He's very good at making complaints!' snapped Pru.

'But this time,' I couldn't resist adding, 'he does not wish to complain about the quality of the workmanship, do you, Mr Osbourne?'

'It looked very professional to me!' he snapped.

'You did say the tiling work to the garage was extremely well done and I can see that the stripping of the lead has been equally well accomplished,' I smiled. 'It was so good in fact that you never noticed its absence. But the culprits have been arrested – or should I say the suspected culprits have been arrested? However, I don't think you can complain about police action in this instance, Mr Osbourne.'

'I thought you people were considerate of the property of others,' he snapped. 'You've left some dirt on the floor. You should have wiped your boots before you came into the kitchen, PC Rhea, you've paddled soil in from the garden.'

'Shall I write that into your statement?' I asked him. 'Or would you like to write to the chief constable to complain about it?'

Chapter 9

While I was dealing with the range of duties just described, Sergeant Blaketon was preparing for his retirement. Police officers were obliged to give at least one month's notice of their intention to retire on pension, but in Sergeant Blaketon's case, he had reached the statutory age limit. Unless he was granted an extension of service, he (like all constables and sergeants) had to retire at the age of fifty-five – extensions were sometimes granted upon request, for one year at a time, provided the officer passed a medical test to confirm his or her fitness to continue serving. I did hear that Sergeant Blaketon did not wish to submit himself to such a test because his heartbeat was giving him minor problems. His doctor had suggested he take his retirement at the first opportunity, albeit with some less strenuous activity to keep his body and mind occupied. It was that advice which had prompted him to buy Aidensfield Post Office, and it was the fact he was approaching the age limit that enabled us all to become aware of his impending departure some time before it actually happened.

I must admit that none of us really wanted him to leave. Bluff and unyielding though he was, Oscar Blaketon was a thoroughly honest man, as reliable and trustworthy as anyone could be, and he was a very good supervisory officer. He did have a soft spot, especially where children, the handicapped and old folks were concerned, but he could not tolerate fools, law-breakers and thoughtless behaviour. On more than one occasion during my service with him, his rather stern exterior had revealed a true heart of gold.

He expected his subordinates to fulfil their duties with complete professionalism and woe betide any of us who let him down, and yet if a mistake was genuine and not done through carelessness or a lack of preparation, he could be sympathetic and helpful. All of us hoped his successor – as yet unnamed – would be equal to the standards Blaketon had established.

An example of this was shown when I

discovered that Oscar Blaketon had decided to continue serving until the very last minute, i.e. the day of his fifty-fifth birthday. Some officers allowed their annual leave allocation to accumulate so that their last day on duty was two or three weeks before the official retirement date. But, over the months, Blaketon had used most of his leave entitlement for golfing holidays and walking trips to the Yorkshire Dales, as well as a week in the Austrian Tyrol, so his official last day of service would also be his last day on duty.

Happily, that was a Friday which meant it was a splendid time for us to arrange a farewell party in his honour. If it was properly organized, it could be a nice relaxed occasion, something he would remember with affection and, if the party was fixed for that Friday, it meant some of the guests could have a lie-in on the Saturday morning – unlike police officers who worked round the clock. It would also mean that Blaketon could start his first Saturday as a civilian in a leisurely way, and then set about finalizing his departure from the police house he currently occupied, the one which adjoined Ashfordly Police Station which would be needed for his successor. Blaketon could then move into the post office house at Aidensfield over the weekend to begin his new job on the Monday morning.

As I discussed his forthcoming retirement with my colleagues, we began to outline our ideas for his farewell party and decided we should include the presentation of a farewell gift to which we would all subscribe. Because I had offered to organize the party, it was decided to hold it in my local pub at Aidensfield, and part of the deal would be accommodation overnight for Sergeant Blaketon and his wife, so that they would not have the worry of driving home after having drunk alcohol. And, of course, because that event would also be his birthday party, we hoped we could give him a rousing send-off, one he would remember. For his farewell gift, we thought he might appreciate a two-wheeled golf caddie. Our research showed he did not own one but sometimes borrowed one from a friend or hired one from the club house. If his heart-beat was not as sound as it had been in his youth, then it might make his games that much more pleasant and enjoyable. He could wheel his bag of clubs around the course instead of having to carry them. I felt we could raise sufficient money to buy one, provided his friends among the public made a contribution, as we knew they would.

And so we began to crystallize our plans, with me booking a private room in the hotel, arranging the food and ensuring there was dance music. There was an invitation list to compile and I needed someone to make the presentation along with a farewell speech – the divisional superintendent was the obvious choice. So far as the guest list was concerned, I felt we should include not only police officers and their families, but members of the public with whom he had worked over the years, including some Ashfordly townspeople – and, of course, Claude Jeremiah Greengrass.

As the arrangements neared completion, I told Sergeant Blaketon that we had fixed his farewell 'do', confirmed the date which coincided with his final day of service, and asked him to ensure he turned up, along with his wife. He promised he would be there. I knew he would not miss it for the world! The final day of one's police service is unavoidably emotional, particularly after serving for some thirty years. Such intense work among members of the public is sometimes more of a vocation than an ordinary job and these farewell parties did help soften the blow of departure. If nothing else, they provided the outgoing officer with an opportunity to reminisce with colleagues whose careers had mirrored his own. However, that final day heralds not only the end of a long and worthwhile career, but the beginning of a completely new style of life. Sometimes, that new life is an anti-climax because police work is unrivalled in terms of powerful human interest, variety and excitement. Few jobs can compete with it in terms of worthiness and all of us knew he would miss his work.

One of the saddest aspects of that final day is the surrender of one's uniform which has to be returned to the police stores along with accoutrements like one's truncheon, whistle, various books and statutes, and, of course, one's warrant card. It is the handing in of the warrant card which marks the final break – without it, one is no longer a police officer. In return, one receives a certificate of service and the return of one's fingerprints on a white card – these are taken from every recruit upon joining the police service and returned upon leaving.

On that final Friday, however, Sergeant Blaketon was due to officiate at Eltering Magistrates' Court where he would be clearing the last remnants of his work by prosecuting his final few cases – motoring offences mainly, such as careless driving, or driving without third party insurance. The Magistrates would wish him well in his new career and thank him for his past and efficient service. In those days, the police prosecuted most of their own cases in magistrates' courts, the local sergeant being the one who presented the facts to the bench.

And so it was, on that Friday afternoon, I

took some papers into Ashfordly Police Station for signature by Blaketon before he departed to Police Headquarters to hand in his uniform. His court duties had concluded before lunch and he had been treated to a farewell meal by the magistrates, but he did return to work! Businesslike to the end, he'd told all his rural officers to ensure they submitted any outstanding work because he wanted to clear his in-tray before he departed to Police Headquarters on what would be his final act as a police officer. He did not wish to leave any outstanding business for his successor, who by now had been confirmed as Sergeant Raymond Craddock of Brantsford, and so I went along with a couple of completed accident reports, a report for summons, two reports of minor crimes and a request for an officer of Leeds City Police to interview an accident witness for me. All routine stuff.

While I was finalizing some paperwork, Blaketon, now dressed in civilian clothes, was loading his private car with items of his uniform. As Mrs Blaketon was packing household goods for their move to Aidensfield, I offered to help him.

It was amazing how much one accumulated during one's service – we loaded two summer uniforms each with two tunics, two winter uniforms also with two tunics, four spare sets of trousers, one greatcoat, one waterproof overcoat and leggings, one British warm, two capes, countless pairs of white cotton gloves, countless pairs of black woollen gloves, umpteen blue shirts, some still in their wrappers, black ties in their wrappers, two peaked caps, a night duty helmet which none of us wore, a truncheon, a whistle, booklets of all kinds, including a copy of Standing Orders, Police Regulations, Disease of Animals statutes, North Riding byelaws, a Civil Defence manual and a list of police stations throughout the county. There was enough to fill the rear seat, the boot and the passenger seat.

'Not quite all my worldly goods, Rhea,' – he spoke softly and I could detect a note of emotion in his voice – 'but it does clear a lot of space in my wardrobes.'

'You're not hanging on to your old uniforms for gardening then, or working about the house?'

We were allowed to buy some used items of clothing, but all unused items had to be returned, such as shirts and ties.

'No, I could have bought some of my better shirts and trousers, but I think it's best if I make a clean break, don't you? I think it's best to get rid of the lot!'

'I think so,' I nodded. While helping with this task, I did feel rather sorry for him – I was the only person with him during those final moments of his service, although there would be a large gathering at his party. Somehow, though, I felt those last moments at his own station were rather sorrowful.

When everything was loaded into his Hillman Minx, he took a deep breath, climbed into the driving seat and closed the door. The window had been lowered.

'See you tonight,' I said because I could not think of anything else.

'Yes,' was his brief reply. 'Eight o'clockish?'

'Fine,' I nodded.

'I'll be there. Now, where's Ventress?' he asked as he started the engine. 'He's taken the section car, I see, so I'll use my own for this last job. After all, when I hand in my warrant card, I'll not be a policeman anyway. I don't want to be driving a police car when I'm a brand new civilian – you never know what I might have to deal with. But soon, I'll have no power to involve myself with any police matter. It's a bit like a one-way ticket – copper one way, civilian the other.'

'I asked Alf to check the food for tonight,' I told him in answer to his question. 'He asked me to hold the fort here until he got back, he's due soon. I thought he'd have been back before now, something must have delayed him.'

In fact, Alf had gone to collect the golf

caddie for tonight's presentation and needed the car to transport it back, to his home address where he'd keep it until this evening, secure from Blaketon's sight.

'He'll be here when I return, I expect, but he'll be there tonight, won't he, at my party?' He closed the window and I knew it was a very sad moment for him, so I said nothing, other than to confirm that Alf Ventress would be at his party. At that moment, I thought he looked so much alone, so isolated in those final hours and I could only guess what was going through his mind.

To be honest, I had no idea what to say because a tide of emotion threatened to overwhelm me. In my own sadness, therefore, I watched him drive out of Ashfordly Police Station yard for the final time as a police officer. When he returned, it would be without the status and power he'd enjoyed while in command of this small but active police station. I continued to watch until his car was out of sight among the town's traffic, then turned to leave for Aidensfield and home. It was quite moving to think that no longer would Oscar Blaketon be my section commander; I wasn't quite sure how to react to those new circumstances.

After tea, I went down to the hotel ahead of the other guests so that I could check the final details of tonight's party; I'd done everything, I was sure. The superintendent had agreed to come along and make the presentation of the golf caddie, along with a suitable farewell speech; the food was being prepared and laid out in a private room – it was a buffet supper for a hundred guests. The pub had arranged a special bar for our private party along with a barman and barmaid, and the band of three musicians had arrived to set up their amplifiers and other equipment, saying they'd play to suit all tastes and would play records during their supper interval. They had been booked until 1 a.m., and the landlord had arranged the necessary extension of hours so we could buy alcohol until 12.30 a.m. For a police party, one had to be sure one obeyed the law!

I'd specified eight o'clock as the commencement time and so, by ten minutes to eight, the guests were beginning to arrive. Mary, my wife, arrived about ten to eight, having arranged a baby-sitter and by half past eight, the place was almost full.

I reckoned everyone would be here by nine so I suggested to the landlord that we had supper at 9.30, with the presentation to Blaketon during that interval. But as the clock ticked away and the musicians began to fill the place with their music, I began to feel anxious and worried because three guests were noticeably absent. One was Oscar Blaketon himself, the other was his wife and the third was Claude Jeremiah Greengrass. I wasn't too concerned about Greengrass's absence, but the star of the evening should have been here at eight, with his wife, if only to welcome his guests. But there had been no word to explain his late arrival. I must admit I began to grow concerned, especially when people like the superintendent and other fairly important guests began to ask, 'So where is he, PC Rhea? Don't tell me Blaketon's forgotten his own party! It's not like him to be late...'

As my worries began to increase, at about a quarter to nine I received a telephone call at the pub. The landlord, George Ward, called me and said, 'Nick, there's a telephone call for you. Take it in the office.'

In the comparative peace of the office, I lifted the receiver and announced my name, when the woman's voice said, 'It's Mrs Blaketon, Nick. Is Oscar there?'

'No,' I told her. 'We're all getting worried. He's not here, Mrs Blaketon, I expected him before now. He must have been delayed. He did say he was coming, I saw him this afternoon and he confirmed he'd be here at eight. I'm still expecting him, and you, of course.'

'He was looking forward to it,' she said. 'And I am too, I'm really looking forward to

301

seeing everybody, but I don't know where he is.'

'You don't?' I was horrified at this. 'What do you mean?'

'Well, he went off to Northallerton with his uniform this afternoon and he's not come home. I rang them at Headquarters, but all the admin. offices are closed now, and Control Room hasn't heard anything, and there's been no accident. When I told them why I was ringing, they contacted the stores manager at home and he said Oscar had been in this afternoon, to return his uniform. Then he left Headquarters to come home. That's all he could tell us. Control Room were very good, they checked the hospitals to see if he'd collapsed or anything, but he's not been admitted. They made a note of his car number in case their patrols come across it, but I said I felt it was too early to make a big official search. I mean, he might just have popped in to see an old friend and forgotten what time it is. But it is rather odd there's no word from him. He seems to have vanished into thin air. I just don't know where he is or what to do. It's very worrying. I wondered if he'd come to see you about something connected with his party; you know what he's like, wanting to check everything or see to some last minute change, he's such a stickler for detail.'

'There's been no word from him and he's

not been here,' I had to tell her. 'I just don't know what can have happened. He's not depressed, is he? About having to retire?'

'No, not at all. He'll miss the police, of course he will, but he has the post office to look forward to and he was looking forward to his party as well, I know that. No, Nick, he won't have done anything silly, like going off to sit in his car on the moors to brood or weep, or worse, he's much stronger than that.'

'He was all right when he left Ashfordly office to go to Headquarters,' I said. 'And he said he was looking forward to this evening.'

'If he told you he'd be there at eight, then that's what he would intend doing. It's all so strange, on his very last day as well.'

'I could bring you here to await developments, you'd be among friends,' I said to her, 'but I think you'd be better sitting by your own telephone in case he tries to make contact at home.'

'Yes, you're right, of course. I'll just sit and wait, but you will try to find out something, won't you?'

'I will,' I reassured her.

When I returned to the party room, it was evident that several people had noticed I'd been called away, and because they'd also noted the absence of our star guest, they linked the two incidents. It was Inspector Harry Breckon, the officer in charge of our

303

Sub-Division at Eltering, who approached me.

'Everything all right, Nick?' he asked and I could see the concern on his face. 'Has something happened to Sergeant Blaketon? He's not arrived yet, has he?'

'He's disappeared,' I had to tell him quietly. 'He went to Headquarters this afternoon to hand in his uniform, and his wife hasn't seen him, or had word from him since he left home. She's checked with Control Room; he arrived at the clothing store and handed in his stuff, then he left to return home but there's no report of an accident and he's not been admitted to any of the hospitals. They've got his car number in case their patrols come across it. He's not rung me either.'

'He's not done something stupid, has he? Jumped off a cliff or gassed himself with his car exhaust?'

'She says he wasn't depressed about retiring and she doesn't think he'd do anything silly. There must be some logical explanation, sir.'

'I agree, he's not the sort to end things like that. Well, if Control Room's been alerted and done those checks, and if his wife is sitting at home expecting him to ring, there's not a lot we can do. We'll just have to await developments, but it's not like Oscar Blaketon to miss his own party!'

'Shouldn't we do something, sir?' I asked. 'Like raise the alarm, or organize a search?'

'We don't want to create unnecessary panic, Nick, and where would we search? There's a lot of countryside between here and Northallerton. Control Room has details of his car so if that's found somewhere, it'll give us a starting point.'

'Mrs Blaketon wondered if he had popped in to see an old friend while he was at Northallerton, perhaps losing track of time?'

'That's the sort of thing some of us would do, but not Blaketon. I agree with his wife – if he said he'd be here at eight, then he would be here at eight. Let's give him another half-hour, Nick, then we might have to consider a search of some kind.'

'Yes, sir.' I was pleased someone of more senior rank had the responsibility for deciding about future action, and I returned to the festivities. Word of Blaketon's non-appearance had circulated to everyone by this time and both Inspector Breckon and myself began to field enquiries, each trying to play down the situation.

But we were worried and very soon that air of concern began to affect the party atmosphere. Happy gossip and cheerful reminiscing turned into worried speculation about the missing sergeant and it was Alf Ventress who reminded me of another matter.

'Greengrass is missing too,' he told me. 'I saw him in Ashfordly this afternoon and he said he wouldn't miss Blaketon's farewell party for anything! He laughed and said wild horses couldn't keep him away because he wanted to be sure Blaketon was actually leaving! He thought it might be just a mischievous rumour.'

'That is odd, isn't it?' I said. 'Even if this wasn't Blaketon's farewell party, Greengrass would be in the bar by this time. He's never away from the pub at this time of night.'

I told Alf what had transpired between Mrs Blaketon and Control Room, and of Inspector Breckon's decision, and he shrugged his shoulders. 'Well, what else can we do? You will keep in touch, Nick, you will let us know if you hear anything? Everyone's getting very concerned.'

'Sure, Alf,' I promised.

At this stage, in order to keep the narrative in some kind of chronological sequence, I shall now relate what happened to Sergeant Blaketon, as later told to me in his own words. He told me about a long-running series of incidents which had been occurring over the past months on the A19 trunk road and also on the Great North Road, otherwise known as the A1. All these occurrences had happened in the North Riding Constabulary area but well away from Ashfordly and Aidensfield.

My local officers and myself had no part in this – the scenes of those incidents were many miles to the west. This is what was happening. On many reported occasions, and, we believe in many instances which were never reported to the police, motorists on those two arterial roads had been stopped apparently by a uniformed police officer in a marked police car, and after suffering a fierce reprimand from the officer, had been fined on the spot for whatever minor traffic offences had been committed. The offences included things like dirty registration plates, broken or in-effective headlights or side lights, defective tyres, exceeding the speed limit, faulty windscreen wipers and washers, out-of-date excise licences, defective exhausts and failing to obey mandatory traffic signs.

It was difficult to know how long this series of incidents had been occurring because I am sure some of those fined drivers felt they had got off lightly – they did not have to appear in court, their roadside fines were modest – £10, £15 and £20 or thereabouts and, according to the 'constable' who'd booked them, their willingness to pay their fine on the spot meant their licences would not be endorsed or put at risk. In their minds, they were guilty because they had offended and were relieved they had been swiftly dealt with in a very fair manner.

But motorists do talk to each other and some of them talk to police officers. After a time, it became evident that this road traffic officer was not a genuine policeman. The fixed penalty system did not embrace on-the-spot fines and in any case, it was not applicable to moving traffic offences; it was restricted to minor breaches of the parking regulations, lighting offences and highway obstruction.

No British police officer or traffic warden would or should accept cash from an offender. In the fixed penalty system, offenders were issued with a ticket which they had to produce when they paid their fine at the Magistrates' Clerk's Office, and the alternative was to contest the case in open court. This traffic "constable" did not give his motorists that opportunity – he demanded cash immediately and I think he made quite a lot of money from his activities.

Eventually, some motorists did begin to suspect he was a fake – his uniform did not seem quite right, his language when dealing with the "offending" drivers was most certainly not correct, and the forms he produced when demanding his spot fines were not official police documents. They were poor imitations – and of course, he should not have been accepting cash from his 'customers'.

A senior officer from the North Riding

Constabulary had been made aware of the growing incidence of these fake cases, and had decided not to publicize the matter. Indeed, even the majority of serving officers were not informed about this man in case knowledge of our interest reached him – there was always a possibility he had links with a serving officer. Publicity would alert motorists to the danger from this man, but it meant we would also alert him and that might mean we would never bring him to justice – whoever he was. It was felt we should do our best to catch him in action and then to make an example of him through the courts, with maximum publicity so that his earlier 'customers' might come forward. We felt that few would come forward – perhaps thinking they might be fined again for the relevant offence by the real police!

A softly-softly approach was decided, which is why so few of us were aware of this man and his blitz on motorists. One problem with restricting information to a few real officers was that one had to be literally on the scene if we were to catch him – clearly, he would never operate if a police car was patrolling in the area and even an undercover car might not provide the right kind of trap to catch him.

What had been learned from those who had spoken to the real constabulary, was that he drove a black Ford Zephyr in immaculate condition and it bore a blue flashing light with a POLICE sign on the roof. It looked just like a police car; indeed, the North Riding Constabulary used black Zephyrs for their road traffic patrols. The driver wore a police uniform complete with silver numerals and buttons, and a black peaked cap sporting a silver police badge. His age was difficult to estimate because he wore the cap with its peak well down, but it was thought he was in his early forties with dark hair, clean shaven, about five feet ten in height and of average build. He had no discernible accent, but when booking a motorist, he became extremely agitated and excited. His MO was to suddenly appear behind a driver in the Zephyr, overtake the car and wave the driver into the side of the road or perhaps a lay-by or minor road, there to levy his fine for whatever offence he had allegedly discovered. It was thought he waited in a private side road until a suitable victim appeared, although the known cases had occurred on differing stretches of both the A1 and A19. Clearly, he had his own hunting ground with which he appeared to be very familiar. He might even have access to police broadcasts.

And that is what happened to Sergeant Blaketon.

He told me he'd been driving home in his

own car along the A19. As Mrs Blaketon had guessed, he had called upon a former colleague in Northallerton and so it was around 6.30 p.m. when he'd left. He reckoned he'd be home about 7.15 p.m. which allowed enough time to prepare for his party. As he'd been driving along the A19, around 6.45 p.m. he'd suddenly become aware of a police car in his rear view mirror. It was a black Ford Zephyr with a blue flashing light, and it roared past him with the driver making waving signals which were incomprehensible to Blaketon. But eventually, the Zephyr pulled a considerable distance ahead of him and eased into the entrance to a caravan and camping site. That entrance was very wide, almost like a lay-by, and the driver leapt out to flag down Blaketon. Puzzled, Blaketon had obeyed, pulling his own car off the road and on to the parking space. He'd then got out of his car but had left his driver's door standing open and his engine running while he went to confront the policeman.

'I knew he was a fake,' he told me. 'The minute he got out of his car, I could see things weren't right. Dirty shoes instead of polished boots, a uniform that had been found in a theatre, I think, because it looked more like a 1930s style than the 1960s, and the numerals on his epaulettes had a divisional letter before them, like the

311

London Met police; we don't use divisional letters like that. And I could see the car was fake too, the sign was held on by a magnet, I think, and there was a wire running from it through the window and into the car. I think the Zephyr might have been a former police car, it was just like our fleet and good enough to fool a nervous motorist in the heat of the moment. But he wasn't going to fool me, Nick!'

'So what did he do?' I asked.

'He started to give me the dressing down of a lifetime, saying I'd been driving carelessly – I did swerve suddenly to avoid a dog but caused no danger to anyone. He was highly agitated, manic almost, then he said one of my brake lights wasn't working and after he'd got really worked up with me trying to say my piece and him refusing to let me get a word in – he said he would have to fine me. He said I could pay a fixed penalty of fifteen pounds cash, in which case I would not have to attend court and my licence would not be endorsed. If I paid him the cash, that would be the end of the matter. He told me that was the new system. And he began to write out some kind of notice on what appeared to be a printed pad of paper. By this stage, I had stopped trying to compete with his verbal outburst and I was observing him and his car, taking note of his appearance, his uniform and so forth.'

'You were behaving like a real policeman, Sarge!' I smiled.

'Yes, but when he asked me for my money, I told him he was under arrest for demanding money with menaces and impersonating a police officer, in addition to any other offences which might be disclosed. I told him I was Sergeant Blaketon of the North Riding Constabulary, stationed at Ashfordly.'

'And?'

'He demanded proof! And I did not have a warrant card – I'd handed it in and so I could not prove who I was, and I was in my own private car! He didn't believe me! Damn it, Nick, I was a policeman until midnight on my last day of service – I was a policeman during all that carry on, even if I didn't have my warrant card!'

'So what did he do?'

'He said he was going to arrest me! Him arrest me! And him a fake... God, he had a nerve. I said no way am I going to be treated like that, I told him I knew he was a fake and I was going to drive away and circulate his description, and that of his "police" car, to my mobile colleagues. I told him I had my certificate of service in the car if he wanted proof of my claim, but at that he pulled a knife which he'd got hidden up his sleeve and before I could react, it was at my throat and he was marching me towards his car. He made me get into the rear seat and lie down, then he handcuffed my hands behind my back, slammed the doors, removed the blue light with its POLICE sign from the roof and put it in the boot, then drove away.'

'Where to?' I asked.

'I had no idea. I was face down on the back seat with my hands handcuffed behind me and my legs jammed sideways down the front of the rear seat and trapped in that position when he moved the front seat backwards. There was no way I could sit up and do anything except shout like hell, and I couldn't see where I was being taken. It wasn't far, though; we drove for only a very short time and the next thing I knew we were entering a barn or a garage and when we were inside, he got out, locked the car doors and then closed the barn door. He left me where I was. It was dark inside, and try as I might, I couldn't budge. And my legs were aching like hell, they were twisted, you see, and jammed... I'll tell you what, Nick, I was getting pretty worried by this time. The man was a maniac, I was sure of that, I had no idea what he was going to do to me.'

'And that's when Claude Jeremiah Greengrass came to your rescue?'

'It seems I had been incarcerated in an outbuilding of a former stately home. The entire complex has been transformed into a caravan and camping site, as well as sporting some holiday cottages and a pond for water sports. Claude goes there regularly selling eggs and vegetables and so on to the tourists. He'd been leaving the complex in that old truck of his when he'd seen the "policeman" rushing away from the barn, pulling off his tie as he ran, and then removing his jacket while trying to carry his cap. All most ungainly! Claude thought it odd and let's face it, he can recognize a genuine policeman even if he's miles away. He thought something was fishy but decided not to interfere, but as he left the complex, he saw my car parked outside the entrance to the site, with the door standing open and the engine still running. He knows my private car, of course – so instead of alerting the fake copper by rushing back to rescue me, he had the good sense to telephone Force Headquarters from that kiosk near the entrance. They told him to wait there and do nothing further until the police arrived. They did arrive – within about ten minutes – and caught the imposter as he was packing his things. He was using a cottage in the grounds and had rented the garage, but he had another plain car in which he proposed to get away. I think he was going to leave me there, although he did say he would have telephoned someone to release me, once he was

315

safely away. I'd panicked him. All he wanted to do was to get away before he was caught.'

'Thank God for Greengrass!' I smiled.

'I never thought I'd have to thank that old rogue, Nick, but I do have to thank him now. Then, of course, I heard that our chaps had been looking for this fake copper for months – it seems he left the Zephyr in that lock-up at the caravan site while he was away from the place and then came back from time to time to conduct his blitz on erring drivers.'

'He's been doing it for years, I believe?'

'No one knows for certain how long he's been at it, but we think he's been doing similar scams in other parts of Britain. He's a fanatic of some kind, it seems he's been turned down by the recruiting departments of regular Forces on several occasions. He's applied to lots of Forces up and down the country, always without success. Not even the Metropolitan Police would take him! His name is Edwin Juggins and he hails from Wolverhampton. He's got no previous criminal record, though. A weird chap. I'm glad he's been caught.'

'Your last big case then?'

'I claim no credit for the arrest, and the real hero was Claude. He could have ignored my car ... but he didn't.'

'So both of you were late for your party?'

'We had to stay and give statements and

be interviewed by the team who were seeking that fake policeman. I couldn't alert anyone for ages, it was all hush-hush at the time but, as you know, I did ask Control Room to ring you the moment we were given the all-clear.'

And that's how it was. As I was beginning to think we would have to raise a search party for Sergeant Blaketon, the chief inspector in charge of the Control Room rang me at the pub to explain what had happened. He gave me a good account of the incident so that I could acquaint the party guests, and said that both Blaketon and Greengrass were on their way home. After freshening themselves, they would soon be joining us. I told Mrs Blaketon about it and she said something to the effect that Oscar couldn't leave the job alone, even in the final minutes of his career, but she did seem very proud of him. She said he was a copper to the bitter end but hoped he'd change in retirement.

With this knowledge, I asked Inspector Breckon to inform the gathering of the drama. It goes without saying that when Sergeant Blaketon and Claude Jeremiah Greengrass walked into that party side by side the place erupted in a huge cheer and more than a few of us had tears in our eyes.

This Large Print Book for the partially sighted, who cannot read normal print, is published under the auspices of

THE ULVERSCROFT FOUNDATION